SOLYRA'S LIBERTY

SOLYRA'S LIBERTY

KEATES NELSON

to all women
struggling to shine
in our tough, beautiful world

CONTENTS

SOLYRA'S LIBERTY

THE DEAL

SOLYRA PAUSED IN THE HALLWAY and drew a deep breath. She simply had to calm down. To face Terring, shaking like a leaf with her stomach all a-tizzle—it just wouldn't do.

She gave a breathless laugh. How could she *possibly* calm down? In just a few minutes, five years of laborious chicanery and penny-pinching would climax in a deal that would dissolve a mountain of debt and bring the security she longed for with all her heart.

Security she'd fought for, tooth and nail.

She drew another breath outside her "conference room" — the front parlor of her house primped up with a large, well-worn and well-polished table, a cheap carpet, and various machines that appeared to be fulgu-powered but whose fulgus had long-since been removed and sold. She had to smile. Fist-sized lumps that looked, at best, like a rock crossed with an oyster, the fulgus she was about to acquire would brighten her house and positively dazzle her fortune.

Terring politely stood as she entered. Handsome as ever, despite his dated frock coat and run-down boots, he looked nervous, too.

They exchanged a few tense pleasantries. Solyra poured coffee. Terring barely got a sip down before Solyra began to draw the contracts out of their folder. Maybe she shouldn't rush a man about to sell every last one of his fulgus — to sign his business away, basically. But surely he, too, wanted to conclude things as quickly as possible.

Terring reached over the conference table, took the folder from her, and put it back on the table unopened.

She looked at him, eyebrows raised. So he wanted to haggle.

"I'm sorry, zizera Solyra," he said, "but I must inform you that our business arrangement is over."

"I will be happy to discuss terms, zizero." She forced a smile. "Though it will mar the clerk's beautiful contracts."

"No, zizera Solyra, you don't understand. I said, our business arrangement is over." His tone remained gentlemanly. "As we sit at this handsome table, my inventory is being liquidated."

"Your inventory is...." Solyra swallowed.

"Being liquidated. Every last fulgu of it. In short, I got a better deal."

Solyra's heart seemed to crash to a stop — then burst into a gallop. The crystal beads on her dress clattered and flashed as she fought to control her breath, even as her mind leaped every which way.

It couldn't be.... He couldn't....

No!

He was bluffing. He must be bluffing.

Right?

Wrong, his face said.

Solyra's house and everything in it, her last fulgus, her very soul, not to mention possessions she no longer possessed, had been mortgaged to get the cash for this deal.

She was ruined.

But that couldn't stop her from trying to save herself, any more than a bicycle brake could halt a runaway coach-and-four.

"Zizero Terring, you can't possibly mean...." She mustn't

plead. "Surely you understand that — that our contract...."
That their contract lay yet unsigned in its folder. "That is, you
are ruining your own—"

"Zizera Solyra, despite appearances — yes, I'm aware that
my wardrobe hardly passes muster in fashionable circles. But
despite that, what my family realizes or doesn't realize from
the sale of my fulgus is just a...." Terring shrugged. "Just a little
corner. A little corner passed down from my grandfather to my
father to me." His voice hardened. "*My* corner."

Solyra bit down the impulse to rejoice at how *nice* it was
that Terring's business failure would cause him no pecuniary
embarrassment. "I certainly sympathize, zizero. My business,
too, was passed to me. From my husband."

To her dismay, her voice trembled. Well, let it tremble.
Terring could read it as grief or something like that. For Solyra, the memory of her husband alive caused more pain than
the memory of his death in a brothel, humiliating as that had
been. Solyra rarely spoke of either, but this was a rare occasion.
Everything she'd built her life on was slipping away.

Solyra pressed on. "Zizero Terring, if you will halt the sale
to the other party, I will handle your legacy with the utmost
integrity, and—"

"I made Terring Fulgus the most advanced concern of its
kind." His hand clenched, unclenched. "And I spent ten years
raising my fulgu frame. You know. The one that crashed. The
one that *actually* crashed."

"All the industry mourned your loss." Solyra aimed for a
look of concern, even as her mind raced.

Raising a frame to cultivate fulgus required a huge investment. Therefore, a crashed frame spelled complete and utter
disaster. That is, unless you could wangle a huge insurance settlement out of it, as had Solyra's husband — for a frame that
never *actually* crashed, because it was never *actually* raised.

Dahn's humongous insurance claim had driven premiums
to near-ruinous heights for everyone else, including Terring.

If Terring knew that Dahn's claim was fraudulent — if that's what he was hinting at — he probably assumed she'd colluded, buying gewgaws and pretty gowns with the money. But the "crash" happened before she got involved in the business. And Dahn had spent the proceeds of his claim on two months of solid debauchery — with other women, thankfully.

Solyra craved to go upstairs, crawl in bed, and pull the blankets over her head. But that wasn't an option.

"Zizero Terring, name your price. I will—"

Terring gave a snort. "No, you won't."

"Zizero, on your honor—"

"Honor!" Terring's fist slammed the table.

The only sounds were the tinkling of crystal beads and the traffic outside.

And Solyra's heart pounding like a race horse. She half-held her breath, trying not to pant, trying to quiet the beads on her frock. Terring, on the other hand, huffed and puffed as his face slowly returned from maroon to its usual mahogany.

A tiny part of Solyra whispered, *Here's your chance.* He'd lost control, and he was the kind of man to regret that, his face already troubled. But the small, practical voice that bid her to exploit the moment was stifled by swelling rage. Terring's outburst had jetted her with terror, weakened her limbs and set her quaking. And in this strategic moment, blinking down the humiliation of hot tears, Solyra hated him with all her heart.

She leaped up and dashed her hands over the table, scattering paper, sending china crashing. Terring jumped away, knocking his chair over, barely avoiding a cascade of coffee, but not the spray of ink that caught his shirt front.

"Good Bih!" Terring stared at Solyra.

She drew herself up tall. At least the frock hid her shaking legs, even if the tinkling beads betrayed her.

"That concludes this meeting, zizero Terring," she said with all the haughtiness she could summon. "And you may take each and every one of your fulgus — and cram them up your caboose!"

Incredibly, Terring's eyes softened and crinkled at the corners.

Solyra marched to the casement window, her back stiff, head high. She kept her back turned as Terring left, watched through the window as he entered a cab, watched as the cab rolled away in billows of dust and a crowd of shouting urchins.

A little girl lagged behind, staring back at the house. She looked wistful, her hair dirty and tangled, her dress orphan gray, too tight and too short. Solyra had begun laying plans to adopt such a one, having a daughter to love and care for, maybe a son, too. Making unwanted children wanted, giving them a home.

No more.

Terring had canceled the deal.

The reality hit like a punch to the gut.

By morning, Dunning & Sons would be tromping over her shoddy carpets, taking inventory of every stick of furniture in her house, down to the simple wicker rockers lined up on her porch.

They wouldn't find, however, her fulgu-powered lamps and braziers. Nor the fulgu-matic copier, the fulgu'd coffee service, the imported rugs and dishes, and all the other valuables offered as collateral in the loan. All those trinkets were long since sold away. Most of all, Dunning wouldn't find four lockers of energy fulgus, ready to be installed in any device, from gadgets like "Bicycle for a Feeble Man" or "Goggles to Light the Way" to more practical machines like clocks that ran without winding and ovens that heated without fire. Instead, they'd find four lockers of worthless pod fulgus.

Dunning & Sons could take everything she had — which they would — from her pod fulgus to the crystal beads on the dress she wore, not to mention the dress itself, and it would not equal what she owed.

She had no family. Her friends were barely more solvent than she. Dahn's machinations and, yes, her own, had chilled others in the fulgu trade, dooming to failure any action she might take against Terring. Debtors prison, not solvency, would be the outcome of the deal she'd worked so hard to bring about.

A friend of hers had been imprisoned for defaulting on a loan far smaller than the one Solyra had taken out. Solyra had visited her every week. One time Renna showed up with both her eyes blacked. Another time with a broken finger. Another time with a limp. She wouldn't talk about it. She told Solyra not to bring her anything. Solyra guessed she didn't want to attract the jealousy of other inmates or maybe of the guards. On coming home, Solyra had always worked lamp oil through her hair, against the lice and fleas. The last time Solyra saw her, Renna announced, her eyes hollow, that she was pregnant. The next time Solyra visited…. The guards told her Renna had hung herself.

Solyra found herself sitting on her cheap carpet. She didn't know if she'd collapsed or just sunk down, her limbs numbed. She forced herself to rise, sit at the conference table, her fingers absently worrying the dent made by Terring's ring. She forced herself to put aside terror, to quench all emotion. She had to think.

The first payment on the loan wasn't due for nearly a whole month. If only she hadn't lost control with Terring, she might have begged him at least to keep quiet about their collapsed deal, give her some time to save herself.

Yet she knew, somehow, he wouldn't boast of it. Not out of kindness, particularly, but because he'd finished his business with her. Finished her. Solyra put her face in her hands as a sob welled up in her chest — she swallowed it down. She didn't have time for self-pity.

The only thing she had time for was to flee.

>> <<

Revenge was supposed to be sweet. Yet the brandy Terring gulped down failed to chase the sour taste from his mouth.

Feeling like a cad didn't help. But she was the cad, wasn't she? If a woman could be a cad. She and Dahn had undermined his and everyone else's business with that fraudulent insurance claim. And Dahn's ignoble demise hadn't slowed her down one bit. She'd fixed prices, she'd sold fulgus on the black market. She'd pulled every under-handed trick in the book.

He had to admit, though, the finishing touch to his own demise had been his own. He'd held on to Terring Fulgus until the bitter end — past the bitter end. He'd been forced to sell out in haste just to keep out of debtor's jail. He'd flaunted the advice of his aide Figgo and just about everyone else, including his oldest brother. Figgo, at least, didn't rub it in. Elder and wiser brother certainly did. His fully fulgu'd house apparently proclaiming him lord of the family, he'd summoned Terring to the sacred precincts of his parlor to intone, "You need to learn a lesson, Terring."

The lesson being that little brother must sink, now that he could no longer swim. No doubt they would eventually have thrown him a line, brought pies and clean linens to his debtor's cell, perhaps even bailed him out before he lost his teeth to scurvy or beatings. They would certainly not invest in him again. His role, henceforth, was to be a desk ornament at the family firm. A chastened desk ornament.

He would suffocate. He would go mad.

But the thing was.... He hadn't meant to devastate Solyra. If that was what he had done.

Terring strode into the office, or what was left of it. Most of the furniture had been sold, and ten years of files now collected dust in a grudgingly granted corner of his brother's investment offices.

Figgo, sitting at the desk, raised his face, his copper goggles glinting, and put his pen down. His fingers slid to the edge of the ledger page and with his nail he made a small dent to mark his place.

"She has fulgus, doesn't she?" Terring demanded. "Several lockers full, if I'm not mistaken."

Figgo believed, and was likely right, as usual, that she and a handful of other dealers in the region had hoarded energy fulgus to keep prices up. No one could get into the business these days without lots of money. That would have worked for Terring, if he had lots of money. He didn't, though. After his own frame crashed, he'd courted bankruptcy to buy his way back in.

"She has four lockers of energy fulgus," Figgo said, "according to her agreement with Dunning & Sons."

"Why in the world would she do business with Dunning?"

"Her credit record is not without blemish. But two or three lockers of energy fulgus will cover the loan quite comfortably." Figgo picked up his pen again, then paused. "Three, I should think, given that prices will drop with your inventory on market."

Figgo had uncovered Solyra's chicanery through a network of business associates and industrial spies. Yet while he showed no sympathy for her, neither did he show glee. He didn't show much of anything, really. Terring knew little about Figgo's family, except that they had been wiped out by the Death Bringers in his homeland. Terring was probably the closest to kin Figgo had. In a way, Figgo was the same for him. Unlike blood, Figgo had stood by him through success and through more than one devastating failure.

Which brought Terring back to the uncomfortable memory of Solyra's face when he'd informed her their deal was off.

Why had he gone to meet her? He could have let her know by courier that he'd found a buyer willing to pay more. But that had seemed the coward's way out.

He'd had to see her, one last time.

Before today, they hadn't met for, what, six years now? They hadn't outright avoided each other since he'd come back east, but they hadn't gone out of their way to cross paths, either. The last time he'd spent any time with Solyra, beyond a nod at a function or business gathering, had been at the fulgu convention in Booton. Where she and her dearly departed husband had stolen a customer that Terring could not afford to lose.

At the convention's ball, she'd been tippled up on the finest bubbly and half-naked in the latest fashion, a long rope of jewels glimmering between her bare breasts. All through it Terring had throbbed red-hot with lust and something like jealousy. He hadn't dared go near her, though every other man with a heartbeat had turned her on the floor, pressed her as close as audacity allowed. Her partners had included Terring's most important customer. At breakfast the next day, Dahn made a point of joining him and Figgo to gloat over having snatched the account, and probably to gloat again over having snatched the woman. Solyra herself had barely granted Terring a glance.

It's business, Terring had told himself. No point being a sore loser.

But today, with Solyra.... He should have apologized, at least, for not notifying her sooner, should have explained that the sale had been touch and go until the very last minute. Instead, he'd acted above it all, rolling in family lucre.

He'd been out for revenge. Which pointed to the sour reality that he'd been, yes, a cad.

When he'd told her the deal was off, her beautiful face had gone from blithe to ... something else. Her mouth had trembled, until she bit down on her lower lip.

Terring thumped his fist on the window frame — somehow he'd ended up at the window though night had fallen and the glass revealed only his own reflection. Himself, in the dated suit that had raised zizera Solyra's brows.

The dark sloping arches over those incredible eyes.

Terring sensed Figgo turn toward him, then bend to his work again. Tallying the final account, lines of pinprick bumps guiding his pen. They'd cleared their debts with a bit left over. Not enough to make a new start in the fulgu business. That was finished. But enough to get him out of town and on to a new business. Anything would be better than moldering at the corporate offices of the family business.

Such were the tides of fortune. Solyra certainly understood. It was all about getting money and, when things didn't work out, losing money.

Just business. That was all.

She had looked that way at Booton, at that hang-over breakfast after the ball. Something her husband said. Terring couldn't remember what it was, but it had caused her lips to tremble, even as she'd held her head up high on that exquisite neck, and bitten down on her lower lip to steady it.

FLIGHT

SOLYRA SLID THE COACH SHUTTER open a crack and gulped in a precious lungful of fresh, cool air—

"Eek!"

She slammed the shutter as something buzzed and whirred out of the night. The shutter vibrated with a thump that somehow sounded disappointed.

"That cursed moth or bat or whatever was going for my hair. I just know it." She couldn't stop herself from checking, then rubbed her arms against the goose bumps that had sprung up. "I'll be glad when the sun rises."

"I wonder if they'd survive if we just let them go," Zago mused, as he had mused for the last several bone-jouncing hours. "They" weren't amorous bats or moths, but the pod fulgus tucked in four lockers under their feet. "After waking them a little, of course," he added.

The usual term for powering pod fulgus was to activate, not to awaken. But like many fulgu keepers, Zago fervently believed that his charges were alive. Solyra knew they were just dumb rocks. Wondrous dumb rocks, but dumb rocks all the same.

They were also dangerous. Solyra wasn't sure how combustible pod fulgus were, but she certainly wasn't willing to chance blowing up the coach and themselves. Not to mention destroying her last chance of getting back on her feet.

"You can't take a chance like that, Zago," she said. "You could kill them. And us."

"All those sentient beings, torn away from each other," Zago said. "Trafficked."

"We're not trafficking them, Zago," Solyra tried. "We're cultivating them. Making more fulgus."

"Even worse." Zago shook his head. "Solyra, I know you think I'm a madman, a fool, a child. But I'm not. I hear them speaking. I don't know what they're saying, not yet, but they are speaking. It's not just body functions. They're people. And I'm exploiting them!"

Zago's fretting used to merely annoy her. Now, it prodded her exhausted panic to new life. She needed not only her fulgus, she needed their keeper. He was one of the best in the business. More important, he was the only one she'd dared talk into coming with her.

To the average person, keeping fulgus seemed less demanding than tending a potted plant. But watering them, the spacing in their lockers, exposure to air, and myriad other subtleties elevated fulgu-keeping to a science, an art. Solyra could tend them for a week or so, but without a skilled keeper, they would eventually "die," their precious energy mysteriously dispelled, leaving only a rotten egg smell.

Like most fulgu keepers, Zago was a bit cracked, but if he mutinied, she was sunk, pure and simple.

"Zago, you have to understand…." Inspiration struck. "We can't just let them go. It would be cruel. We'll liberate them out in the Zhengahk. They'll be free in their native land. That's why it's called a Liberty."

That wasn't why the property, which lay at the far end of beyond, was called a Liberty. Or maybe that was why. Solyra had no idea. But in the dim, flickering light — the coach not fulgu'd — Zago's face filled completely with joy and hope.

Then he lunged at her.

Solyra cringed into her seat before realizing he meant to hug her. He bounced back into his seat. "Sorry, zizera, but — that's so wonderful! Why did you tell me we were going out to cultivate them?"

Solyra gave a shaky laugh. He'd startled her badly. "I — well, I was still working it out in my head. But first things first." She unhooked the speaking tube. "Sirrah, may I ask how far the border is from here?"

The tube responded with a honk, then, "About tenkeh oakens, zizera."

Solyra put the mouthpiece of the speaking tube in her lap. "Tenkeh oakens," she repeated. "What does that mean?"

"I don't—" Zago began.

The speaking tube honked. "Tenkeh oakens is, arrrr, about thirty minutes by your time."

"Thank you, sirrah."

"Much welcome."

Solyra hung up the speaking tube, discomfited. It didn't have a plug, but she'd assumed that unless she spoke directly into it, the driver couldn't hear her. He'd probably been listening to them the whole ride. Never mind. It was too late to worry about the driver. The thing to worry about now was getting across the border with over a hundred fulgus that, technically, the bank owned.

She'd traveled enough with Dahn to know that border checkpoints bristled with uniformed men armed with musketoons, pikes, and swords, and equipped with capacious purses. Dahn always carried enough gold to pay them off. Solyra had enough doubloons, she guessed, to pass this border.

But she, her fulgus, and hopefully Zago had many more borders to pass. Her "Liberty" in the Zhengahk, with its cultivation fields, lay so far away, it seemed mythical. She'd never been there herself, not even near. With four lockers of fulgus that law-enforcement types could consider stolen, Solyra didn't see how she'd ever make it....

Never mind. Remember what a friend said as the Collectors began circling Solyra like vultures after Dahn died: Get through this day. Then get through the next. And the next. And she had. Only in this case it was: Get through this border. Then get through the next. And the next and the next.

Meanwhile, it wouldn't hurt to tidy up. She combed and netted her hair, refreshed her face and hands with witch hazel water, and shook and straightened her green wool caftan. She would have felt cleaner breathing outside air, but she wasn't willing to risk the amours of moths with foot-wide wingspans. Zago didn't need freshening up. Like other fulgu keepers, he had a pleasant dry-earthy body odor, and though he was a little fly-away, he was never sloppy.

Dawn grayed the cracks around the shutters as they pulled up at the border station. Solyra opened her shutter, ready to slam it shut if something flew at her. Nothing did. The sight that met her eyes made her gasp with relief. Rather than a swarm of uniformed guards, the only person at the crude turnstile was a paunchy man who had just rolled out of bed, judging by his yawning mouth and mashed hair.

Not a man. A troll! Solyra stared in fascination shading to disappointment. She'd heard that trolls were spectacularly hideous, but while the troll didn't approach handsome, he was merely extraordinarily ugly and dirty.

The driver had advised Solyra to stay in the coach and let him do the talking, but too much rode on this crossing to trust to a stranger. Solyra needed to use the facilities, anyway, and stretch her legs.

As she stepped from the coach, the troll's eyes, or one of them — the other permanently eyed the heavens — slewed toward her and a grin spread across his stubbly face.

"Yaieeee!" The troll followed that with what sounded like a complicated, rattling yawn.

The driver translated, his face glum. "Arrrr, zizera, he asks you to do the honor of, arrrr, attending tea."

If the troll's ugliness fell short before, Solyra could hardly be disappointed seeing — and smelling — his grin close up. She considered pleading fatigue or lady trouble, always a trusty excuse to avoid men's company. But she decided to tough it out. Zago had dozed off; she was on her own. Solyra followed the driver and the troll inside the trollhouse.

The building might have been respectable, once upon a time. Since then, it had lapsed into little more than four stone walls with a moldering thatched roof. The driver grew even more glum when a trollette, polishing glasses behind the bar, cheerfully greeted them. Though chunks of food and straw studded her dingy rag, the glasses would be about the cleanest things in the place. The prize for filth would have to go to the two men sleeping or passed out on benches pushed against the wall. Solyra had grown up humble, but never had she seen such squalor.

All for the best. The place was obviously a kind of smuggler's cove. The troll barked something at the trollette and ushered his guests to a grimy table under an unglazed window. He and the driver engaged in a mutual haranguing yawn, punctuated by longer or shorter "arrrr's" and "yaieee's." For all Solyra knew, it was a perfectly amiable conversation. The troll broke off to shout something over his shoulder, presumably at the trollette, who'd disappeared through a door behind the bar.

When no answer came back, the troll threw his towel on the table, sending an insect scurrying over the edge, and stomped back through the door. A dialogue of shouting, snarling, snorting and yowling ended with a catlike screech. A few minutes later the trollette bore out a tray laden with coarse crockery and food. Tears reddened her eyes and streaked her grimy face. The troll looked smug.

"The lady an' her gentlemen friends are welcome to our house," the trollette said in a trembling voice as she eased the tray down onto the adjoining table. She served out a pale purple drink — no tea — bowls of grease-clotted stew, and a hunk of dried up bread. "I fed the coachman," she said.

Solyra wondered if the "coachman" — who must be Zago — got all the choice morsels from the stew. Her own bowl held a watery brown gravy, some carrot stumps and coarse greens, and what looked like the spine of a small mammal. Or maybe a chicken. Whatever its species, Solyra sorely regretted not following the driver's advice. Twice-given, in fact: "Zizera, again, I strongly advise you to remain in the coach and allow me to negotiate at the border…."

Solyra took a deep breath and looked up to see the trollette watching her. Despite the bruise — a bite mark, Solyra realized — surfacing on her cheek, her eyes brimmed sympathy. "Lady all right?" she asked.

Solyra forced a smile. "Yes, I'm all right, thank you."

The woman serving wasn't a trollette after all. The catlike vibration to her voice, the curling corners of her mouth, the slightly pointed, tufted ears, showed her to be an onza. Solyra had never seen such a one before. But onza or trollette, the server was a woman in trouble.

"What about you?" Solyra touched her own cheek, in a place that corresponded to the onza's bruise. "Did the — the man do that to you?"

"My husband." The onza gave a soft hiss. "I hate 'im!"

The troll muttered and clattered glasses and cups behind the bar, and the onza hastily collected the still-full dishes. The driver watched without protest. As the onza began to heft the tray to her shoulder, Solyra put a hand on her arm and said, "Come out west with us." Even as the impulsive words tumbled from her lips, her mind raced to think of how she could take them back.

But the onza's radiant smile banished regret. She winked,

then re-assumed her gloom and scuttled back to the bar, the crockery clattering on her tray.

The driver put his face in his hands and started laughing.

THE WUDU

"I won't be a Collector," Terring said.

The head of Bull Security & Collecting pushed his lips out with a sigh. "You're turning down good money, man."

When Terring didn't answer, Bull shrugged and turned to the wall map, darkened from countless cigars and cheap lamp oil. No fulgus lit this heap. Bull jabbed his finger at the main road through the Wudu.

"Couple of caravans taken by pirates. Gang of a dozen or so. Think you can handle it?"

The deep, unmapped forests of the Wudu made it a bandit's delight. Still, only a truly audacious outfit would attack travelers on the main road. Although the Wudu had neither police nor armed forces, its governors used hired thugs to guard their territories.

Which Terring, if he took the job, would be. A hired thug.

"How many men will I have?" he asked.

Bull relit his cigar. "A dozen. And some gals, if you don't mind that."

Terring studied the map. He didn't mind "gals," but fighting pirates was hardly his specialty. As if he had a specialty, besides fulgus. He'd commanded a unit of Zhengahk militia at the tail end of the War, though. Taking care of a band of pirates could hardly rival fighting Death Bringers. And a job like this would be easier on Figgo.

Terring had offered Figgo as generous a severance as he could. But they both knew it wasn't enough. Figgo had never become part of the little exile community from his homeland and, worse, he was unregistered. Even if Terring wangled a clerkship for him from his brother, nothing in heaven or on earth would get Figgo a work permit. The Norvadale government simply no longer issued them. Terring couldn't abandon Figgo, severance or no severance. For this job, though, he could put him up safely at the various lodges along the road. Pirates preferred the easier pickings of caravans. Figgo would be safe.

"I'll take it," Terring said.

"You'll be doing the world a favor, so to speak. These ones aren't happy with just loot. Or let's say they consider women loot." He puffed the cigar, sending out a foul cloud. "Then they kill 'em."

>> <<

ONCE UPON A TIME, SOLYRA might have found the Beechen Lodge over-rustic. But after a week riding in a coach whose springs were evidently wrecked, and nights spent in moldy way stations, the tiny pine-paneled room the steward showed her epitomized gracious comfort. And if the Beechen was a bit musty — well, it lay in the Wudu Forest, right? Hewn from the pines that towered around it. The place was clean, and the staff, from the stableboy to the clerks to the steward were efficient and courteous, in a brusque, woodsy way.

"Ye privy chamber be at th'end of ye hall, mahm." The steward's eyes roamed the room as he spoke. "There be bathing pools near ye grand..." He whipped out a rag and snapped down a small cobweb over the window. "Bathing pools near ye grand porch," he resumed complacently, "a poker parlor, sewer for ye clothes—" it sounded as if he meant midden, but he must have referred to a tailor, or maybe a laundry "—and all business services. May I do ought else for ye, mahm?"

"No, thank you." She over-tipped him, judging by his raised eyebrows and smug nod.

"I'll leave ye, then, mahm, and just ask whom ye see if ye need ought else."

Above "ought else," Solyra craved a bath, but first she couldn't resist lying down on the moss-stuffed mattress. Extending her limbs fully was paradise after the dwarfish rope beds at the way stations. And solitude was sweet. From here on out, privacy would be extinct.

If there were a "here on out." The driver had turned back when they arrived at the Lodge. Only caravans continued west.

Solyra had not the faintest idea what caravaning involved. Would she need her own conveyance and animals — mules? horses? camels? She'd never driven a team of any kind; she'd always rolled around town in a rackety gig drawn by a plac-id old mare. Zago certainly didn't drive, and her new friend Diaa, when asked, giggled something about a dog-cart — a cart drawn by a dog? Even a mastiff couldn't drag them and their fulgus over prairies, mountains, and desert. Supplies brought to mind vague coils of rope, burlap sacks of beans, slabs of bacon, buckets of axle grease.

But never mind business for the blissful moment. The vermin-free bed gave deliciously to her body, and the screened, open window let in cool air, the burble of a stream, and the songs of forest birds settling in for the night.

Solyra opened her eyes again to twilight, and a soft knock at the door.

"Solyra?" Diaa called.

Solyra sat up. Her head felt boggy. "Come in."

The door cracked open and Diaa peeked in. "You asleep? It's dinner time."

"Oh." Solyra rubbed her face. "Come on in, Diaa, but brace

yourself. I must look...." She stopped herself from saying, she must look like a troll.

The onza could hardly take that personally, though. She was very pretty, with rosy round cheeks — the purple and blue teeth marks nearly faded away — and bright golden eyes. The tufts at the top of her ears and at the inside ends of her eyebrows, her silky soft, pinkish-orange hair, and the catlike resonance of her voice made her all the more charming. Her lips concealed the sharp, fanglike incisors most of the time.

Solyra pulled her hair into a net and they went to eat. Nearly full, the dining room clattered with noise and conversation. The last time Solyra had seen such an array of people had been at the fulgus convention in Booton that Dahn had dragged her to. The Beechen array was quite a bit more rustic, and foreign.

Rather, she was foreign. She wore a caftan, while most of the other women, like the men, wore short tunics and trousers tucked into their boots. Parties of trekkers sported leather shorts and knit jerseys.

At the fulgus convention, Solyra had been embarrassed by the evening dress on some of the women: nothing but jewelry and slinky ankle-length skirts that rested low at the hips. She'd been even more embarrassed after Dahn bullied her to adopt the fashion, though that had turned out to be only the preliminary humiliation.

Never mind. The most appalling sight in the Beechen dining room, fashionwise, was knobby knees and hairy calves. The homey, wholesome scene made her almost light-hearted.

After a meal of broiled trout and tender green stalks — "fairns" as the waiter called them — and a shared bottle of wine, her heart grew lighter still. And it just about floated free when Diaa claimed among her Lodge friends several caravan captains.

"We need a caravan captain, badly," Solyra said.

"Don't you worry," Diaa purred. "I will fix us up with a nice, brawny man."

Solyra wasn't quite sure it was a good idea. It had turned out, Diaa had run from the trollhouse several times before, each time returning to her husband. The troll had basically sold Diaa for a gold doubloon, and repeat flights could be lucrative. But Solyra understood Diaa returning to her husband, troll that he was. She herself had never gathered the courage even to try leaving Dahn.

So, maybe Diaa had deceived them, a bit, to stage her escape, but Solyra had detected no viciousness in her. And she was proving to be clever and hardworking.

Solyra put a hand on Diaa's arm. "Diaa, I can't pay you wages."

Diaa must have guessed what was coming, for her face lit up, and she gave a little purring trill.

"But if you help me with business," Solyra continued, "I'll cover your expenses to come with us. And I can also give you a good reference." Solyra would have liked to extend the promise of a big, fat bonus, once they got the fulgu cultivation frame raised, but she didn't want to reveal her plan for fear of Zago finding out.

Diaa's golden eyes shone. "I'll work hard for you, zizera. Like a aide, eh?"

"Like an aide," Solyra agreed.

>> <<

TERRING HAD HOPED NEVER TO see a sight like this again: a scattering of the dead, killed in violence. Seven men, two elderly women, and three children. Theoretically, he'd seen worse. Battlefields, sacked villages. But any slaughter was sickening.

The young woman they had found, not far into the woods, only added to the misery. She had been left, accidentally, alive. Three days on, she still crouched naked in a bramble thicket with the corpse of another young woman. Lady Liberty had her now. Heaven grant that her body and mind be healed. With face slack, eyes staring blank, she'd told what happened.

The caravan had been struck at nightfall. A ruthless attack, and efficient, if that was the right word. The pirates, their heads completely hooded, made quick work of killing the men, elders, and children. They looted the wagons. Then they raped the young women, then killed them. Except for the one.

Unfortunately, she had been unable to offer any description of the men, except that the leader had a big, bushy beard. "And he laughed a lot," she said. Terring had ended the interview at that point. When she began to shudder uncontrollably.

As his crew set to work burying the poor souls, Terring circled the area again, mostly on his hands and knees, searching for a print of man or horse, something dropped, a button, anything. The place the pirates brought the women was littered with bottles and the remains of a feast, but nothing revealed where their lair might be.

They were clever, even if each attack was more audacious than the last. When they'd finished their debauchery, they'd left the area via the road, rather than going immediately off into the forest. Three days' traffic and a heavy rainfall erased their path.

As in the other raids, the pirates struck exactly when a vulnerable caravan — and no other traffic — traveled that disputed and hence unguarded stretch of road. They also hit caravans carrying valuable, portable and easily resold goods. Such precision and the fact that every attacked caravan had come from the Beechen surely meant that a staff member at the Lodge was in league with the pirates.

Terring and his company had traveled from the trollhouse at the border nearly without stopping. Terring wanted to push on, but the horses simply had to rest.

"We'll head toward the Beechen at first light," Terring told his lieutenant, Cynta. "With any luck, we'll get there before the next caravan takes off."

Lying on a lumpy bedroll in a moldy tent, Terring had to wonder why he was doing this. Had he not had enough of violence? Of hunting men? Hunting bad men. Killers and rapists. There were easier ways to make money, but at least here he might do some good, rather than rotting away at the family business.

He'd fought four long years, in the Zhengahk. When it was over, he had nothing left at his ranch but a hero's welcome. His fulgu frame had long since crashed. He'd blamed Dahn's maneuvers for his subsequent woes, but the reason the insurance adjuster denied Terring's claims had nothing to do with Dahn. Neglect had crashed Terring's fulgu frame.

Fighting the Death Bringers instead of tending the frame had seemed right, at the time. It still did, even if it had destroyed his life's work and left memories that would haunt him forever.

He closed his eyes against his thoughts, against the tide of self-pity.

And saw Solyra. Not biting her lips. He saw her as she first came into the conference room, that last time they were together. She had looked like a woman convinced that all her troubles were at an end.

He grasped the image of her, eyes glowing, cheeks pink with excitement, her lips trembling not with chagrin but with a barely contained excitement.

Once upon a time, he would have given his life to bring that look to her face....

Not a good idea to brood over that. Just let the memory of that moment, her fragile joy, drown this day's anguish.

>> <<

ON SEEING THAT THE BATHING pools at the Beechen were mixed-sex, Solyra almost decided she could do without. But the bathing costume given out by the dressing room attendant surely preserved decencies.

The pools, lobes off a meandering channel, had benches around their walls, so that bathers could sit and be submerged more or less neck-deep. The pools closest to the source looked boiling hot. At the further end, the pools were lukewarm and shallow, apparently designed for children, though at this hour no families visited the pool. In fact, most of the pools were empty and the little bandstand was dark.

"Look, there's my friends!" Diaa pointed to a noisy pool at the hot end of the pool, filled with bearded men and rimmed with glasses and bottles. "We'll have a caravan captain before the night is done." Before Solyra had a chance to answer, Diaa darted off, tearing off her swimming costume as she went.

Solyra was torn between the certainty that she should get Diaa out of that pool and the impulse to slink back to her room.

"Solyra!" Zago waved at her from a pool about midway. She hesitated, then went and eased into the pool with him.

He wore only skivvy shorts. Solyra looked away from his hairless chest, then beckoned to an attendant. "Can you please bring me soap? And shampoo?"

"Yes, mahm."

"And a bottle of bubbly," Zago put in.

"O' course, sarr."

Zago looked as if he'd already had more than his share of bubbly, his eyes half-mast and his head lolling on a sponge pillow at the edge of the pool.

The attendant brought the bottle and glasses then left, hopefully to fetch the soap and shampoo. Solyra sipped the bubbly. She'd had similar wines, but this tasted particularly pleasant: sweet and pearlike, refreshing rather than cloying.

The soap and shampoo arrived in little flasks on a tray, along with a fuzzy towel. Solyra scrubbed and rinsed, reaching under the bathing costume as discreetly as she could, and all the dirt and lather flowed out of drains set around the pool rim. The tensions of the week, too, seemed to flow gently away.

"This is lovely," Solyra sighed. "Like being in a big cup of warm bubbly." She giggled. "Or tea." She put her head back on a pillow that had appeared as if by magic, and gazed up at the

star-filled sky. The breeze carried the scent of the tall dark ev-
ergreens, and though the air chilled, the water warmed Solyra's
body.

"Why don't we go up a pool?" Zago asked.

Solyra could have stayed in their pool forever, but if Zago
wanted.... "Good idea."

Out of the water, the true nature of the bathing costume
became evident. It clung to her skin, revealing every bulge,
curve, nook and cranny of her goose-bumped body. The men
in Diaa's pool swiveled to look as Solyra, hunched over, darted
to the next pool, then to the next at Zago's, "No, let's try that
one." A burst of laughter came from the hot pool and Diaa's
high, hoarse voice scolding. At least Solyra could blame the hot
water for her blush.

Relative to the men in Diaa's pool, Zago made but a poor,
scrawny specimen, but he was enviably unselfconscious in
his skimpy skivvy shorts. The bubbly might have helped. He
dipped in beside her and handed her a full glass. The cold air
had sobered her; still, she wasn't sure she wanted any more
bubbly. She sipped it anyway.

"Ah, that's good," she said. Last one, she told herself.

Zago muttered something in reply.

"What did you say?" Solyra asked.

He shot the rest of his glass as if it were liquor. "You can
take it off, you know." He mumbled again, but this time Solyra
heard him. "To get cleaner, you know."

His suggestion was hardly in interest of hygiene. But the
bathing costume did feel awkward. And heavy. Solyra slowly
pulled the tunic over her head, dropped it on the side of the
pool, pulled off the trousers and put them atop the tunic.

"Kapow!" Diaa's high, hoarse voice made her start as she
settled back. "My head spun like a rolehpoleh!" Her voice
dropped again into the laughter of the men in the pool with
her.

Out the corner of her eye, Solyra saw the attendant collect

the bathing costume and Zago's shorts and leave a couple of napped white caftans. So this is what people did, and Diaa's friends had been laughing at her keeping the bathing costume on all this time. She gave a laugh at herself and put her head back on the cushion. A shooting star traced white overhead. Surely an auspicious omen.

The warm water lapped on her bare skin. It really did feel better in this pool—

A hand touched her thigh.

She curled up so fast she almost dunked her face, her knees pulled up, her arms wrapping around them.

"Did I hurt you?" Zago sounded dismayed, even frightened.

You're no wife, Dahn had said. *You're a tight little prude.*

Solyra could have wept with shame and chagrin, just as she had when Dahn said those words to her.

But that was then. She forced herself to uncoil. She was no longer the girl that Dahn tried to break. And Zago wasn't Dahn. Far from it.

Comparing Zago to Dahn chased back Solyra's tears and nearly brought a smile to her face, relaxing Zago's worried frown to a tentative smile.

"I was just startled." Then she whispered, "Let me have more bubbly."

Zago began to refill Solyra's glass. But she took the bottle from him and drank straight from it. They killed the rest of it that way. As the last of it tickled down her throat, Solyra felt Zago's hand again, this time on her breast. She forced herself not to flinch away, and maybe he thought her shudder was pleasure.

Maybe it was, too. Solyra's feelings didn't match the passion in the penny-novels she'd read, as Zago caressed her and kissed her and finally entered her. But it didn't hurt, either. His gentle touch comforted, in a way, and she found herself happy when Zago settled back in his seat with a deep sigh of gratification.

"Thank you, Solyra," he whispered. "That meant a lot to me."

"Me, too," she whispered back.

"Did you… Did you enjoy it at all?"

The question nipped a rough edge into her pleasure. "Of course I enjoyed it." She sounded like a child defending herself. "It was nice, Zago. Really."

She reached for the bottle, then remembered it was all drunk up.

CAPTAIN REDBEARD & CAP'N FROGBELLY

SOLYRA DIDN'T FEEL ANY BETTER or worse than could be expected, as she staggered to "ye privy" down the hall, considering how much she'd drunk the night before. Head like a cracked bowling ball; stomach like a dozen coarsely chopped lemons, peel and all; icepicks chipping at her eyeballs; limbs palsied and weak. She'd never been a big drinker, but she knew first-hand the cost of a bender.

The cure was to knock down some coffee or the local equivalent, and to get something hot and salty in her stomach. Given the level of efficiency she'd seen so far from the Beechen staff, they'd probably take one look at her and supply just what she needed.

Just as they had for Zagu last night. A few bottles of bubbly and the lady jumped into his lap. But wasn't that just what she'd needed, too?

Her marriage had been not about love. It had been about pain and shame. Widowhood followed, and panic. Yet Dahn had done her a favor, in a perverse way, by leaving a financial

shambles. In reviving the fulgus business, Solyra had rediscov-
ered a spark of pride. Being unable to find her parents had cast
a deep shadow; Dahn had severed contact with them. Yet, busy
and challenged, she'd discovered a kind of happiness, even
without the joys of love — whatever they might be. A friend
asked once how she could stand living in the building where
she worked. She'd loved it. She'd loved the feeling of being
cradled in the security of her business, her own little empire.

Her own little empire that Terring demolished as easily as
a baby knocking down a pile of blocks. Her home was now just
an item to be auctioned, though the building and everything
in it would never cover her debts. But they hadn't nabbed her
fulgu pods, and when she returned home, by gum, she'd return
in grand old style.

For now, she'd settle for not looking too much the trollette. She made herself presentable with the help of a maid, a
basin and pitcher of warm water, and — blessing of blessings
— a little gourd of matte tea. It wasn't coffee, but it rendered
Solyra nearly human by the time she entered the dining room.

The waiter did, indeed, bring her just what she needed
as soon as she sat down: scrambled eggs covered with toma-
to sauce so spicy it made her eyes water, another gourd of
matte, and dry toast. She would hardly have been surprised if
they kept a roster somewhere of how much each guest drank,
cross-referenced with their age, weight and gender. Zago must
have already gotten a treatment; he looked chipper and the
uncertainty of his smile relaxed when she met his eyes with a
smile of her own.

They didn't speak of the night before, but touched hands,
once, and smiled at each other again. It was all wrong, consort-
ing with an employee, but it sure felt nice.

"Where's Diaa?" Solyra asked as she pushed her plate away.

"Asleep, I guess. She was still carousing when we left the
pool."

"I bet."

It had been a fool's hope after all, to think that one of Diaa's hairy men would save Solyra the ordeal of finding a captain herself.

The waiter began to clear the table. "Sirrah," Solyra said to him, "is there a — a bureau of wagon train organization at the Lodge?"

"Yay, mahm. In ye business center, ote by ye livery yard, there be a caravansary, where such like arrangements be made, and ye jobbers and so on."

"Thank you so much."

A series of neat fingerposts pointed the way to the business center, a log-made building like the Lodge itself, but newer, with a big front window framed by pillars of rustic stonework. From its porch, Solyra could hear animals lowing, mooing, roaring, braying, clucking and barking in a coral out of sight but not out of smell. A post in the lobby bristled with more fingerposts pointing in various directions for various functions; Solyra and Zago followed CARAVANSARY.

Solyra recognized one of the men lounging around the un-lit stove in the center of the room. His bushy red beard had floated above the waters of Diaa's pool last night. The moment he set eyes on Solyra and Zago, his face split into a knowing grin. Solyra disliked him immediately.

He bustled over before any of his companions had a chance to stir. "A good friend tells me you are looking for a caravan captain, sirrah, and I am pleased to offer the best terms."

Knowing grin, wild beard and all, the man was well-spoken, even if he had addressed Zago, not herself. Solyra was used to that, though, and it wouldn't hurt to interview him. If nothing else, they could get a feel for the business.

"We can talk, Captain — is that your correct title, sirrah?"

"Aye, mahm, Captain it is." He led them to a table by the window. The other men around the stove fell silent as they passed, watching them with an air of resignation mixed with idle interest. They were a scruffy lot — just as she would be, a week or so out from the amenities of Beechen Lodge.

The discussion with Redbeard dragged, and the previous night's bubbly, together with the past week's flight numbed her mind, but Solyra didn't let her guard down. The gourds of matte that a waiter brought to the table helped.

Redbeard produced a list of supplies down to the last bit of straw. He knew the business, no doubt of that. He claimed they would travel in comfort and style; a wealthy prince and his entourage would be part of the train. Solyra hadn't seen anyone fitting that description, but likely they were keeping private quarters. Three gourds later, winding up with the "extras" Redbeard had on offer — coffee the only one Solyra even considered — he pounded lightly on the table.

"Now come and look at my beautiful beasts and be convinced that I am the best captain you can find."

As they passed the circle of men, Solyra happened to catch the eye of one of them, an unkempt dark-hair with a pallid wedge of paunch hanging between a grimy jersey shirt and baggy shorts. He lifted one finger and wagged it back and forth, then turned back to his friends.

It was a private signal, just to her, but what the meaning was, she surely couldn't say. Was it obscene? Was he one of the men who had gawked at her last night at the pool? Comfy as Beechen Lodge was, the sooner she got away, the better.

Zago winced at the cacophony of sounds as they went in the barnyard. "We can't use mules," he whispered in Solyra's ear.

"The fulgus will just have to put up with it," she whispered back. She hated the hoarse roar and bray of mules as much as any self-respecting fulgu might, but picking and choosing what kind of animals would haul their freight was not on Redbeard's list of extras.

"And here, sirrah and mahm, is my string of lovelies." Redbeard swept his hand over a stinking pen crowded with donkeys, mules, dogs and horses. "My lords of the road, my trustworthy and submissive beasts."

When Solyra gently held a hand toward a donkey at the edge of the crowded pen, it bared its teeth. Redbeard flicked the animal's nose with the whip he carried. The donkey flinched back, its eyes watering.

"Be not dismayed, mahm," Redbeard said. "Such confinement disheartens them. All are friendly enough, friendly enough." He thumped the donkey's flank. "Be nice to the lady, Hildinga."

Solyra's dislike of the man resurfaced. And something was wrong with his animals.

"They're perfect," Zago whispered to her. "Just perfect."

That was it. Surrounded by strange animals, jumbled together, the donkey flicked and thumped by its keepers, none made a sound beyond woofs of breath and clops of hooves. Solyra bent to look at the donkey's neck. Sure enough, a scar zigged along it. The animal's voice had been cut.

"Thank you, sirrah," she said. "I'll let you know my decision this evening."

Redbeard bowed. "As mahm wishes."

"What are you thinking, Solyra?" Zago hissed as they left the barnyard.

Solyra considered sending Zago off somewhere, anywhere, but she couldn't take a chance on some critical fulgu need being left out of the negotiations. "Just leave it to me," she said.

The men at the cold stove turned when she and Zago came back in the business center, then huddled together, maybe drawing lots for the next chance.

The potbellied man stood, hitched up his shorts, and came over to their table. A wiry young man and a fat, glossy black and brown dog trailed him.

"Cap'n Frogbelly, and my nephew Tad, at your service. And Queenie."

"Captain Frogbelly? I'm—"

"Cap'n Frogbelly, mahm."

"Captain—"

"Cap'n, mahm. Frogbelly. Cap'n Frogbelly. At your service, mahm."

Solyra nearly sent him away. But among the men lounging around the stove, Cap'n Frogbelly had been the only one to give her a warning about Redbeard, if that's what the finger waggle had been. And she liked the smile crinkles at the corners of his eyes.

"Let's talk then, if you please, Cap'n." Solyra laid her map on the table. "We're going to the Zhengahk."

Frogbelly pushed the map in front of Tad, who bent over it. The map's labels were in Zhi'nging'ha!, but the symbols were clear enough. Dahn had outlined the property in red, when he'd boasted of carrying her out there "to a new life."

"You really want to go to the Zhengahk?" Tad asked without looking up from the map.

"That's correct." Solyra spoke with an air of assurance. She hoped.

"The Zhengahk," Tad said thoughtfully. "Land of Shining Orchards. That's what it used to be called. But now it's the Taglimagan, the Waste Land."

"Isn't that something," Solyra said, as if they were gossiping about a stage actor's secret baby. She pointed to Solyra Liberty. "That's my property, and my destination."

"Huh." Tad and Cap'n Frogbelly exchanged a look that held a whole conversation which, unfortunately, Solyra could not decipher. Then they leaned over the map, muttering in a jingly, sneezy language. Zhi'nging'ha!, Solyra guessed.

They might hope that since she possessed a Liberty bigger than the Wudu Forest they could soak her for loads of money. If so, they were doomed to disappointment. Drought and a decade of vicious lawlessness had rendered the vast property valueless — except for fulgu cultivation.

Supposedly, order had been restored in the region. Even

so, Dahn's contacts there could be long dead or moved on. She would have to recruit new engineers and linemen and purchase supplies from strangers.

But labor would be cheap, wouldn't it, in a region so hard set? She needed the labor to be cheap. She needed equipment to be cheap, too. And officials. And supplies. She needed everything to be cheap. Her gold coins, snuggled in a pouch slung around her neck, could only go so far.

Never mind. She'd go as far as she could, and then she'd go the rest of the way.

"You're picking a long, hard road, mahm," Frogbelly said. "And a harsh—"

"Nevertheless, I intend to go to the Taglima — the Zhengahk. So, what will it cost? That is, if you gentleman will take me there."

Frogbelly slipped his dog a dab of butter from the dish on the table while Tad asked the inevitable, dreaded question, "Are you carrying freight?"

Captain Redbeard had pretty much breezed over the freight question. Zago had gone to the loo, leaving it to Solyra to sweat out the negotiations. She lowered her voice while trying not to sound like a smuggler, which would offer yet another opportunity for extortion. "I'm carrying fulgus. Pod grade, that is. Not valuable, particularly, nor do they take much room."

She handed over the manifests, and Tad and Frogbelly had another exchange in Zhi'nging'ha!. Solyra didn't understand the language, but she thought she caught her name and "fulgus." She'd had to put her name on the manifests, but did she hear Frogbelly say "Dahn Fulgus"?

Her heart jumped into double-time. She'd left off the corporate name, in the hope of throwing her creditors off the scent.

"And your personal baggage, mahm?" Frogbelly asked.

Slowly, quietly, Solyra let out her breath. "My two assistants and I have a carpetbag each."

"Traveling light, eh?" Tad asked.

Solyra resisted the temptation to spin an explanation of why she was going to the back of beyond with just a carryall. This time she would stick to the driver's advice: *Keep it simple, zizera.*

"Traveling light," she echoed. "And one more thing. The fulgu pods need to be watered regularly. So we'll need to carry water." She tried hard to keep the whine out of her voice.

"No need to carry water, mahm, except at the very end," Frogbelly said. "Animals and people need to drink. We'll take roads with water at hand."

"Oh. Of course." Redbeard hadn't bothered to explain that. "So what will your rate be?" She started as the dog's cold wet nose prodded her fingers.

"Sit down, Queenie." Frogbelly gave the dog another dab of butter. "As I said, it's a rugged stretch. Everyone will have to bear a hand, crew and passengers alike."

"I understand," Solyra said.

After more discussion in Zhi'nging'ha!, Frogbelly offered a price of passage half that of Redbeard's. Solyra went over the terms again. They were the same, except the need to "bear a hand." Given that he and his nephew exuded competence, rather than oiliness, Solyra was inclined to go with him. She only wished Frogbelly had availed himself of the bathing pools of the Lodge. He gave off a potent combination of animal and human body odor.

"May I take a look at your animals and conveyances?" she asked.

"Yes, mahm."

Zago came back, and they went to the hostelry.

Frogbelly carried freight in what he called "ships," big-wheeled wagons with high sides and hooped tarp covers. His draft horses, kept in the stable, were huger even than the draft horses back home. The saddle and pack animals, an assortment of mules, horses, ponies, and donkeys, milled in their own corral.

When Solyra reached cautiously into the corral, a donkey and a mule took turns butting their heads against her hands. A pony shoved its face into Frogbelly's armpit, tickling him into helpless laughter. Solyra could have sworn that the other animals started braying and neighing with laughter, too.

"It's too noisy," Zago muttered.

"It's fine," Solyra said.

"There's only one more possible hitch," Frogbelly said.

Solyra swallowed a groan. "What is that?"

"We're looking to set out this afternoon."

Solyra could have wept with relief. Instead, she beamed. "We'll be ready."

PIRATES!

SOLYRA AND DIAA ARRIVED LAST to the caravan, meaning they got last pick of the saddle animals. The prince and his entourage, evidently having decided on Frogbelly instead of Redbeard, had reserved the best mounts.

It made no difference. The tea-server at the Beechen had let drop that this would be the last caravan of the year, heading to the Zhengahk. No one crossed the mountains in the winter. Solyra would ride a badger out if she had to.

Diaa wouldn't pick an animal, badger, donkey, or horse. "I will walk."

Frogbelly, passing by, paused. "You'd be better off riding."

"No way." She was still pouty over Solyra passing over her chum Redbeard.

"Mahm," Frogbelly said, "you'd best—"

"She'll ride," Solyra broke in quickly. She waited until Frogbelly was out of range. "Why not, Diaa?"

"I like to walk." She hunched her shoulders as a hostler led a horse by.

"All the animals are nice, and you need to get used to riding. Later, we might not have a choice."

A strapping young crewman with a thin braid hanging over one eye and a ring in his lip, led up a donkey. "Come, little lady," he said to Diaa. "I, Bo, will lesson you in riding."

Where Solyra had no sway, a rascally looking hostler did. Diaa let Bo help her mount the animal. Slight as Diaa was, her feet dangled only about a foot-length from the ground, but she wouldn't put them in the stirrups. "Ah keep 'em ready to jump off." Solyra didn't bother to persuade. Once the animal got moving, Diaa would gladly use the stirrups.

Solyra went to her own mount, an aged gelding. The tack was ugly, but well-maintained, and the saddle reasonably comfortable. Solyra asked one of the hostlers to tether her horse to the main wagon, so she could read as they went.

The fat portfolio she pulled from her luggage was Hoggins' Log. Not riveting, but as Solyra opened it, she silently sent thanks over the miles to her clerk, who'd had the presence of mind to stick it in her baggage during those frantic hours before the flight from Norvadale. The Log was worth more than her paltry handful of jewels and doubloons.

Hoggins, the first engineer to raise a fulgu frame, had kept meticulous record of his trials and tribulations, and though his frame had crashed over fifteen years ago, frame engineers still lived by his tome. His Log was not a mere log or business diary. The book encompassed the entire business. Copies of invoices recorded all the things men needed for living in an unforgiving terrain — food, clothes, tools, livestock, charcoal, various sundries, and the frame materials themselves. Payroll records, schematics, and construction schedules added to its value. Hoggins' daily entries completed the picture.

Each entry began with a note on the weather. The Norvadale papers had carried stories of the horrendous drought that had scoured the Zhengahk, but Hoggins had been there in better times. Many of his weather notes read *Hot, dry, clear* or *Hot, dry, dust storm*, but many also recorded *rainfall* and *cool and pleasant*.

The entries included the names of workers, if any, down with illness or injury — heatstroke and frostbite, a horrible burn from mishandling the frame, several injured in an explosion. Deaths, too: *RIP, Barney, lightning; RIP, Holmes, bloody flux.* Gempy whose foot was crushed by fulgu crate, became *RIP, Gempy, gangrene.* Solyra didn't know if the death toll was appalling, or sad but not unusual.

She really didn't know much about fulgu frame raising at all. Hoggins Log meant that at least she'd have the knowledge to hire the right people to get the frame up and running.

Although her father had clerked for a bank that invested in fulgus, Solyra had grown up with the vague idea that fulgus were stones that grew like crops in fields out west. It was an average layman's ignorance. It wasn't until Dahn died that she plumbed the depths of that ignorance, struggling against sleep, night after night, to read everything she could about fulgus.

Fulguologists called the fulgus "fulguic petrites," a waffling way to say they didn't know exactly what fulgus were, since the mineral content mingled with organic components. The "fields" — the rare tracts of land where fulgus could be cultivated — lay in the Zhengahk, and energy fulgus, the kind that could be used by people, grew not on the ground but on "frames," wire netting stretched between upright posts about chest-high to a man. Each post was capped by a pod fulgu, the kind Solyra had.

Not even advanced fulguologists understood the process by which energy fulgus appeared and "ripened" in the frame's netting. Somehow the currency emitted by pod fulgus drew them. Zago's fulgu rights movement pamphlets had it that, "the infant fulgus burgeon in the bliss of their elders, never knowing the devastating truth: that those elders themselves are enslaved in turn to enslave them…."

Fulgu rights nuts could, mostly be ignored. A dented frame post could be ignored. The nets were heartbreakingly expensive, but a tear in them was easily fixed. However, if the current got wobbly — because of too many new fulgus, a lightning strike, a sloppily installed or poorly maintained pod fulgu, or if new fulgus stayed in the net too long — it had to be corrected immediately. Otherwise, the resulting oscillations would bring down the whole system: the frame would crash.

And that was the end of the field. The frame materials could be reused, but not on the same field, and given the rarity of fulgu fields, a crash usually meant the end of a business.

It had happened to Terring.

>> <<

TERRING'S COMPANY MOVED QUICKLY — he prayed quickly enough.

On arriving at the Beechen the night before, he could have punched a hole clear through the stout stone wall of the caravansary when he'd learned that a caravan had left that afternoon. He'd been too late to save the previous caravan. He might be too late, again, to save this one.

The Beechen clerk had confirmed that a wealthy prince was traveling with the caravan. A tea server had gleaned the impression that the departing caravan carried something contraband. That would mean, something valuable. Never mind that the bearers were breaking the law. What the bandits dealt out was no kind of justice, and no one deserved it. There were a couple of women on the caravan, too. So much the worse.

Each time the pirates struck, they struck with precision, hitting the richest caravans at just the right time and place. That, and the description offered by the woman who'd survived the most recent depredation pointed to a caravan captain called Redbeard. As a caravaner, he would have access to exactly the right information. He was audacious, this Redbeard, hiding in plain sight. Except attacking unarmed or lightly armed men, women and children was anything but audacious.

It reminded Terring of the Deathbringers. A shudder took him. He'd left Figgo at the Beechen, though, absurdly, his assistant had wanted to come along. Terring just told him no. He didn't want to rub in the fact, obvious as it was, that Figgo would be a hindrance, that his exquisite skills as a scribe, an accountant, a preternaturally savvy business manager had no place in stalking bandits. Figgo had offered that he could hear and smell things the sighted could not. He might sense the presence of the bandits before the others.

But Terring didn't give in. He couldn't bring himself to drag Figgo into a scene like the shambles of the previous raid. As Figgo himself said, his other senses filled in his lack of sight. He would smell the blood, hear the sobs — if any lived to weep. Whether or not Figgo had been present when the Death-bringers sacked his village and did away with his family, Terring wasn't going to risk exposing Figgo to another scene of slaughter and misery.

Terring didn't want to expose himself to another scene of slaughter and misery.

His patrol was surely more nimble than a band of thieves. And his men and women were more than satisfactory. Strong and able and eager to nab the pirates. Not only for the reward, though that helped. They were genuinely bent on justice.

When Terring's lieutenant Cynta, a woman with a deceptively soft face, held up a hand, the company halted. No buzz of question, no complaints. Well-trained and well-disciplined, they listened.

An infection during the War had dulled Terring's hearing, and fleetingly, he wished he'd brought Figgo after all. But it took only a few moments to read in their faces what the others were hearing. An attack.

Terring had only to bark "Go!" and the company charged up the road.

Redbeard was immediately recognizable: a huge red beard hung below his mask. And he was laughing. A woman was slung over the withers of his horse — dead? Or unconscious? Redbeard lashed a riding crop down on the thighs of the woman.

She might have quivered, or just been stirred by the force of the blow, for as Redbeard raised his arm again, she remained utterly limp. Were it not for the risk of hitting the woman, Terring would have sent a bolt from his crossbow right into the man's chest.

Absorbed in his sport, Redbeard didn't notice Terring's company until they were nearly upon him. Still, he had enough time to dump the woman on the road and take off into the trees.

Terring wasn't concerned. His troops were already in pursuit. Then his heart lurched to a stop and his mind froze.

The woman sprawled on the road was Solyra.

Terring snapped back to awareness. Cynta had already dismounted, and she knelt beside Solyra.

That allowed Terring to pursue Redbeard personally.

>> <<

A HORSE HOOF STOMPED IN front of Solyra's face and she curled into a ball. She waited for it to be over.

She barely felt the injuries she knew she'd sustained. When the masked leader — Redbeard, she knew — had pulled her up, her body had slammed across his lap, the saddle edge hitting her belly and ribs like a club. One hand gripped her hair, pulling her head back, while another hand plunged down her dress to find, seize, and tear away the pouch of doubloons hidden there, and on the way out to squeeze her breasts so hard, she screamed. Her hair still wound in the rough fist, Solyra screamed again as a burning line seared the back of her legs, another her buttocks, and another and another. Above the shouting of men and horses and the clash and thumps and blows of fighting, above her own sobs: Redbeard's growling laughter.

She went quiet and limp. That was how to make the whipping stop soonest.

And suddenly she was sprawled on the road. She knew she should get up, run, get out from this battle churn of thuds and cries, horses stamping and neighing. Instead, she curled into a ball. The sounds grew fainter as Solyra sank into something like sleep. A cocoon of oblivion.

"Mahm?" A woman's voice, a hand gently touching her back. "You're safe now. You're safe."

Solyra believed it, with her mind. But she couldn't seem to uncoil herself. Then another voice. Tad.

"Zizera Solyra?"

Solyra let herself take in the sounds around her. Not screams and thuds and trampling hooves, but voices issuing orders, sobs, footsteps. The prince spewed shrill threats against the people who, Solyra realized, had rescued them. Tad helped her to her feet.

"Everyone all right?" Her voice was so faint, she could barely hear herself.

"Yeah. Well, we are. Not the pirates."

Solyra's stomach heaved when she looked around. Several men, still hooded, lay dead. One had been trampled and his entrails mixed with the dust of the road.

Tad held her arm. "What about you, zizera?"

Solyra forced a smile and nodded, though she couldn't meet his eyes. "Just…bruised."

He pointed to a enclosed wagon. "Get Peg to take a look at you."

Solyra was limping toward the wagon when Zago ran to her. "Solyra! Thank Bih you're all right!"

"Solyra! Solyra!" Diaa joined them, her face flushed and clothes tousled.

"Careful, don't hug me," Solyra said. "I think my ribs might be cracked. What about you?"

"I was so scared," Diaa whimpered. "I thought that Red-beard killed you." Her voice rose into a snarl. "And that other one who touched you!" She whirled away and ran to where a few of the Frogbellies were shoveling the horse-trampled bandit off the road.

The men backed off, daunted by her fury. Her hair stood up in a ridge from her brow to the nape of her neck and her lips were drawn back in a snarl as she hunched over the dead bandit. "You are cursed!" Her screaming yowl nearly drowned her own words. She kicked the head, sending a gobbet of brain flying, and then spat on the body with all her might.

"Diaa, Diaa, come here, come here," Solyra crooned. She couldn't bear more violence. "Come here, honey, come here."

Diaa panted and stared, then ran back to Solyra and Zago, her lips barely covering her fangs. They all stood embraced, lightly, favoring Solyra's ribs, while around them Frogbelly's crew got the caravan back together. The prince had moved from complaint to loud boasts of slaying the largest of the bandits.

Diaa gave a growl. "I'd like to wring his lying lips. All he did was hide in the—"

Zago cut in. "Are you hurt anywhere else, Solyra?"

"I don't know." She bit her lip, as if that would steady her voice. "Are the fulgus all right?"

Zago nodded. "Luckily those fiends didn't set the wagons on fire."

"My things! We need to find my saddlebags. And the pouch."

But though they combed the area, they didn't turn up Solyra's pouch of doubloons or her saddlebags.

Her money was lost. So was Hoggins' Log.

AN UNEXPECTED MEETING

THE SETTING SUN WASHED THE sky pink and blue and gleamed gold over the grass that stretched in every direction as Terring and his company rode through the gate of the Oaks Wayside. A few survivors of Redbeard's outfit were headed for justice, trussed up tight and under guard. Terring's best mounted guardsman had gone back to the Beechen to get Figgo.

"No bubbly here, sir," Cynta said.

Terring grunted a laugh. The Beechen's proprietor had promised them bubbly, hot baths and sex workers of every persuasion if they would nab the bandits who threatened to put a serious dent in his business.

Unlike the Beechen, though, the Wayside was no resort. It was completely devoted to caravansary. The livery stable dwarfed the brick lodge, and the drovers lounging on the porch were scruffy and road-worn. Corrals and humpy pastures surrounded a collection of sheds and barns.

A couple of crew members from the raided caravan, staying back to search for the passengers' belongings, had assured Terring that everyone from the caravan was all right. So instead of galloping straight into the lodge to search for Solyra, Terring led his lathered, thirsty horse to water.

At one end of the tank, a young man arranged crates on some planks he'd laid in a cross hatch. The boxes, about an arm's length in all dimensions, had grids top and bottom, and were built to carry heavy cargo. If the design of the crates hadn't been a give-away, the young man would have. He had a typical fulgu keeper's look: dreamy eyes that belied the under-lying competence that it took to maintain fulgus, and a noodly body that belied the strength it took to lift fulgu lockers.

But where would Solyra — assuming these were hers — be bringing fulgus? The market for them, such as it was at the moment, was back in Norvadale. No one brought fulgus out west.

Unless….

"Mind if I take a look?" The young man completely ig-nored Terring. Rather, he was probably not even aware of him.

Terring swallowed hard at what he saw. A locker full of pod fulgus, fresh as harvest day. Not a wisp of steam or stench as the keeper sprinkled water over them. Prime. Three more lockers besides.

Terring could hardly breathe. He had not even suspected that Solyra inherited from her husband not only energy ful-gus but pods. She had also inherited Dahn's huge property out in the Zhengahk. A virgin property, for all of Dahn's claims of having suffered a frame crash there. She was bringing four lockers of frame fulgus to the Zhengahk to raise a frame.

Never in life had Terring expected an opportunity like this to come his way.

If it was an opportunity.

That would be up to Solyra. And Figgo, because since Terring didn't have a penny to his name, he'd need every bit of Figgo's know-how to wangle himself into this venture. If Figgo even agreed to try.

Terring's horse nosed him, as if to say, I'm done here, let's eat.

In the stables, Terring met the captain of the caravan, a sloppy man with the improbable name of Frogbelly. "Let my crew take care of your animals," Frogbelly said. "It's the least we can do. You go on and wash up. There's plenty of hot water for you all."

The man's animals looked glossy and content. Terring relinquished the reins. "Thanks."

As he crossed to the lodge, Terring went over Frogbelly's face in his mind. He couldn't shake the feeling he'd met the man before — under a different name. Or had he seen his face in the stack of WANTED posters he'd gone through, back at Bull Security? That was the problem with working security. You looked at everyone as a potential criminal. A smuggler? The tea-bearer at Beechen had been half-way sure the caravan was carrying contraband.

Ah. Terring stopped in the middle of the yard, then went on up the porch steps. Frogbelly — aka Carl Ruah — had owned a transportation company, back in Norvadale. When Ruah suddenly sold out last winter for less than what everyone thought the business was worth, it cast a little ripple in the community.

Maybe Ruah had found something more profitable than freighting. Like smuggling. No one would know better than a transportation man how to pull it off.

Whether or not Frogbelly and Carl Ruah were indeed the same person, if Frogbelly was moving contraband, even just untaxed rugs or porcelain, Terring, as a lawman, was honor and duty bound to report him.

Terring stopped again. Summer was just beginning here. But any caravan leaving now would barely reach the Zhengahk before winter snow blocked the mountain passes. If Frogbelly got stuck, Solyra would get stuck, too. She might reconsider the whole venture. Sell her pod fulgus to someone else.

"Cynta!" Terring called.

His deputy turned from the pump, where she was rinsing her hands. Rinsing off Redbeard's blood. "Yes, sir?"

Terring gestured her over.

"Sir?"

He took off the badge and handed it over. "I've just re-signed, and you're now Marshall. I'll send a message to Bull and let him know. Congratulations."

She stammered out a thanks, they shook hands, and he headed back toward the barn.

He had no money — he'd used even his pay advance to get mounts for himself and Figgo. He was surely the last person Solyra would want to do business with, except maybe Figgo. And speaking of Figgo, he undoubtedly would throw down his pen at the prospect of going into business with her, not to mention returning to his homeland, even if the Deathbringers had been defeated.

Cynta had stepped up. He'd stepped off a cliff.

Oh, well.

A couple of hours and several pots of tea later, Terring had been hired as security officer for Cap'n Frogbelly & Caravan. The pay was crap, but he and Figgo had their passage west. Not that Figgo even knew about this mad venture. He still had to talk him around. And bring Solyra around. But his step was lighter as he headed into the lodge.

>> <<

THE OAKS WAS A STEP or three down from the Beechen. Solyra didn't give a snuffed fulgu. All she wanted was a hot bath. And to hide. Forever.

Neither was an option. On arriving, Frogbelly set the car-avan to work. Diaa and Zago were tending the animals. Out of deference for Solyra's injury, presumably, Frogbelly sent her to the kitchen, where she was set to chopping onions. Even that was painful to her bruised ribs, but Solyra didn't want to be idle. If she was idle, she might think.

First of all, about what Terring was doing here. She'd gone out the side door to dump a dish of water into the wastewater barrel, and there he was at the tank, chatting with Zago.

Incredible. Perhaps terrifying. Definitely irritating.

He hadn't seen her, she was sure. Maybe he would think Zago was traveling on his own. More likely he'd figured out whose fulgus Zago was tending. And had she glimpsed a badge in his hand? The woman he spoke with, before heading to the lodge — sending Solyra scampering back into the kitchen — stood suspiciously straight. As if at attention, all but saluting. As if Terring was a Marshall, and she his lieutenant.

Solyra returned her attention to onions.

Frogbelly's cook was a gaunt and peg-legged woman — called Peg, of course — black-haired, then egg-bald after she stuffed her wig in her apron pocket. As they worked, she discussed Frogbelly's caravan, working her way methodically down the ranks.

"Did you see the Cap'n with his crossbow?" Peg asked as she briskly checked the chickens over for pinfeathers.

"No, I—"

"Gar, deadly. And his husband with that saber. You wouldn't think a stringbean like Tad would have it in him." It took Solyra a few moments to figure it out. The euphemisms of "nephew" and "uncle" didn't come into play with Peg.

"I suppose—"

"Not like that, Darklocks. Gar, that hair of yours would make me a nice wig." She gave a bark of laughter. "Chop the pieces nice and even. Big and small means some raw, some overcooked. You haven't done much kitchen work, have you?"

"I've baked—"

"Well, no matter. Let's see you try, now.

Solyra took up the next onion and chopped it carefully and evenly. Her kitchen at home was fulgu-powered, a sort of showroom, and she hadn't chopped anything so crude as an onion for years. Her eyes already watered, with a mountain of onions unpeeled at hand. Not quite like slivering a half cup of blanched almonds for tea cookies.

"Lovely. There's art for you," Peg said. "Remember: beauty before speed. Not that our Cap'n's blessed slubberty-gullions will know the difference. Just the same, we'll keep up standards, even under the boughs, eh? Or in a sea of grass, rather."

"You think we'll reach—"

"Raid or no raid, Cap'n Frogbelly's known for having the best chow on the road. And after all, Redbeard's devils didn't get any of the food, though I do believe they nabbed some baggage."

Solyra remembered a streak of blue the color of her beaded frock disappearing into the woods with the pirates who'd escaped, not to mention Hoggins' Log. And her gold. But she just couldn't think about that. Not yet, at least.

"We'll comfort the poor Cap'n with a proud feast," Peg continued. "He's in a right old-fashioned funk. Never heard of anyone raided this close to Beechen, and by a friend. Not that he and that pirate were true friends, of course. But friends don't raid friends, right? Don't you think that's cutting it a bit low?"

"Yes," Solyra said simply.

"So do I. But our Jerzy—" the head hostler "—did handsomely, and didn't his boys come on like heroes? Even that sorry old mutt of theirs got a good nip in."

Solyra wouldn't have called fat, complacent Queenie "sorry," but she didn't bother to say so.

"Only Brid got his pinky mangled on a line," Peg went on. "Poor lad. I think I'll have to chop it off. He didn't even notice when it happened, his blood was up so. I thought Jerzy would never be able to call the boys back. And you, gar, Darklocks, you were dead brave, you were. That nasty old Redbeard."

Solyra was glad the onions covered the tears that might have sprung to her eyes, had they not already been streaming down her face. Through the blur, she saw Peg shoot her a penetrating look.

"Go easy, now, Darklocks, cutting onions is tricky business. Remember, beauty before speed. And keep your knife sharp. Let me show you."

Solyra's kitchen had been equipped with a fulgu-powered Whirl-a-Whet. Peg demonstrated, with an ice-pick-like instrument, how to strop the knife, then watched as Solyra did it, dictating little corrections to the angles and sweep.

"Ai, Darklocks, you were a dangerous woman; now you're a right menace."

Solyra gave a sniffling laugh. "Beware, ye onions!" she cried.

"That's the spirit, my heart."

Peg made no other references to Solyra herself, but as Solyra worked through the onions, feeling as if all of the fluid in her body was streaming out her nose and eyes, she realized that the cook wasn't just gossiping about Frogbelly's entourage. She was offering comfort, reestablishing the caravan as a moving home that could defend itself, and placing Solyra in it by showing her the machinery of its relations.

It was but cold comfort. Solyra was soon to be spit out of that machinery. With her gold gone, she could no longer pay Frogbelly. She didn't even know how she'd pay her lodgings here. And what would she do about Zago and Diaa?

Poor Diaa, cheery as a bird. The attack, rather than unnerving her, seemed to have made her more fearless, and she'd graduated to riding a pony. For most of the hours it took to arrive at the Wayside, she stayed at the rear of the caravan, the caboose, as Frogbelly called it, chatting with her ring-lipped chum. Now and then she raced up to check on Solyra, her pinkish hair sticking up around her head like porcupine quills.

In Zago's world, as long as the fulgus were all right, everything and everyone else was all right. Well, that wasn't true.

He had been truly worried about her. But he didn't grasp the extent of her losses this day.

The two of them depended on her, and her bad luck was worse luck for them. Real tears threatened again to mingle with onion tears. She conquered Onion Mountain and was moving on to Potato Peaks when Peg put a hand on her arm.

"You rest, Darklocks. I'll take care of the potatoes."

Solyra gave a sigh. "Thanks, Peg. Do you mind if I take a couple of cold pies to my room? I don't know if I can make it to dinner." What she really meant was, she didn't know if she could face Frogbelly, and Diaa, and Zago, not to mention Terring — and his shadow Figgo, whom she'd glimpsed on the porch.

"You go right ahead."

As Solyra pulled off her apron, the scullery boy whose place she'd taken appeared at the door. "Mahm Solyra?"

"What is it, young sirrah?"

"Sirrah Terring asked me to say…." He licked his lips and shut his eyes. "Um…. Zizera Solyra, if you please, may we meet for breakfast after business…. I mean, for business. After breakfast. On the porch. The front porch. Um. Right. On the front porch of the lodge. Tomorrow morning."

Solyra owed Terring her life. Still, she was tempted to send back a message the boy would have no trouble remembering: No. But she nodded. "Tell zizero Terring, yes, I'll be there."

The boy started to leave, then turned back. "Oh! And this." He held out a bundle of cloth. "He said this is yours."

Solyra forced a smile. "Thank you."

In the room she and Diaa were sharing, Solyra spread the bundle on the bed. Her blue frock. Her "lucky" blue frock. It looked as if it had been in a tug of war between a thorn bush and a pirate. Snagged, stained, torn nearly in two, the crystal beads dangling, the embroidery ripped. Past repair.

Solyra slipped onto the back porch and sat alone on a

rough log bench, the plundered dress bunched to her face, her soft keen muffled in the blue silk.

After a while, she let the dress slide into her lap and stared, her eyes burning, into the dark trees.

Just a dress, and yet so emblematic of herself: her pride tattered, her luck unraveled, her confidence torn, perhaps damaged past repair. Long since damaged past repair. The idea that she'd remade herself after Dahn's death was no more substantial than a length of sky-blue silk.

"Solyra?" Zago sat beside her and gently put a hand on her back. "Don't be sad, Solyra. We'll fix it."

She sat up painfully, her ribs stiffened from just a few minutes of stillness. "It's not the dress."

"What a horrible day. Horrible." He gave a sob himself, shuddered with an effort of holding back, then broke down completely, gulping and gasping and groaning into his bandanna.

"Oh, Zago." She stroked his back. Even in the face of events, she wouldn't have thought Zago had such intense emotions in him. And after all, he'd been in the wagon throughout the worst of it.

"It's over now," she murmured. "All over, and we're safe."

"No, it's not over." He straightened, wiping his face. "I have to live with myself." He added savagely, "I hate myself!"

"Zago!"

"When those pirates crashed out of the woods, I — I burrowed under the straw in the wagon. I hid. Even better than the prince." He gave a rough laugh. "I didn't even think of defending the fulgus, let alone you or Diaa. All I thought of was saving my own hide."

She took his hand. "Zago, do you know what I was doing while you hid out?"

"Diaa told me that Redbeard grabbed you and was going to abduct you." Zago spoke slowly, as if forcing every word out. "And I just... cowered. I can hardly stand to think about it, but it's all I can think about. Solyra, don't tell Diaa, please. She thinks I stayed in the wagon to defend the prince's people. But why should you save my sorry face?" He started crying again, more softly this time. "I'm glad they're not continuing west. The prince. So I won't have to face them, day after day."

"Zago, listen. While you cowered, I... I submitted. Redbeard beat me and I just let him, hoping he would stop. I was paralyzed. I couldn't even defend myself, let alone anyone else."

They held hands. Kissed. Zago's gentle touch unraveled a little of Solyra's cares.

She sighed and broke away. "Diaa should be back... might be back any minute now."

Zago smirked. "No way. She's with her new friend. Bo."

Solyra had been planning to have a talk with Diaa about fraternizing with the crew. As if she had room to talk. Though it seemed different with Zago...though it wasn't.

When they got up to go inside, she left the dress on the bench. "No, it's beyond repair," she said as Zago reached to pick it up. She pushed down the grief that threatened to well up. Foolish it was to mourn a dress, especially given the much graver loss of the Log. And the still greater loss of her coin.

As she and Zago made love, flashes of pain from her ribs kept physical pleasure at bay. But what she really liked, anyway, was cuddling afterwards. Gradually she slipped into that cozy borderland, a drowsy dreamy passage to sleep.

Her hand on Terring's chest. His eyes crinkling with a smile.

She popped wide awake. What a dream. Terring, smiling. Just as he had when she told him to shove his fulgus up his caboose, after he informed her he was selling them to someone else.

Now, he would have the last laugh. She'd have to sell her pod fulgus to him — no doubt, that was exactly what he had in mind, with his morning meeting. Figgo no doubt knew she had exactly nothing to her name; Terring had only to name his price.

They wouldn't know, at least, that actually she had less than nothing to her name. No one did, yet. Her house note was due — today, as a matter of fact. She had a week before the Dunning & Sons' grace period expired, and they unleashed Collectors on her.

She had to get enough out of Terring to send Zago and Diaa safely home. From there, Zago would have to take care of Diaa until she could get work.

For herself, she could see no way forward and no way back. Without references, she wouldn't be able to get any kind of respectable job — not even cutting onions. And without the means to pay off Dunning & Sons, if she headed home, she'd be collected the moment she set foot over the Norvadale line. They liked to make examples out of defaulters. Just as they had her friend who'd died in prison.

SURRENDER

Zago was already gone when Solyra woke. She had fed Peg's pies to some stripy-tailed little wild animals, the night before, but she still wasn't hungry. She had no appetite at all. Today would be remembered as the Day of Surrender.

Frogbelly intercepted her on the way to the dining hall.

"Mahm Solyra, if I could speak with you."

Solyra swallowed and nodded, and they went through her room onto the back porch.

Before she could form the words to tell him that she would be off his caravan from today, he handed her a paper. "Take a look at this, mahm."

Solyra assumed he was handing over a bill for the next leg of the journey. But with a sickening lurch of her stomach, she saw it was even worse. Much worse.

To Marshals whom it may concern:
You are hereby commanded and directed to arrest
SOLYRA DAHN
wanted on charges of fraud and theft

AND HER ACCOMPLICE
ZAGO BROLWA

Physical descriptions of the two of them followed. An addendum stenciled in red at the top offered a reward of 100 doubloons for information leading to her arrest.

Solyra sat back, leaning on one elbow, a hand over her face. She panted; she felt faint.

She'd been telling herself the lie that as long as she didn't get caught at a border, as long as she kept away from Norvadale, she was safe. But she wasn't. And now she'd pulled Zago in.

Frogbelly touched her hand. "Mahm Solyra, if you take a look at that warrant, you'll see it's issued by bankmen, not lawmen." He added, "So Tad tells me."

Solyra raised her head. He was right. Dunning & Sons. Signed and sealed. How Dunning found out she fled…didn't matter. The troll, the driver, one of her former staff: anyone could have given her away, innocently or maliciously.

"These so-called charges are just big words," Frogbelly continued. "A bank can't command and direct Marshals. That doesn't mean Collectors won't take it up, but it does give us more latitude in our response."

"And what…" Solyra swallowed and tried again. "What is your response?"

Frogbelly rubbed his chin, which was, as usual, stubbly. "I'm not sure. But for now, we don't need to worry. Not many Collectors like to play their tricks in Lady's Liberty."

If Solyra ever reached her own Liberty, she vowed, she would get that same reputation.

Solyra forced herself to say, "I believe a marshal arrived here last night."

"No worries. They left at daybreak."

"Not all of them. A dark gentleman…."

"Mister Terring. He's security on our caravan now. Wants to come out west."

Solyra nearly laughed, though she couldn't say why. Relief? Terring might make the caravan safer, but he wouldn't be much good for her. "Cap'n, you know, don't you, that all my money was stolen during the raid?"

"Oh, yes." Frogbelly looked pained at the reminder. "Well, Mister Terring's not proof against an army, but he'll be drilling the crew against fire and mayhem, and altogether I believe we'll be safer."

"It's not that, Cap'n. It's…. I won't be able to pay. Anything. I mean I have some jewels…."

The Captain looked less than sympathetic. "If you think I'm out to blackmail you—"

"No! No." Solyra swallowed and pushed on. "But if you can find in yourself the kindness to just leave me. I mean, don't turn me in. It's my creditors…." Her throat closed and she couldn't go on. She could barely stop herself from sobbing.

The clouds on Frogbelly's face cleared. "Now, mahm Solyra, I'm no Collector. I'm Cap'n Frogbelly, and my aim is to get safe and sound to the Zhengahk with my freight and crew and what passengers choose to go so far. That includes you and your property."

"But with no money…."

"Peg's scullery boy jumped ship and she could use a hand. She says you're willing and able. Not just scullery," he added quickly, as if Solyra wasn't willing and more or less able to chop every onion, peel every potato, and scrub every burned pot under heaven to reach her Liberty in the Zhengahk. "She's quite a chef. So it's not as coarse as it may—"

"I'll be very glad to help," she said. "And my assistants? Diaa and Zago? I can't leave them…. Can they come along? I'm sure they can help in some capacity."

Frogbelly hesitated, then shrugged. "All right. They seem

to have a way with the animals. But I hope they understand the need to be low-key, if you take my meaning."

"I certainly will tell them," Solyra assured him fervently. "But, Cap'n...."

He raised his eyebrows.

"Won't this be, well, risky for you?"

The long scrutiny he gave Solyra's face gave her plenty of time to regret asking.

"No worries, mahm. Now, if you'll excuse me, I need to get back to packing up for our next leg. If you would save me a few steps, tell your employees to pack their things and be ready to go first thing in the morning."

Frogbelly stood and meditatively rubbed his big stomach. "Caravan life is much different from land life, mahm, as you've noticed. It takes learning. We'll be in yet more challenging places further down the road, so we all need to do our part in keeping order."

"I'll do my best," Solyra promised. Even if her personal life was way out of order.

"One more thing. If you'd show our new passengers the ropes, I'd be obliged. Nothing like a woman's touch."

"I'll be glad to help." She hardly knew the ropes herself, but it wasn't a request she could turn down, whether the new passengers were a gang of trolls, or Terring and Figgo, or just a family group heading, with her, to the ends of the world.

And "Frogbelly" was no more illiterate, despite his act, than Tad was his "nephew." Clearly, the two had their own reasons for hurrying out west.

Solyra could only hope they weren't wanted for crimes more nefarious than hers.

>> <<

SOLYRA BARELY HAD A CHANCE to savor her relief at Frogbelly's mercy before encountering Diaa at the entry of the dining hall. The onza had on a turbanlike headdress made of red jersey wound to a peak, its end trailing over one eye. Solyra lifted the tail, and Diaa snatched it back with a hiss, but not before Solyra saw that, sure enough, Diaa had a black eye, well-ripened.

"Did Bo do that to you?" Solyra demanded, low-key.

"I ran into a door." Scowling, Diaa rearranged the tail, then forced her mouth into a wide grin. "I'm starving." Before Solyra could question her again, Diaa went ahead into the dining room.

"Good morning, zizera Solyra." Terring caught up with Solyra. He wore dark leather pants, a coarse linen collarless shirt, a black waistcoat, and a canvas frock coat with lots of pockets and tarnished brass buttons.

"Good morning, zizero," Solyra answered. Next to Diaa — ridiculous coif, shiner and all — she felt a drab broomstick of a woman. She'd been called beautiful once upon a time, but her glow had been snuffed by Dahn, by working all hours to rebuild the business, by worrying about her missing parents, by holding all that in for too long. By missing the joys of love, for earth's sake. Not to mention that her face and hair, hands and feet longed for the company of her Norvadale dressing table. Abandon that fantasy of vanity. She and her looks likely hadn't nearly hit bottom yet.

But so what? This afternoon, she and her fulgus would be lurching to yet another border. Thank earth Frogbelly had snagged her before she met with Terring! She might have sold out, never knowing that the road had re-opened for her. Granted, she would have to share that road with Terring, but they'd both learn to live with that.

The Wayside dining hall was not nearly on a scale with the Beechen's, but to Solyra the food smelled heavenly.

Zago gave her a puppy dog look as she came to the table, but the seats on either side of him were already taken. Diaa sat at the end next to Bo, and they kissed each other as cosily as husband and wife.

Solyra didn't know what to do. Report Bo to his boss?

She'd have to talk to Diaa first, get what really happened out of her. Frogbelly wasn't at table anyway.

Solyra sat in the only seat left. It hurt, and not only because it was next to Figgo. To compound the misery of her ribs, her legs were chafed raw from riding, and her buttocks and thighs burned from the welts Redbeard laid on them.

Terring sat down and surveyed the table, then rose again. "My excuses. I forgot something." He left.

At least Figgo wouldn't expect witty conversation. He sat still and straight as a good schoolboy while the servers brought out the food. A neatly trimmed beard fringed his dark, lean face, and his tightly curling, shiny dark hair was close-cropped. The copper goggles covering his eyes were polished to a soft sheen.

How would this place seem to him? She closed her eyes.

Voices and snatches of conversation, the clatter of dishes and utensils, a squeaking trolley wheel, chairs scraping, a dog barking outside somewhere, a burst of shouting and clattering that suddenly disappeared: the kitchen door opening and closing. All intermingled with the smells of people and food and wood smoke. The fragrance of rosewater.

"That smells good," she said unthinking as she opened her eyes again.

Figgo's head turned slightly toward her, and another waft of rosewater made her realize that it was his scent. Just in time, the server put before her a plate of the biggest eggs she'd ever seen, along with gravy and mashed potatoes.

"The food," she said quickly.

"Yes." He had kept his hands in his lap, now they rose to the table, so that his fingertips touched the utensils and the plate. Watching him, she could almost feel for herself the polished wood of the table, the smooth bone handles of the fork and knife, the rough clay underside of the plate and the smooth glazed top. His hands crept further up onto the table, feeling around, not tentatively, but rather like intelligent ants. Then they paused. "Is there a napkin?" he asked very quietly.

For Solyra, a napkin placed in a tea cup was an oddity. For Figgo, it was missing; and napkins would be important to him. He would never want the sighted to see gravy on his chin, or on his immaculate clothes. She reached to hand him the napkin, stopped herself and said, "In the teacup, top right of your plate."

Figgo said something, adding, "That means thank you in Zhi'nging'ha!"

"Shew'wah," Solyra tried.

"Shhh'u'wah," Figgo repeated.

Solyra closed her eyes. "Say it a few more times, please, zizero Figgo."

"Shhh'u'wah. Shhh'u'wah. Shhh'u'wah."

Solyra tried again.

"Good."

"Shhh'u'wah, zizero Figgo, for teaching me such a pleasing word."

"You're welcome, zizera Solyra." He placed the napkin in his lap and began eating in a deliberate, measured way, a marked contrast to the general scarfing around them.

Diaa, or Diaa's voice, rather, caught her attention from down the table. She was regaling her companions with a story, something about a goat, a Bihst master, a baker woman, and a bottle of booze.

Hopefully, whatever she was saying wouldn't offend the people behind her: a Bihst master and his small group of followers. None of them were talking, and one, a lean woman somewhere between middle and old age, turned to look at Diaa then faced her group again. When Diaa wound up, her audience roared with laughter — and the Bihst master joined in with a merry hooting not loud but carrying.

Terring burst back in the dining room with Frogbelly and Tad. Solyra couldn't imagine why they looked so hard and grim — but Bo did. He leaped from his chair. Terring and Tad grabbed him before he got far and half-dragged him out. After exchanging looks, the other crew members followed.

Diaa stood gaping after them, then glared up the table at Solyra. Her growl rose into a snarl, then a scream. "You snitch!" She ran out.

After staring, and some chuckling, the other people in the dining hall turned back to their food and the murmur of conversation rose to the buzz of an agitated hive.

With Figgo a silent witness, Solyra finished her coffee, then excused herself with as much dignity as she could muster.

She found Diaa in the room she evidently shared with Bo, his clothes and hers mingled on the floor. The onza drooped on her bed like a broken marionette. She started up, eyes wide, as Solyra came in — then slumped again to utter dejection.

"I'm sorry, Solyra," she whispered.

Solyra sat on the bed. She'd come in furious, but Diaa's pathetic apology defused her. "It was Bo?"

"He didn't mean it! He's not like that troll of a husband of mine. He was sorry. He really was."

Solyra touched her hair. "Diaa, if you could have seen your own face when I came in — you looked scared until you saw it was me."

"You don't understand. I'm really, really sorry for yelling at you, but you just don't understand."

"I understand more than you think I do. Once it starts…. Well, it just gets worse."

Diaa growled, even as she took Solyra's hand. "I'm done with him." She gave the trousers on the floor a little kick. "I wish I got rid of him before I fight with you."

"I wish you'd gotten rid of him before he hurt you."

Diaa gave her a little hug.

"Now, Diaa, listen. Frogbelly's letting us come with him, even though I can't pay anymore. We have to be low key, though. We can't get in fights with his crew."

"*Letting* us come with him! Oh, so nice, after you was robbed on his caravan."

Solyra hadn't thought of it that way, but she was hardly in a position to sue for damages. "Still, we have to work our passage," she said. "It's only fair."

"I don't mind working," Diaa said. "I like the horses now."

"But you can't have relations.... Frogbelly doesn't like his men interfered with." Solyra took Diaa's hands. "We've got a long, hard journey ahead. If we want to make it all the way, we have to get along with the crew." And pray Frogbelly would overlook the latest incident.

"I like 'em all. Except Figgo, and he ain't the fightin' kind. But, zizera, I have to show you something." She gave a gleeful purr. "Zago and Peg will be mad as troll-ticks that I ruined the surprise, but you and me have to make up. And I can't wait!"

Diaa reached under the bed and pulled out a package. "Open it!" she cried.

Solyra opened it, and barely kept herself from wailing aloud.

It was her dress. Or what had once been her dress. It was now a motley frock coat, with sleeves made of a folksy woven material, the frock's silver piping spiraling down the arms. The beads were gone, every last one of them. Diaa had somehow gotten hold of some leather riding trousers, probably traded the beads for them. A slouch hat with a hat band made of the frock's embroidered trim completed the ensemble.

Diaa, Zago, and Peg, and who knew who else must have worked all night to put it together. Tears filled Solyra's eyes.

Diaa plopped onto the bed. "Don't you like it, zizera?"

"Diaa, I'm just so.... I'm so touched. It's beautiful. More beautiful than it ever was before!"

"Try it on!"

Solyra tried it on. It was the most outlandish thing she'd ever worn. At least the riding trousers would stand her in good stead. "Perfect! I'll be so proud to wear it."

By gum, she would, too.

Diaa purred, all bitterness forgotten, and prinked at the lapels.

Solyra got up with a sigh. "I'd better see what's happening with Bo."

"No, don't." Diaa caught her hand. "You won't like it, Solyra. Leave the boys to sort it out."

Tempting, but Solyra felt a sense of responsibility. "No, I need to deal with it. You get Peg to look after that eye. That's an order."

Solyra headed for the barnyard. Instinct told her that the stables would be where the caravan men would deal justice.

Not the stables themselves, but the tackle shed was the seat of justice. When she peered in the open double doors, unnoticed by the men crowded inside, the trial had already taken place, verdict rendered, and sentence handed down.

Bo cringed against the far wall while Tad faced him, *contemplated* him, gloved fists on his hips. Blood poured from Bo's nose over his mouth and jaw, vomit covered his shirt and chin, and, in perfect justice, his right eye was swelling shut. Bo suddenly kicked out with his legs. Tad let him, then calmly darted in and dealt him a blow to the ribs that looked like a mere kiss but caused Bo to scream out and stagger, before lunging at Tad again and crying out at the pain he'd just inflicted on himself.

The men watching, mostly Frogbelly's crew, gave a collective groan, part sympathy, part bloodlust. Otherwise, they were quiet, as if respecting the dignity of the court. Tad lashed out, this time toward Bo's jaw—

Solyra backed away, not wanting to see anymore, not wanting to be seen. With Bo's wrenching groan quivering in her ears, she scurried back across the stableyard, heading for the gate when she remembered Peg saying something about bringing a snack out to one of the barn mousers who'd had kittens.

Following the sound of mewing, Solyra climbed up to the loft to find the little family tumbled in a corner. One of the hostlers, in a fit of tenderness, had thrown down a wad of old underwear to make a nest for them. Solyra befriended the mama with a palmful of cream begged from the dairymaid below, then settled down to play with the kittens. Their sharp little claws and teeth would someday be as brutal as Tad's fists, but holding their soft cuddly warmth in her hands and letting them suckle and nip at her fingertips soothed her spirits.

Diaa had been right, warning Solyra to leave the men to their devices. But Solyra also felt she'd been right, to see first-hand what happened. Whether she liked it or not, this was her world now. On the road, justice had to be swift and physical. At least Frogbelly and his crew cared enough to make Bo pay for striking Diaa — of course they would. A caravan crew that assaulted its passengers would go out of business in a hurry.

Now Solyra had to decide whether to bring Diaa to the meeting with Terring. On one hand, it would be good to present a united front. On the other hand, Diaa needed to learn a lesson or two about business decorum, and, even passing over the scene in the dining room, her black eye and makeshift turban were an embarrassment.

In the event, booted steps coming up the loft ladder informed Solyra that she didn't need to decide. She just knew it was Terring; she was right.

"Awwww," he said as his head came through the opening. His eyes ran over the kittens exploring her new jacket skirts and the mama cat purring in her lap. "Isn't that cute?" He sat on a hay bale across from her. "And could I have heard you of all people purring?

She had, in fact, been purring back to the kittens and mother. She kissed the nose of the one she had in her hand and settled it back on her lap. "If this is your idea of flirting, it's a bust," she said. "If you're trying to insult me, count yourself nearly successful."

He shrugged. "The only women who understand my wit are whores."

She would have liked to have grasped a kitten in each hand and raked his face with their little claws. Instead, she gently picked the kittens off of her and put them and their mother back in the nest, then stood, brushing hay off herself.

"Insulting and coarse, what a gentleman you are." She tried to hold a bantering tone, but her voice shook. "Let's consider this meeting adjourned."

She began toward the ladder, but he blocked her. "Solyra, I beg your pardon. That came out wrong."

She tried to side-step him, but he followed. "Solyra."

A burst of panic weakened her limbs, wilted her… No!

She grabbed a pitchfork stuck in a mound of hay and jabbed at Terring as if he were a mad dog. "Get out of my way!"

He raised his hands and stepped back — into the opening. With one foot still on the loft floor, he teetered, then grabbed wildly at the pitchfork, pulling her forward. She collected her wits just in time to pull back with all her might. He managed to thrust the pitchfork aside to keep from being impaled, and stumbled into her, knocking her down and nearly burying them both in a mound of hay.

After some mutual thrashing around, they sprang apart as if they were both red hot. His face, in fact, looked red hot. Solyra knew hers was. Even so, a little teeny sliver of herself noticed that his body, unlike Zago's, was heavy and hard-muscled. An even teeny-weenier sliver of her wanted to pull that body back with her into the hay.

She got busy dusting herself off, swatting away Terring's attempts at help.

"It's a good thing we didn't crush your little pussies," he said when they'd both recovered their dignity.

She had to laugh. She picked a piece of hay from the end of one of her braids. "What was it you wanted to meet about?"

"How about we discuss it over a cup of coffee? I need fortitude after our roll in the — our, ah, rollup with disaster."

ALONE

Terring's men — or Cynta's men, now — loafing over a game of cards, turned to stare at Terring and Solyra as they came in the canteen, still dusted with hay. A couple of them did a double-take, looked at each other and laughed. Cynta winked at Terring, another woman gave a knowing grin. A man sighed theatrically, mournfully; another slapped his hand over his heart. When Terring gave them the evil eye, they sobered up and hunched over their cards.

Then he caught sight of Zago at the entrance of the lobby, staring, stricken, his hand pressed over his heart without a trace of facetiousness. Solyra waved him over, but he left, nearly at a run. What a confounded fool.

Why Zago's besotted swain act irritated him so, Terring couldn't say. Maybe because it wasn't an act. Terring had glimpsed Zago slipping out of Solyra's room last night. That had done more than irritate him. He had wanted to pull the little noodle apart. Still wanted to, unmanly as it would be to dismember such a milk-toast.

They got coffees, Solyra adding to her plate a roll and a sausage — a kind so spicy, it had just about sent steam out of

Terring's ears the night before — and they went out to the porch.

After the confines of the Wudu, the grasslands gleamed in endless green waves. Hidden in swales and crevices were countless streams to cross and tedious hills to climb and then precariously roll down. Yet for all the mud bogs they'd have to churn through, Terring relished the sight. The grasslands marked the beginning of the frontier. The beginning of freedom. A wide open space that made him feel as if chains were dropping away from him.

"Where's your aide?" Solyra asked as they settled down.

"Enjoying a little time off," Terring answered.

"I see." She bit into the sausage roll, then her eyes popped wide.

"Are you all right?" Terring asked. He was a cad, wasn't he, holding back a laugh as tears ran down her cheeks. And he wouldn't have warned her for the world.

"I'm just crazy about hot sausages." She took another bite, chewing as daintily as if she had a bite of cucumber sandwich in her mouth. Crusts cut off, of course.

Difficult, very difficult not to respond to that line, but best move on to business. But the crazy thing was that despite her absurd bravado and the even more absurd remake of her blue gown, he would have given a locker full of grade 01 energy fulgus for a good kiss from her. A good hot kiss.

Back to business.

"I have a proposition for you, zizera Solyra."

"Propose away, sirrah."

"I understand that you're going out west with the idea that you can raise a frame on Dahn's fulgu field."

"My fulgu field."

He didn't remark that if a frame had crashed on that land, as Dahn claimed, the field would be too unstable to use. As useless as Terring's land, which really had suffered a frame crash.

"And you're bringing pod fulgus with you," he continued.

"What if I am?"

"We partner and split the profits. Your land, your fulgus. My equipment, and I'll engineer the project and recruit an experienced crew. Figgo's already worked up a contract." He drew a rolled longpaper from his coat pocket.

He had taken her by surprise. Had her big eyes on him not been so exquisitely distracting, he might have relished the moment.

She took the paper from him without a word and got to reading.

Figgo hadn't been happy about writing it up. In fact, he'd been almost wrathful, though only a slight tightening of his voice had revealed his emotion.

"I cannot believe, zizero Terring," he'd said, "that you would consider going into business with a woman who cheated you, ruined you. A woman of low moral—"

"That's enough," Terring had snapped.

The heavy silence gave Terring, and maybe Figgo, too, the chance to contemplate the fact that this was the first time they'd quarreled, and the first time Terring had spoken harshly to Figgo. He wasn't sure he could say theirs was a close friendship, or a friendship at all. It was a relationship founded on mutual need and gratitude. On Terring's part, more than a dollop of pity, though he hoped he never let that show. Not for Figgo's blindness. It was the loneliness that enveloped him, like a shroud.

Terring had finally broken the silence himself. "I'll never get a chance like this again. Neither will you. Write up a contract that's foolproof and watertight."

Which was exactly what Figgo had done. He'd worked all night. Now he was "enjoying some time off" by sleeping. Or maybe brooding on how, due to his utter dependence on Terring, he was getting roped into what was by any measure a dubious enterprise. As for being dragged back to his homeland, Terring had offered that the jobs generated by the frame would help Figgo's people recover from the War. Maybe he'd been persuaded, or maybe he'd given in. He wrote up the contract, and an elegant masterpiece of legalism it was.

"Looks sound." Solyra brushed her fingers over the page, and over again. It had a texture from the lines of pinpricks that Terring had made to guide Figgo's writing. "But why not offer to buy me out? Land and fulgus?"

Buying her out was certainly the logical thing to do. If he had money. Which he didn't. Which he wasn't about to admit. He shrugged. "Why waste capital?"

"You and Figgo must be cocksure I would sign this."

"Why wouldn't we be? Your chances of raising a frame without our help are next to nil."

"I don't know about that." She gave a smile. A smirk. She must know he was broke.

Terring own smile tightened. "You won't say no this time."

Her smile faltered, her lips trembled. That look came over her face. The look that destroyed Terring's game.

She nipped in her lower lip, and raised her brows and her chin. "I'll let you know my decision this evening." She left, head high.

Years ago, and what seemed a world away, Terring had asked her to marry him. Begged her. She'd said no.

This time, her answer would be yes.

His confidence tasted like ashes.

>> <<

THE MAN DIDN'T MISS A beat. From reneging on the deal to sell her his fulgus, to policing up the disaster between Diaa and Bo, to witnessing Zago's hangdog look, he seemed to be watching her every stumble.

Her folly, his enjoyment. She seemed to amuse him, like a cute little kitten. Maybe that's all it had been, back when she was a naive girl and he'd gone down on one knee to her.

She'd already accepted Dahn. How distressed and

saddened she'd been over having to hurt Terring. What a child she'd been! Terring likely stood up, dusted off his knees, and went on to the next amusement. Actually, he'd gone out to the Zhengahk and raised his fulgu frame. Meanwhile, as the shock and misery of her wedding night repeated itself over and over, she'd gnawed up her own insides over the biggest mistake of her life.

No doubt, Terring would have treated her better. Life with him would have been more materially secure as well, with his family behind him, even if at the resort they had paraded their contempt for Solyra and her parents with any number of snubs. But as far as missing out on love, current events did offer one bonus. She now knew that love was not in Terring's nature. He was a player, that was all, and he didn't like to lose, whether in courtship or business.

Solyra unrolled the contract. She wasn't about to lose either, this round.

Looked at objectively, Terring's offer was a supreme piece of good fortune. Even his irksome stipulation that the business be named after himself meant less of a trail for her creditors.

The main point was, he had raised and cultivated a fulgu frame in the Zhengahk. Her own business had operated on a retail basis in the civilized comfort of Norvadale. It was the difference between manufacturing goods and selling them.

Without Hoggins' Log or even with it, she would be at the mercy of any man who knew enough fulgu lingo to spout off a stream of competent-sounding nonsense.

It was join Terring or be licked.

Tears caught Solyra unaware. She quickly dabbed her eyes dry. It must be her courses coming on.

She only wished....

She wasn't sure what she wished. That she didn't have to stand alone.

Zago was wonderfully competent as a fulgu keeper. As a lover, he was sweet, and she was genuinely fond of him. But his arms offered no shelter. She would have to take care of him, on this journey. She could hardly lean on Diaa, either. The trouble with Bo would not be the last.

She was going it alone. No, not alone. She had two dependents.

If only Terring weren't her enemy.

The feel of his body hugged against her enveloped her again. His strength, his warmth. He could sustain her, and in turn, maybe, she could encourage him, take away that bleakness that would suddenly flood his eyes. Instead, he and she seemed doomed to parry and poke, all too often drawing blood. She didn't blame him. The bitterness of the past, from their courtship to their business dealings, tainted their every interaction.

As tears threatened again, Solyra pulled her bath things out of her bag. Frogbelly had changed their departure time from the next morning to late this afternoon, and she wasn't about to miss what might be a last chance for a hot bath, especially since the hay made her itchy. She got out a fresh sea sponge, too. Her courses weren't tempestuous, but she hated the melty messiness, along with the constant fear of leaks. What it would be like further down the road, far from relatively civilized baths and privies, simply didn't bear thinking on. But at least she didn't have to worry about Zago getting her pregnant. Keeping fulgus rendered men unable to make babies.

Before going to the bath, she got Diaa and Zago together in the cramped confines of her room and explained the partnership with Terring.

"Huh, so you were actually talking in the barn," Zago said poutily. Diaa giggled.

Solyra could have shaken them both.

"Zizero Figgo's contract looks fair and tidy," she said evenly. She took it out and handed it to Diaa. "I know you're not used to contracts, but we can go over it together before we meet with the gentlemen."

All merriment fled Diaa's face. Studying the scroll intently, she nodded. "Let me read in my room. To concentrate."

So it was true, Solyra thought as Diaa left. She couldn't read. A business aide who couldn't read.

Zago heaved a deep sigh. "How could you throw me over like this, Solyra?"

"I have not…" Solyra stopped. She had to get her and Zago's relationship on a different footing. But she couldn't bear to hurt him. "Zago, just for the record, Terring and I…. I was playing with some kittens in the barn loft, and he came in and, well, accidentally fell on me. No foul play was done or intended."

Zago gave another sigh. "Oh, Solyra." Then he laughed. "I've been moping for two solid hours." He knelt in front of her and softly stroked her inner thighs. "We have enough time to make up with each other."

His hands gave her a shivery pleasure, but she removed them. "I'm in my courses, Zago."

That had always fended off Dahn, but Zago shrugged. "I don't mind."

"No, it's too messy." Against her better judgment, she added, "Later, when we have more time."

"Oh, Solyra." His sigh as he left was cheerily melodramatic.

Why had she promised herself to him? It wasn't the sex so much as the hugging and kissing, the physical closeness. And if she had to pay for that with sex, it wasn't such a bad deal. She'd not experienced much cuddliness in her marriage.

So much for employer-employee relations.

Never mind. They'd have plenty of time to work things out on the way, and when all was said and done, intrigues and amours were inevitable on a journey of this magnitude. Solyra gathered her bath things, started to stand, and sat again.

A journey of this magnitude.

It hadn't really hit her, until this moment. The avalanche of events had nearly buried her over-arching fear: that even if she reached her property, she would fail at raising the frame and be stuck far from home, withering away in a strange land, impoverished, separated forever from her parents.

What she wanted more than anything was to sit on the porch of an oceanside cottage with her mother and father, the three of them safe and happy. Just that. Simple. The complications of wealth had little appeal. Even when her affairs thrived, she'd adopted only the luxuries needed to lubricate her way in business and society.

However, to buy a cottage by the sea, not to mention tracing her parents and paying off her debts, she had to get rich. And to get rich, she had to wager everything she had — namely, her pod fulgus — on this enterprise. No doubt about it, Terring's appearance was blessed.

Never mind love.

LADY LIBERTY

THE CARAVAN WAITED AT THE top of the driveway, animals laden, saddled, or harnessed. Thankfully, the prince was not continuing, nor was Bo to be seen, but some new people besides Terring and Figgo had joined: the Bihst group who had overheard, and thankfully laughed at, Diaa's ribald story, and a pair of identical-looking women two heads taller than Terring — giants more foreign in these parts than Solyra herself. Since the twins seemed to be part of the crew, Solyra went to the Bihsts to "show them the ropes."

Solyra bowed to the master with a hazy memory that this is what one did when greeting a Bihst. "Would the master and his disciples please bless us and our animals before we start?"

The master smiled, his face crinkling and his eyes nearly disappearing. "We will be very happy to bless," he answered in a nasal, clipped accent.

A boy of about thirteen scrambled into their wagon, a smaller version of one of Frogbelly's "ships," and handed down several cloth-wrapped bundles. A middle-aged couple placed the bundles on the tailgate, and a young girl of about eleven carefully put down a lidded basket and darted to the roadside to pick some flowers. The basket meowed and a pair of cat's eyes appeared in a slot on its side. A young couple arranged two silk-wrapped shapes, while a young man lined up seven little crystal bowls and filled them alternately with gems and gold-tinted water. They worked smoothly and cheerfully together.

Frogbelly, walking back from the head wagon, took in the scene, glanced at the sky striped with sunset pink and yellow clouds, and murmured something to Tad, who made a gesture back: be patient.

Finally, the master removed the silk cloth on the shapes to reveal two bronze statues. He adjusted the statues, lovingly smoothed the skirt of the female, then began chanting something tuneful though not quite a song. After a few phrases, the other Bihsts joined in, eyes closed or half-closed. Solyra gazed at the statues.

One was a laughing man sitting with his legs stretched out in a V in front of him and his hands spread on his fat belly. He wore baggy white pants of real cloth, and a garland of cloth flowers. The other statue was a slender woman sitting cross-legged, her body undulating slightly. She was clad only in a flowing skirt made of red silk satin, and necklaces and bracelets.

The female statue's outfit was very much like the one Dahn made Solyra wear at the Booton conference, the very lowest point, humiliation-wise, of a humiliating marriage.

She pulled her eyes from the statues and studied the group. While the Bihst priest was their spiritual guide, she sensed that the middle-aged couple, Jaleen and Baloos, led the group. The boy and girl looked too young to be their children and too old to be the children of the other couple. The pouty young man might have been theirs, though Solyra didn't see much resemblance.

Two tears slipped from the young girl's closed eyes and she gave a sniff. Jaleen put an arm around her shoulders and the girl leaned into her. The man, Baloos, opened his eyes to glance at them, caught Solyra's gaze and smiled politely, then gave a sigh and closed his eyes again.

The service didn't take more than ten or so minutes, but as the Master fell silent, the clouds had faded to gray and a few stars poked through the sky. The Bihsts repacked and closed their altar.

Solyra smiled her thanks and mounted Toggly, the mare she'd switched to. Toggly was prone to wander toward the roadside for unauthorized snacks, but she had a smoother gait than the gelding.

The crew walked the length of the caravan, adjusting tack here and there, checking that the animals were loaded properly, and tallying with each other their count of the passengers. Brid, at the caboose, gave a two-note whistle that meant, "Ready!"

"Ayyyyyup!" Frogbelly cried.

With wheels creaking, horses neighing, donkeys and mules braying, and a few people cheering, the caravan set off down the dusky road.

>> <<

ANY CHEER THAT MARKED THEIR start fell quickly by the roadside. Most of the passengers focused on staying awake, as the caravan moved too quickly for dozing in the saddle. Only their lamps lit the way along the muddy road.

For himself, Terring found it all too easy to stay awake. He couldn't get rid of the feeling of Solyra pressed against him, up in the hay loft. She'd sneezed, her body spasming against his body. That, he couldn't forget either.

"Do you know why we're traveling at night?"

He turned as she rode up alongside him. Her outfit was as outlandish as the frock coat she'd worn earlier, a caftan split up the front and back to allow her to ride.

"Yes, I do," he said, and left it at that. Why it was so much fun to tease her — when only moments ago he could have fried an egg in his britches.

"Are you willing to share?" she asked.

"We've been summoned. It happens that Bo is the Liberty's cousin."

"The Liberty's...cousin? How can a place have a cousin?"

"The governor of the Liberty is called the Liberty. You'll be the Solyra Liberty, when you reach your property."

Her smile looked more wistful than amused. "Hard to imagine," she said.

A few minutes later, Queenie started barking and whining, and straining at her tether, her tail wagging furiously.

Frogbelly and Tad looked at each other.

"It's the Liberty," Frogbelly said.

It sounded like a distant riot of birds. A glow of light appeared over a rise.

The sound and sight resolved itself into torches and a chaos of men and women, not rioting but ululating. Terring had not met Lady Liberty before, but no one could mistake which one she was.

A mountain of a woman rode a kind of throne, complete with lanterns on posts, atop the biggest horse Terring had ever seen. She descended, rather than dismounted, by a set of folding stairs placed and secured by several men and women who scrambled and jostled for the privilege. Meanwhile, others set up a canopy whose floor was spread with rugs and seating cushions.

After ordering a seat higher than her own for the Bihst master, insisting over his polite refusals, Lady Liberty ensconced herself on a mound of fleeces. She gestured Frogbelly to her right hand, Terring to her left. Queenie settled decorously at her side and gave her fingers a little lick.

Once tea and snacks were served and consumed, Lady Liberty took Terring's hand. Her hand was soft, warm, dog-damp. "You and your lieutenant did me a great service getting rid of that pestilence Red Beard and his scurvy scum." The Lady's voice was nasal, high-pitched, and tremulous, though certainly not out of timidity.

"It was my job, Lady, and I'm very glad to have done it."

She said very quietly, just to him, "You turned the reward over to your crew, but I shall add something for you." Then aloud, "Tell us about the battle."

Terring told the tale as briefly and dryly as possible, leaving out the sickening realities of it, the thuds and screams and gore. Even the Bihst children seemed to take it all right, but when Terring's gaze swept Solyra, he saw that, rather than look impressed, or just unimpressed, she looked ... mortified. Terring knew she'd been hurt, but he never considered how painfully humiliating the assault must have been to her.

Terring wished he could wind up, but he hadn't yet gotten to the real point of the rendezvous.

"The worst of it, Lady, was that Bo conspired with Redbeard, letting him know when the caravan left Beechen, how fast we were traveling, and where certain valuables were to be found."

A shocked buzz rippled among the gathering.

Frogbelly continued, "Besides some cargo of inestimable value," a glance at Solyra, "one of my men lost a finger."

Brid held up his hand, with its bandaged half finger.

"Another of my boys lost a tooth." Frogbelly continued with a list of the other injuries: slashes, a foot pierced by an arrow. "My passengers were also hurt. One suffered gashes on his legs and arms. Another sustained severe bruising and lacerations. The prince was badly shaken and... well, he'll sue for sure. In a separate incident, Bo assaulted one of my passengers, which incident brought the rest to light."

Lady Liberty's gaze roved over the assembly as Frogbelly spoke, pausing on Diaa, who raised her chin defiantly. Solyra put an arm around her.

"The damage to my reputation," Frogbelly wound up, "not

to mention my outlay for reparation, is negligible next to the injuries of the people in my charge. But I got in a few blows for it, all the same."

"I take it you have good evidence that Bo was in league with Redbeard."

"Yes, Lady, we do." Frogbelly handed an envelope to Lady Liberty's aide, a young woman approaching the girth of the Lady herself. "A notarized confession from Bo."

"Hm." Lady Liberty glanced over it, then handed it back to the aide. "I can imagine how this was gotten."

"Fairly, Lady," Terring said. It was true — they hadn't turned Tad loose on him until he signed and sealed his confession. In any event, the Lady seemed satisfied. Terring guessed that Bo had run to her with a self-justifying story that, to anyone intelligent, would incriminate him more than the confession itself.

"I suppose you'll be long gone before my little cousin is able to do more than merely wish for revenge," the Lady said. "I'll do my best to contain him, but he's got friends from the Wudu to the Ihm."

Terring repressed the wish that they'd killed him. He'd believed Bo's oath that he'd thought Redbeard would only rob, not kill. Still, they'd worked him over thoroughly, and should Bo hanker for revenge, a message to one of his pals on the road ahead could bear unpleasant results.

>> <<

FROGBELLY INTRODUCED SOLYRA AND DIAA as businesswomen traveling out west, and the Lady invited them near.

"And what's your business, may I ask?" Lady Liberty fixed small, dark eyes that Solyra found acute, but friendly.

"I'm owner of — of... I mean, partner in Terring Fulgus. Diaa is my aide."

"Fulgus.... We don't have fulgu power around here, but one

of my cousins lived in a fulgu'd house. Frankly, it seemed more a fad than an industry. You think there's growth potential?"

"Most certainly," Solyra said. At Lady Liberty's questions, she explained the process, from raising the frame to harvest, to home installation and use. She must have made some sense; Terring, who'd joined them, didn't laugh or butt in.

"The main damper on the industry," she finished, "is the risk of failure in cultivation. However, zizero Terring is a brilliant frame engineer, and with some innovations in the process, we can bring the costs down and make fulgu power available in countless applications."

Lady Liberty chuckled. "Until now, you were down to earth. But that last bit sounds like an advertising brochure. No offense, Terring. I'm sure you're as brilliant as your lovely partner says. But it all sounds mighty vague and promising."

Solyra had to laugh, too. She also couldn't help notice that Terring had blushed. "The details are less vague and even more promising, but I'm afraid all the more boring."

She felt certain that the Lady would not find the details boring, though. In fact, Solyra sniffed a deal in the making. She elaborated on the potential of fulgus, then Terring took over with a description of cultivating them. He didn't make it sound exactly easy or risk-free, but his confidence inspired confidence. Solyra glanced toward Zago. Luckily he was occupied in a weapons lesson being given by one of the Lady's men. He wouldn't be happy at the expansion of fulgu exploitation.

Lady Liberty had just proposed buying a license for installation of fulgus throughout her Liberty when Diaa asked, "What if the fulgus are alive?"

Lady Liberty's eyes went not to Diaa's but to Solyra's face. At least Figgo hadn't been here for that one.

"Lady Liberty, aide Diaa is alluding to a cult that believes fulgus to be sentient," Solyra said as calmly as she could, "even though the latest scientific investigations indicate they are mineral. No more alive than rock. Or fire."

"Zago said their shells are mineral," Diaa said, "but that no one knows exactly what fulgus are inside. Except they seem to be organic."

A month ago Diaa wouldn't have even known the word "organic." She said it now with a maddeningly know-it-all air. Solyra would have liked to take her aside and explain that now was not the time to raise a controversy. Better yet, she would have liked to take her aside and shake her, but a cat fight between a principal and her aide would hardly bolster their cause.

"Zago is a very talented fulgukeeper," she said smilingly, "but he's no scientist."

"He knows all about fulgus," Diaa insisted. "He talks to them. Zago," she called

Solyra caved in to the wish she'd been fighting: that she'd left Diaa back at the trollhouse on the border. It wasn't that Diaa was malicious, mischievous, or stupid; she just happened to make trouble at every turn.

Zago plopped down next to Diaa.

"And you, zizero Terring?" the Lady asked. "What do you believe?"

"Fulgus are things, not beings."

"Fulgus carry the essence of all life," Zago said. "Their language is as yet unknown to man, but it is clear they bear the divine spark within, the divine spark we all share."

"There is a, in my view, hair-brained movement that claims fulgus are sentient," Terring said, "but without a shred of scientific evidence."

"The movement for fulgu rights is not hair-brained, sirrah," Zago said. With that, he got up and left, Diaa trailing him.

Solyra, cheeks burning, drew a deep breath. Thank earth she wasn't wearing her pre-pirated frock. The crystal beads would be positively chattering with agitation.

The Lady made some pretty talk about how she hoped they would bear the Liberty in mind when they had established their enterprise, and so forth and so on, but she backed off from her offer of cash in gold. Terring, his smile obviously pasted on over a scowl, bowed away to help the crew ready the caravan to depart.

Solyra was heading to her horse when one of Lady Liberty's maids caught up with her.

"Zizera Solyra, the Lady would like to see you before you leave."

The Lady, at the foot of the steps to her saddle-throne, took Solyra's hands in hers.

"I can't invest in your business the way it is now," she said. "You understand that, don't you?"

"I'm sorry we wasted your time, Lady. We're new to each other, my employees and I, and we're still working out our processes."

Lady Liberty laughed. "That's one way to put it. At the least, you need to agree on how to disclose this idea that fulgus have souls. But I don't consider my time wasted. I like learning about things, and these fulgus are very interesting. I meant it when I invited you to keep in touch." She gently squeezed Solyra's hands. "I think you'll come through, Solyra. I believe in you."

Solyra bowed her head, the lump in her throat keeping back an answer. No one had ever said those words to her. I believe in you.

"I'm giving you a gift," the Lady continued. "No strings attached." Solyra looked to where Lady Liberty pointed. Several men were loading crates on Frogbelly's biggest wagon.

"Well, it does have strings attached," the Lady said. "It's a cargo balloon. The Cap'n was going to haul it out to one of my copper mines in the Ihm, but I want you to have it. It'll help you raise your frames. The Cap'n can explain how to operate it and I'm sure your handsome engineer can take it from there."

Solyra didn't waste words with polite refusals. If Lady Liberty wanted to give her a cargo balloon, she'd made up her mind. Still holding hands with her, Solyra said, "Lady Liberty,

I've done nothing to earn your generosity, but I hope I will at least repay your faith in me."

"I have no doubt you will succeed, my dear."

They kissed, then Lady Liberty mounted up to her saddle-throne. With a jaunty wave at Frogbelly, she rode off, surrounded by her crowd of ululating men and women.

Solyra stared after the giant horse with its rider, fighting an impulse to chase after them, shouting, "Take me with you!"

It would beat reality: a not-so-former rival, now a partner, armed with a hostile secretary, a pouting keeper who, against all sense, continued to cling to his myth of soulful fulgus, and an illiterate aide with no sense of business or decorum. Not to mention posses of Collectors, and maybe vengeful pirates on their trail.

MUD & MEMORIES

DAY AFTER DAY, THE CARAVAN trundled through grasslands lush under early summer rain. The saddlehorses were reserved for the people on guard; the rest of the animals either pulled wagons or were kept in reserve. No one except drivers rode on the wagons; they jounced so much, their contents had to be roped down.

Solyra enjoyed her position as Peg's "lieutenant" as Peg called her, not least because after a week, Peg invited her to sleep in her small enclosed wagon, a cozy bunkhouse, pantry, and pharmacy on wheels. Solyra's still healing ribs didn't yet allow her to stir the big pots or knead dough, and she used them as an excuse not to pluck fowl, but she chopped veggies, ground spices, mixed condiments and medicines, and listened to Peg's endless monologues on kitchens she'd worked in and caravans she had known.

For all her chatter, Peg spoke little about herself, but Solyra learned that she had been born missing half a leg, and that when she was fourteen her hair fell out for no known reason. She riffed on herself as "a scrawny peg-legged baldy with a face that could stop a buffalumph in its tracks" in crazed pursuit of

Jerzy, the head hostler, a man handsome in a bulky, hairy way. It didn't take Solyra long to figure that Peg's comedy was a self-deprecating fantasy. For all her assurance in the kitchen, she was too shy even to approach Jerzy.

One evening, while Solyra was peeling the huge berries the Bihsts had gathered along the road, Peg dropped the news that Zago and Diaa seemed "enthusiastic" about each other.

Solyra squished a berry. "I didn't—"

"Pinch them gently at the tips," Peg cut in. "Like this." She pinched the papery skin off a few of the berries. "Just like you're pleasuring a man's nippies."

Solyra answered Peg's cackle with a forced giggle. Her memories of pinched nipples were anything but pleasant. But she wasn't going to be thrown off course.

"What makes you say—"

"And then cut them in quarters lengthwise. Gar, these fruits are sour but with a good long simmer and some—"

"What makes you say so?" Solyra finished loudly.

Peg shook her head. "All I'm saying is, Darklocks better make up her mind."

"What do you mean, make up—"

"Gar, what I could do with a nice tub of gwomps and a knob of butter."

>> <<

ZAGO CLAIMED THE FULGUS "LOVED" the constant rain, and so did the "gwomps," a kind of river clam, but no one else did. The animals nipped and bickered. Nearly every day, everyone had to push the wagons through mud. Peg fretted over her herbs and powders, and Baloos and Jaleen fretted over their cargo, four bales of cheap rugs. At every break in the clouds, the couple drew back the tarpaulins so the dampness wouldn't spoil them. They might have a few hours, before the rains came again.

Thanks to Peg's insistence on straining and boiling the

water, and the sour tisane that she forced on everyone nightly, no one was sick, and the rain meant plenty of grass for the animals. The terrain grew more level, too, which meant fewer mud bogs to churn through.

Still, leeches bred in the puddles, adding another task to their daily lot: picking clean their legs and the legs of the horses and donkeys and mules. Queenie rode in one of the wagons most of the time, boxing or snuggling with Snowball the cat.

Just when all except the fulgus and leeches were totally fed up, a day dawned without a cloud to mar the fresh, blue sky. Frogbelly called a rest to celebrate. It wasn't quite a rest day. They rubbed mildew from tack, lubricated axles, and doctored the animals. But a day not spent in motion, Solyra found, was celebration enough.

That evening, rather than huddling under tarpaulins or tents, they ate together around a fire under the still bright but softening sky. They'd left towns and cities far behind and their camp wasn't near one of the scattered farm cottages or villages. The flat expanse of grass was unbroken even by trees.

"It's like the ocean, in a way," Solyra said.

"Wet," said Panno — Panno the Pouty as Solyra secretly called the young Bihst man.

"True." Solyra used her finger to scoop up the last dollop of fruit custard from her plate, then put her finger out, pushing Queenie away with her foot so that Snowball, on his leash, could get it. He shot Queenie a smug glare, then licked Solyra's finger as daintily as could be.

Erin, the youngest of the Bihsts and of the whole caravan, spoke up. "You've been to the Ocean, Auntie?"

Solyra smiled at her and saw out of the corner of her eye Baloos and Jaleen take each other's hand. It was the first time Erin had spoken in company since they'd joined the caravan, maybe longer.

"I grew up on the shore," Solyra said. "My father clerked a while for a chandler — someone who sells supplies especially for ships. We didn't have a ship, but we went sailing sometimes. Once you're away from the land, the ocean sky is just as vast as this, and the water is this flat. Well, unless there's a storm. But my parents never took me out in a storm."

"No, I guess not," Terring said.

Solyra looked quickly at him, but he wasn't mocking.

He'd been fit and brown to start, and so the rigors of their journey hadn't changed him as much as it had Zago. In fact, he seemed to be settling into his element, his dark eyes, wide mouth, and overgrown black hair gentling into rugged tranquility.

And now he had gone from gazing back at her to smirking. Solyra tried to smirk in return, but it probably came across as a grimace and, confound her soul, a silly blush.

"You miss the ocean?" Tad asked.

Solyra shrugged. "It's been a long time since I was there. When my father changed jobs we moved inland."

The chandler went out of business, and they were forced to move in with her mother's parents. The old man, who'd disapproved of his daughter's marriage, took them in with every show of condescension, got her father the job at a bank that was one of the first to invest in fulgus.

"You were, what, eighteen that summer?" Terring asked.

She knew he didn't mean, the summer her family moved inland. He meant, when they'd first met each other, at the resort. "Eighteen I was, that summer." She looked at the fire, a smile fixed on her face.

Her father clerked at the fulgu conference held at the resort, taking her and her mother along. They'd stayed for only a week, yet it felt like a whole season to her. A summer week, a charmed interval between her girlhood and...Dahn.

Looking back, Solyra knew the resort as a second-rate joint, rundown and swanky. But at tea parties in the afternoon, pure white swans glided over a lake to get cake crumbs from her hands. And she had a new dancing gown, and a band played every night. And two wealthy men vied for her hand.

Terring had just returned from the Zhengahk, looking every inch the fulgu rancher, his face weathered dark, his suit well-made but faded and terribly outdated, his feet clad in boots instead of dancing slippers. And Dahn, a gentleman with scented flaxen hair in a ribboned queue, a dandy suit and patent-leather slippers, spun her with such elegant grace on the dance floor.

Two men equally wealthy, equally eligible, but her parents had encouraged Dahn. Ironically, they'd feared that Terring would take her far away from them.

"Solyra?" Terring said.

She got up and quickly left the fireside. Peg said behind her, "No, leave her be."

Solyra stood at the edge of the road staring up at the stars poking through the firmament. The larks had given way to bats flitting against the day's dying glow.

That summer was like a long-ago dream, Dahn and Terring courting her, a young woman yet untouched, taking their tribute with shy delight.

The next time she'd seen Terring and Dahn in one place was at the Booton conference. They'd vied not for her, but for a customer, a married man who'd eyed her and all but smacked his lips as she hung half-naked and drunk on Dahn's arm.

Solyra sighed. She'd fled the fireside thinking tears threatened, but none fell. After a visit to the privy pit, she returned to the fireside. No one questioned her. Secrets might have been hard to keep, but being unobservant at times was a privacy they gave each other. Except Terring stared at her, on the brink of a question.

Solyra wished that Peg hadn't stopped him from coming after her, that he'd come to her and asked, "Why? Why Dahn rather than me?"

Ridiculous thought.

And who was to say that Peg had been talking to him? It could have been Diaa, or Jaleen.

Terring moved to sit next to her. "And you married Dahn that year?" Picking up right where they'd left off, quietly, but Solyra sensed Peg listening.

"Yes."

"You were eighteen," he said, as if she hadn't already said as much. "And you were married for, what, seven years. Then five years ago—"

Peg broke in. "Garr, you don't ask a lady her age, even in such a mathematical way."

Terring didn't take his eyes from Solyra. "Five years ago you were widowed."

"Just so, mister mathematician," she returned.

"You did all right with the business in just five years," he said, "considering the shambles that Dahn left it in."

She searched for a reply, then shrugged again. The near demise of Dahn's business had been well known. And Terring's lack of sympathy for the young widow might not have been callousness. The picture of a proper marriage that she and Dahn had so carefully cultivated had been flimsy — even before Dahn died in a brothel.

The picture of business success that she had so carefully cultivated seemed to have been more believable. She'd been so close to making it real. So close....

"Meanwhile," she said, "you went out west, blew out a fulgu frame, and came back."

He gave a jaunty grin as fake as her attempt at another smirk. "That's pretty much it. Came back to... Well, to be beaten by the competition."

"Such as it was."

They both laughed for real then, and with his dark eyes smiling into hers, Solyra felt her heart lift. She felt, too, the warmth of his body, his arm, with the sleeve rolled up, next to her bare arm. Unexpectedly, he put an arm around her and gave her a little hug, then let her go and stood. "Jerzy. Brid. Robet."

The four men went to make a final check on the animals and what they grandly called the security arrangements: sentry shifts and the configuration of the wagons.

Peg stood. "Solyra. Erin. Tindy." The women burst out laughing.

"I heard that," Terring called back, and another gust of laughter went around the fire.

Giggling, the four women went back to the "kitchen," the tailgate of Peg's wagon.

The beans had already been picked over for stones and twigs; now they were put to soak in a crock that would ride secured in Peg's wagon. When they stopped for lunch the next day, the beans would cook with bacon.

Peg held up two eggs nearly the size of her head. "Look what Brid stole for breakfast." The eggs must have been from the nest of one of the man-tall, long-necked birds that loped through the grass.

"I hope mama bird doesn't come looking for them." Solyra mashed the day's leftover beans into a loaf pan to be congealed into "bean jelly," a treat she never would have thought could be so delicious. Tindy and Erin pulled the iron pot-ovens of bread from the embers of the kitchen fire, up-ended them, and hung the round breakfast loaves in linen bags to cool alongside a net of fresh roots.

"We'll have a nice cobbler from those berries you found," Solyra told Erin. The Bihsts had a knack for foraging every- thing from seeds and berries to tubers, honey, herbs and let- tuces. Solyra was, paradoxically, both more hungry and more well-fed than she'd ever been in her life.

Erin smiled, and though she didn't answer, Solyra was con- tent. From Erin, smiles were rare jewels to be treasured.

Only a year earlier, when she was eleven and her brother Raal was fourteen, their parents were killed in a pirate raid on their remote charcoal manufactory. The two children, foraging in the woods when the pirates struck, returned to their cottage to find it burned to the ground, their parents dead, and the livestock killed or stolen. Carrying a can that held the scavenged, charred remains of their mother and father, and a gunny sack holding Snowball, the only other survivor, they walked to the Bihst commune, about twenty miles away.

Baloos and Jaleen, long-time residents of the commune, had buried Jaleen's own mother, their last parent, only a few months earlier. With no children or close relatives, they'd decided to give in to their hankering to go out west. They asked Gobi to come along to help found a Bihst commune in the Zhengahk. Panno was coming along because, he said, he'd had enough of being persecuted for what he was — a homosexual. The young couple, Tindy and Dan, had also decided to try their fortune out west.

The children were adopted happily into the Bihst group. They called Baloos and Jaleen Gramma and Grampa, Gobi Master Gobi, and everyone else, including Solyra, Auntie or Uncle.

Solyra had just hung up her apron when Baloos and Jaleen came up to her.

"Could you give us a little business advice?" Jaleen asked.

"I can try," she smiled.

"We're planning on selling our rugs in the Ihm," Baloos said, "to get Jaleen enough money to set up a pottery studio while I try to find a job engineering."

"Engineering?" Solyra asked.

He nodded. "Roads and bridges. I've done water systems, too, but I have a feeling that where we're going, sewage systems and indoor plumbing won't be in high demand."

"Irrigation might. Have you talked to Figgo at all?"

"He said the Zhengahk is totally dried up. The water's died, was how he put it. Made me wonder if we're heading in the right direction. But there are still people out there, so, well, we'll just keep going. What Jaleen and I hope is that you can help us set up the books for our business. We both worked for other people back home and never got into the numbers side of things."

"You're going to scare her off," Jaleen said to Baloos, "making out like we know nothing. But we're not total babies," she said to Solyra. "We got a good deal on the rugs. Thanks to me."

"Thanks to me, you mean," Baloos said. Their mutual love was plain to see, but it didn't stop them from bickering. "They're very fine rugs. I'll show you."

He climbed up onto a wagon and pulled a bale of rugs to the edge. "Just a corner will give you the picture." He worked loose a piece of the bombazine covering to expose the rugs inside.

When Solyra had sold the costly imported rugs Dahn had laid over the floor of every room of their house, she'd learned how to value them. Rubbing "just a corner" between her fingers told her that she was not looking at a "very fine" rug.

It had a coarse, crackly feel. She almost expected the dye to rub right off on her hand. Now that she thought of it, the Bihsts all had faintly blue or red bottoms. They sat on the rugs for their services.

"Are all your rugs the same?" she asked.

"Yes," Baloos said, killing her hope that they'd put a low-quality rug on top. "We got a fantastic deal on one of the last shipments to come out of the Zhengahk. The dealer told us that the war brought the costs down, but that would change, with peace. And he said people in the Ihm would pay well for them."

Solyra could have told them it didn't work that way. War boosted the costs of exports; peace caused costs to sink. But it would have made no difference. Baloos's and Jaleen's rugs were not from the Zhengahk. They were knockoffs of tribal rugs, born and bred on industrial looms back east.

They couldn't very well turn back and demand a refund

from the dealer. Solyra decided not to say anything about the rugs' value. They hadn't asked for an appraisal. And she was a coward.

"Terring and I are setting up our business," she said, "and you're welcome to sit in on our meetings if you want. Figgo is an excellent administrator and my Diaa is learning; a few more students will help everyone."

Baloos and Jaleen beamed. "That's very kind of you, Solyra," Jaleen said. They repacked the rugs and returned to the fireside.

Most of the people had some kind of evening handicraft. There was always mending: tack, clothes, or tools. Terring was restoring a mandolin, and Figgo was working on a pair of drums. Gobi made use of the sea of grass around them, weaving baskets and cheerfully throwing his botched efforts into the fire. Baloos and Jaleen made and just as cheerfully mashed up mud pottery. Onyx and Ebony, the twin giants, incongruously knitted delicate lace. They were both deaf, but they understood most of what people said by reading lips and communicated with each other — and increasingly with the other Frogbellies — in their own language of gestures.

Solyra contented herself with mixing medicines, shelling beans — whatever chores Peg had left over. Peg did nightly battle with her wig. Because the hairs had not been laid in the same direction, they snagged and tangled. "Garr, when I get rich I'll buy me a wig as pretty as your hair, Darklocks. No one will recognize me."

"I'd know you anywhere," Jerzy put in.

Peg guffawed without looking up from her wig. His words hadn't held a touch of mockery — though Peg might not believe that.

"You two," Zago said easily.

Their heads jerked up and they stared at each other, then quickly looked down again, blushing, and combing and whittling furiously. Laughter went around the campfire. Jerzy and

Peg pretended nothing was happening, then finally gave in and laughed, too. Peg still wouldn't look up, though.

Solyra knew what her friend would say, next time they were alone with each other. She'd play the buffoon, as she always did, and whatever Solyra said wouldn't talk her out of her fixed notion that she didn't stand a chance to get Jerzy's love.

As the fire died down, they put away their projects and headed to their bedrolls. Most of the caravaners slept in tents or under the wagons. Gobi, Jaleen, Baloos, and the children camped in the Bihst wagon, made as cozy as a cottage once they set it up for the night.

Tiny though Peg's wagon was, Solyra loved its age-polished wooden walls, the faded flowers and designs long ago painted on its ceiling and around the tiny window, the shining copper and tin pots and pans neatly stowed in their racks, and the complicated smell of herbs and medicines, hams, coffee, and soap that escaped from the chests below the narrow sleeping platforms.

Solyra was climbing aboard when she heard Tad: "Holy crap."

He didn't sound panicked, but that didn't stop most everyone from getting up — several grabbing the weapons they never left out of reach — and pouring over to where Tad held a lantern.

At his feet sat the biggest animal skull Solyra had ever seen.

>> <<

"What is it?" Tad asked.

"It's a buffalumph," Baloos said.

"And a big one, at that," Terring added.

Even for a buffalumph, he reckoned, the skull was huge. A normal specimen stood as tall as a draft horse and twice as wide. The hair grew as coarse as porcupine quills, and both male and female had two, sometimes three horns jutting from their brows. A painting of buffalumphs Terring had seen back east portrayed them as peaceful, oversized cattle. In fact, they were stupid, mean, and paranoid.

"I thought buffalumphs lived only west of the Plid," Robet said.

"Hunters must have left the skull here," Frogbelly said. "There's no other bones around."

Figgo had knelt by the skull and felt it over. "I think the captain is correct. This is a trophy."

"Why'd someone leave a trophy like that?" Brid asked.

"How'd you like to carry that around?" Robet said.

"Or they left it as a warning," Baloos said. "If the animals left their normal migration route, they could be dangerous."

"I have been listening to the ground and haven't heard rumblings," Figgo said. "I am sure no herd is nearby. Yet this skull is not more than a few seasons old. If the buffalumphs have been hunted recently, they might have been driven into a new migration pattern." He stood, brushing his hands together.

"I haven't heard big animals either," Zago said.

Something about the way Figgo turned to him caused a curious hush to fall. "You put your ear to the ground, zizero Zago?"

Zago gave an embarrassed laugh. "Sometimes."

"What do you hear when you listen to the earth?"

Zago was silent, then said finally, "Water."

A crease came and went between Figgo's brows. The last time Terring had seen him show this much agitation was when ordered to draw up the contract with Solyra.

"Well, given that we're always by a river," Panno said, "you would hear water, wouldn't you?"

Zago laughed again. "Right."

But that wasn't the water Zago meant, and if Terring could hear the lie in his voice, Figgo would, too.

"And other water?" Figgo asked.

"Tell them, Zago," Diaa prompted.

Zago looked at his feet. "A lake under us."

"How can there be a lake—" Panno began.

"An aquifer is an underground lake," Figgo said. "How do you hear such a thing, Zago?"

"I'm not making it up!"

Solyra put a hand on his back. "Figgo didn't mean it that way. I think he's interested because he's from a desert land, where water is hard to find."

Figgo walked away.

HIDING

W HEN THE ROAD CONVERGED WITH a north-south trunk road, other wagon trains as well as soldiers in dust-colored uniforms passed the Frogbellies several times a day. The soldiers' main concern seemed to be collecting tolls, but they also gave news of other caravans, watering holes, weather patterns and anything else that could be of interest to travelers. No one on the increasingly busy road mentioned bandits, so apparently the soldiers did a good job keeping order as well.

Terring noticed that Frogbelly avoided chumming with the soldiers and the captains of other caravans. He remembered, too, that none of the permits, bills of lading, and registrations for the caravan were in Frogbelly's name, but rather in Lady Liberty's name or held by individual members of the caravan. Before signing on with Frogbelly, Terring had inspected the caravan and its papers thoroughly. He'd even insisted on taking apart personal baggage. While willing to overlook at few untaxed rugs, he wasn't going to be part of an operation smuggling weapons or drugs. But everything had been clean.

His inspection hadn't helped relations with Frogbelly or Tad, nor had the fact that Terring had negotiated the security job while still rattled about Solyra nearly being killed. As the discussion had grown heated, Frogbelly let Terring know that he considered any reference to the attack as a dig. But Terring wasn't about to shield the captain's pride from the fact that his caravan could have been wiped out by the pirate attack.

To cap it all off, at the Oaks Wayside Terring had caught Frogbelly rifling a stack of wanted posters evidently purloined from a mail bag. When Frogbelly looked up and saw Terring at the door, sheer terror fought with the rage that darkened his face. Terring's silence no doubt only bolstered Frogbelly's conviction that Terring was pleased to have something to hold over his head.

Pilfering wanted posters from a mailbag — to find one on himself? Terring would have found out by now if the man was smuggling even so much as a hairpin. Still, something was going on. It was only a matter of time before the truth spilled out. Meanwhile, Terring was watching him — and Frogbelly and Tad knew it.

They kept their bad blood in, though. As colleagues and as caravan mates, they knew how to keep it in.

Terring couldn't fault Frogbelly's skill as a captain. He kept everything rolling. Just as important, he knew when to rest, a not-so-fine point that caravaners often ignored to their peril. Animals, not to mention people, could only work so hard for so long.

If they were near a roadhouse on their break day, some of the crew spent their pay to go in and sleep on a bed, take a bath, and eat trash, as Peg called the cafe offerings. Terring was among them. Greasy, salty food, a real bed, a hot bath: they were worth a few coins from Lady Liberty's reward purse. He left the well-weathered sex-workers alone.

At a roadhouse that nearly qualified as a lodge, Terring treated himself to a deep massage not from a busty woman, but from a blacksmith. A back injury he'd suffered during the war had come back to life after he helped change a wagon wheel.

Once the smith had pummeled, rubbed and kneaded the pain into submission, he commanded Terring, "You bath. Now. Hot bath."

"Where is bath?" Terring asked.

Terring understood enough of the local dialect to get the gist of the directions: look for the building with steam seeping from the eaves.

He also knew the local symbols for men and women. Or he thought he knew. But maybe he didn't, or maybe some prank-ster switched the signs. When he strolled into the bathing area, towel slung over his shoulder, he saw not other men but Diaa.

Oblivious to the male intrusion, she paddled about in the hot spring pool, her back turned. Her buttocks resembled a Back East dessert called floating islands. As momentum and sheer maleness robbed his mind of volition, Terring took a step further. Solyra came in sight.

She stood, eyes closed, legs braced apart, steaming water lapping just above her knees. With arms raised, she held her hair up behind her. Her entire body was streaming with water, flushed and shining, and utterly naked.

Terring's mind puddled. Then the puddle rose into a flood—

A hand at the back of his bathrobe pulled him back, just moments, perhaps, before he charged mindlessly into the water and hurled himself on Solyra.

Peg.

"Women only, my friend." At least she said it quietly.

>> <<

A DAY AFTER THEY PULLED out of the Warrior's Woost Roadhouse — Brid challenging the two children to say it fast three times — a line of wagons came in sight and, at the head of the line, the Plid River, wide and brown. By midmorning they joined the line, moved about twenty footlengths, and stopped.

Frogbelly called a meeting. "Today's gonna be a long day,

stop and go," he said. "We'll probably reach the ferry by late afternoon. If we're ready to cross, we'll make it to the other side tonight. That's my wish." It was Frogbelly's way of saying, everyone better be ready when they reached the ferry.

"Keeping in mind that the wagons will be pulled across by rope pulleys," he continued, "we need to re-stow everything. Jerzy and I will boss you."

Terring didn't trust Frogbelly not to be a criminal of some kind, but he did trust him completely as a caravan captain and had no issue with being bossed by him when it came to transportation.

Frogbelly had ensured that the loads were balanced throughout the journey, to minimize wear on the wagons and animals. During the crossing, though, water would seep in to the wagons, so they had to put whatever must stay dry atop the other things. The fulgus could stay at the bottom to get, as Zago said, "a nice, cool bath." The dish crates also went at the bottom. Clothes and linens made the next layer. Baloos and Jaleen bickered about whether their rugs could be put atop: Baloos was sure the rugs would withstand anything and at any rate, they were wrapped in tarpaulins; Jaleen didn't want to take a chance. Frogbelly settled it by decreeing they would go atop, though he surely knew how worthless the rugs were — everyone did, apparently, except Baloos and Jaleen.

Terring helped Peg and Jerzy wrap the pharmacy tightly in the best tarp and stifled a laugh as Jerzy ogled down Peg's dress while she leaned over the knotwork. Terring had tried to get Jerzy to make a move on Peg, but the man shied off with every excuse in the book, from "it wouldn't be good for relations" to "I'm not her type." Everything but the truth, which was that even after all these miles he was too bashful to do more than joke around with her now and then.

Well, Terring knew for himself how devastating "no" could be from a woman, though he didn't discourage Jerzy by saying so.

They arrived at the crossing by late afternoon, as Frogbelly predicted. Terring made short work of negotiations with the crossing authorities, and they were ready to cross.

Each wagon would be fastened to a system of lines and pulleys operated by a troll with a foursome of froward looking mules. Terring, with Jerzy, Tad and Panno, swam ahead on horseback. The current swept them a good hundred yards down river, and the horses were panting by the time they clambered up the opposite bank.

"It's blasted strong," Terring said to Jerzy.

"Yeah," Jerzy said without lowering the spyglass he was peering through. "Lines look sturdy enough, though."

The first wagon carried Gobi, Jaleen, Tindy and Dan across. Though they were wet to the knees when they climbed out, the passage seemed safe enough.

Solyra got on the next wagon with Baloos, Erin and Raal, and Snowball, who traveled in his cage clutched in Erin's arms.

Terring took the spyglass from Jerzy without asking.

The first thing he happened to focus on was Snowball. The cat had been grumbling and farting since last night; Raal said he'd eaten a rodent that hadn't gone down well. At least the beastie seemed settled down for the ride over the river.

Just as Terring was starting to move the glass to Solyra, the cat swiped at Erin's palm through the edges of the cage. Erin's lips moved, the river's roar covering her ouch!, She lifted her hand to check the scratch — just as the wagon jolted on the pulleys.

The cage flew from her hands. Her scream carried over the current.

Terring shoved the spyglass back in Jerzy's hands, tore to his horse, jumped on, and galloped into the water.

The cat, cage and all, bobbed in the brown torrent. By some miracle it hadn't capsized. But Terring's horse simply couldn't make enough headway to reach it.

Then the cage overturned.

"The rugs!" Jaleen screamed from the bank.

The confounded cat! Terring felt like yelling back. Erin and Raal would be devastated if anything happened to their Snowball. The cheap rugs hardly mattered.

But Baloos understood. He drew his knife and cut loose one of the rug bales, put the end of its rope into Solyra's hands. Then he jumped with the bale into the river.

Baloos managed to grab the cage and pull it onto the bale with him. The bale bobbed precariously. The strain on the rope Solyra held threatened to yank the wagon off the pulleys, but if she let go, the current would take Baloos.

The bale was sinking fast, the water over Baloos's knees. Terring didn't have time to get closer.

He yelled, "Solyra! Let go when I say!" He could only pray she understood as he maneuvered the laboring horse downstream of Baloos.

"Let go!" he shouted.

Solyra released the rope, and the rug raft and Terring came together. Terring grabbed the cage while Baloos dragged himself up behind Terring.

The wagon reached the shore safely, so did Baloos and Terring even if their legs shook as they dismounted.

A hero's welcome pinned Terring and Baloos to the landing. Snowball got hugs, too, though as Peg said, "That rascal doesn't deserve all the fuss." Jaleen harangued the men to get into dry clothes, but when Baloos began to go toward their baggage, she threw her arms around him, wet duds and all.

"Where did Solyra go?" Terring asked Peg. She was rubbing Snowball with a dish towel, and he took advantage of her distraction to whap her with a paw and take over using his tongue.

She stood up. "She needs to be alone." She wiped her hands on her apron. "And you need to...."

Terring didn't stay to hear what he needed to do. He strode to Peg's wagon, threw open the door, grabbed Solyra and pulled her stumbling out. Her face was wet not with river water but with tears.

Terring wrapped her in a bear hug. And she let him. All chill and drenched as he was, she circled him with her arms, pressed herself against his body and sobbed.

He closed his eyes and gave to her his strength. Her sobs subsided. He felt her calming. He knew, somehow, that she could hear his heart beating within him. He felt the moment, too, when she came to herself and began to pull away. It felt a little like heartbreak.

His heart broke a little more when he looked in her face. He'd had a foolish thought that she had been scared that he would drown, that she'd been scared for him. And she looked scared, now.

Scared of him, not for him.

No, it must have been the trauma of the crossing. Terring forced a grin. "Pussy's all right," he said. "No need to take on like that."

The fear left her eyes, and she laughed. "You idiot." She rubbed her face. "I better stop slacking or Frogbelly will make me harness the O team." The nickname for the most ornery animals.

Had it just been a dream? Feeling their hearts beat together. A union deeper than desire.

And she walked away from it, blithe as can be.

Shape up, chump, Terring told himself as he changed into dry clothes. She's just a flitting bird — except toward her business. So stick to business.

>> <<

THEY WERE THE LAST CARAVAN to cross for the day, and the mishap had given the wagon train ahead of them a head start, so when they stopped for camp they were on their own. Peg and Solyra excused Erin from kitchen duty so she could nurse the cat, although as Peg said, "nothing wrong with him other than a bruised ego, and beating up on poor Queenie will take care of that."

Solyra doubted Snowball had taken anything out on Queenie. As she headed back to Peg's wagon after dinner, the two animals were snoozing together.

She found Peg savagely kneading a piece of dough the size of a six-month child, using the tailgate as a counter, a lamp hung overhead.

"What's wrong?" Solyra asked. When Peg kneaded like that, she was upset about something.

"Oh, nothing."

And when she wouldn't talk, she was very upset.

"Tell me, Peg," Solyra asked. "And cut me off a baby piece of that."

Peg cut her a loaf-sized chunk of dough and Solyra began kneading.

"Now tell me—" Solyra began.

"Nay, push your baby boy down in the middle, roll him up, like so, then push, then fold, see?"

"Right. So, Peg, what's—"

"Speed before beauty. Remember?"

"You mean beauty before... Peg." Solyra put her floury hands around Peg's heaving shoulders. "Talk to me, Peg."

Peg stopped her tears almost immediately, but the woe didn't leave her face, even with her forced laugh. "I've got a problem you wouldn't know, Darklocks. Gar, but I'm ugly."

Solyra didn't know what to say, because it was undeniably true: Peg was ugly.

Peg laughed again. "Gotcha stumped, eh, Darklocks?"

"I love you, Peg. So does everyone else. Beauty before speed, but love conquers all."

Peg hugged her. "That means a lot, and don't think I don't believe it. And don't think that I'm ungrateful, but the love of my friends won't nab me a man for my bed. Not a man with honest intentions, anyway. And don't try to fix me up with your blind chum." She cackled. "Not my type. Back to our bread, Darklocks. Yeast waits not for self-pity."

Solyra attacked her little ball of dough again. Dahn had married her for her looks, and no other reason. For her body and her face. And maybe he'd seen through that to something else. He'd seen that she would go limp, rather than fight...

"I hate them all," Solyra said suddenly. "No, not Zago. He's all right. And Jerzy. And... Oh, I don't really. But you know what I mean."

"Men aren't so bad, Darklocks."

Solyra didn't want to bicker with Peg, but just as Figgo had developed his other senses, Solyra had developed a sense of what men thought when they looked over a woman. However nice and warm and strong he could be, Terring was still just like any man.

But not like Dahn. She'd dreaded Dahn's touch.

When Terring and she embraced, she'd wanted to melt to the heat of his body burning through the chill river water soaking him. Her head to his chest, his heart beating in her ear, his arms encircling her.

Then she'd panicked.

"How does your little boy feel?" Peg asked.

"Soft and warm as a baby boy should."

"And fair with little freckles?"

"Just so."

"All right." Peg divided up the dough and showed Solyra how to form loaves. After covering them with a cloth, Peg extinguished the lamp. "Don't worry about me, Darklocks," she said. "I'm happy in my life. I just get a little horny sometimes."

Solyra supposed she felt pretty much the same.

>> <<

A WEEK OUT FROM THE Plid River, the grass grew sparse and dry, and the groves of ash and hickory became cottonwoods along flat, wide stream beds. Figgo, with Terring helping, gave lessons in Zhi'nging'ha! every night. Onyx and Ebony took sentry during the lessons so everyone else could attend, though Zago and Diaa tried to get out of the lessons by volunteering for sentry. Figgo and Terring told about the Zhengahk, too, its customs, its plants and animals and geology, its history and government and economy.

Solyra and Terring also began forming a business plan. Diaa attended the meetings enthusiastically, but as an aide to Solyra, she was a bust. Whenever Solyra tried to teach her anything about business, from how not to break a deal to basic accounting, it was like pouring water on an upside bowl.

When Terring took Diaa in hand, though, which he did more and more often, she was all perked up ears and bright eyes. Even under Figgo's dreaded tutelage she progressed: she could read and write at a basic level, in both Norvadale and Zhi'nging'ha!. Solyra knew she should be glad, but irritation got in the way.

Zago attended the business meetings only because Solyra ordered him to. His listless presence contributed nothing. During his free time, if he wasn't with Diaa or the Bihsts, he was mooning over his fulgu crates. He'd even taken to sleeping with them, doing extra crew work in exchange for a wagon berth.

One evening, Solyra saw Diaa climb up in the wagon after him.

She had gone to the rear to throw out a hunk of meat not fit even for Queenie. In the deepening dusk, she stared at the wagon as if it were riding away with her dearest dream.

She turned back and nearly ran into Terring. "I just don't get what you women see in that fellow," he grinned.

Solyra considered braining him with the meat dish. Instead, she walked around him without a word. After dropping the dish off at Peg's wagon, she continued alone along the track made by a shepherd who had sold them some tough mutton and pungent cheese. She walked far enough away for the wind in the rough grass to shush the voices of her companions.

It shouldn't have surprised her, Diaa bedding with Zago. Certainly it shouldn't have upset her. Zago and she had made love only a few times since they'd entered the Plains. The argument at the meeting with Lady Liberty had frayed the intimacy between them, the intimacy she'd wanted to break away from.

She missed it.

And she wanted to slap Diaa silly for having it.

The horizon deepened into darkness against the dusty orange rim of the indigo sky. Solyra tried to let the dewy fragrance of the world sooth her spirit. Stars sprang forth more quickly than even Figgo could have counted, had he been able to see them. A bird passed low over the road, a shadow in flight.

Solyra didn't know what drew out the tears that wet her cheeks: remorse, self-pity, or just homesickness. She sorely missed her porch buddies, as she and her neighbors used to call each other. She missed the ocean, and groves of oak trees, and buildings, and the horses and rickshaws and carriages bustling by her house. She wished she knew her parents were all right. She wished Dahn had been a good husband, that he hadn't succeeded in flaying her spirit.

She wished she could fly into the deepening night, up to where the stars came from, to lose herself in that immeasurable, jeweled vastness.

But she couldn't. She wiped her face on her shirt tail and returned to the encampment.

Peg read her face, but as they cleaned up the last of the pots and pans, she only chatted about how tough groundpigs were unless they stewed overnight. And one of the men found more eggs, so they'd have a feast of four eggs between near a dozen people. Tomorrow she would show Solyra how to make biscuits with bean flour.

And Peg was the one with a right to mope, her unrequited love for Jerzy weighing on her heart. "I won't make a fool of myself," she'd vowed, and she didn't. She kept her love tucked tight under her laughy-joky manner. Solyra wondered what it would be like, to love a man as Peg did. She'd loved Dahn, for a very short while, or she'd thought she loved him, and she'd thought her love was returned. Illusion or not, any romance was killed on their wedding night, when he'd taken with violence what she would have given freely, even if unskillfully.

"Let's go for a walk," Peg said, grabbing a blanket.

They didn't venture into the grass, where venomous critters lurked. They went down the shepherd's track, a little past where Solyra had stopped before, and sat on the blanket.

"We're a couple of sad sacks, that's for sure," Peg said as she rolled an herbal cigar.

Solyra laughed. "I hope we fool the others better than we fool each other."

"Oh, they don't know beans." Peg inhaled deeply, then passed it to Solyra.

"Peg, why don't you just tell him?" Solyra grunted through her own inhalation. "Tell him how you feel."

"Gar, Darklocks, can you imagine how that would go over? Poor Jerzy. Pursued over the plains by a frightful looking baldy."

"Stop talking that way," Solyra said sharply. "I don't like it."

Peg replied with a forced chuckle and another toke. "You're right. It's getting old."

She passed the herb back to Solyra.

"I'm sure Jerzy likes me fine. As a friend. As a girlfriend? No. And in close quarters like this, you don't want to make mistakes with other people."

"It wouldn't be a mistake."

"Trust me, I've been this way many a time. With Jerzy and without."

"I've made one mistake after another since I started this trip," Solyra said. "My latest being to let my business become a free roadhouse."

Peg's exhalation turned into a long raspberry, and they both went into a gale of laughter. Peg knocked the ember off the cigar and put the stub in a little tin.

"I think we've had enough smoke."

That set off another burst of laughter. They sat for a long time, pointing out constellations they knew, making up others, crying out when they saw a shooting star. Solyra didn't often smoke herb; it tended to make her broody. This time it had the opposite effect, though she did feel unusually sensitive about lurking snakes.

At the encampment, only the lookouts were still awake. Solyra had already decided to forgo Peg's wagon tonight in favor of sleeping under the open sky.

Someone had smoothed the ground, laid out a canvas and her bedroll for her. She shook out the sleeping bag, a reflex against creatures, then lay down. Sure enough, the brooding set in.

Not that she hadn't already brooded out the topic: about how, step by sure step, her machinations against Terring dogged her. Like a pack of dogs, yes, one nipping here, another nipping there, barks worse than their bites maybe, or maybe not. The dog she wrestled with now was an old one, but bigger than ever. Because it threatened her friendship with Peg.

What would she say if she knew that Solyra had coldly, calculatedly, undermined Terring's business then jumped to grab it when it was finally destroyed?

Terring hadn't let on, nor had Figgo. They wouldn't, most likely. Having exacted his revenge, Terring contented himself with jabbing at her now and then. Figgo was sated with his own righteousness. Besides, if they undermined her integrity they'd foul their own nest. But if Diaa figured something out, would she tell others? If she told even one of them, sure as the sun rose and set, Peg would find out.

Funny, how the threat of exposure sharpened shame. Solyra had felt only fear and fury when Terring spoiled their deal.

Even after he told her what his business meant to him — *a little corner passed down from my grandfather to my father to me* — she'd felt only a grain of remorse, a grain she'd shoved down to the very bottom of her heart, then buried with excuses. He had plenty of money; she had more important things to tend to; it hadn't really been her fault that his business had gone under — the frame crash was to blame.

All technically true, but it didn't change what she'd done. She'd hit a man when he was down, not by honest competition but with underhanded intrigues. However she turned it, that's the way it was. What her father and mother would think of their daughter's methods didn't bear contemplating.

It wasn't her own sobs she heard, muffled in a bedroll. She sat up silently. Stars softly illuminated the camp, the world.

"Tad?" she whispered.

He stopped: he might have been holding his breath. She got out of her bedroll and pulled her caftan over her long underwear, then crept over to him. Brid, on lookout, glanced back, then out again. "Let's talk," Solyra whispered.

Tad slipped out of his bedroll, pulled on trousers and boots, and they crept up front of the camp. Robet, on prow lookout, murmured a greeting as they passed.

"Don't tell anyone," Tad said as soon as they could talk without being overheard. "That's all they need: the feh crying in his pillow."

Solyra couldn't imagine who he meant by "they." No one on the caravan had a problem with Frogbelly's and Tad's relationship. But he would be used to prejudice, even persecution

"I almost thought it was me," Solyra said. "I was feeling that miserable. It's what I get for smoking hemp."

"You've got hemp?"

"No, sorry. It was Peg's."

He gave a laugh. "Peg and her herb jars." Then he heaved a sigh. "So what's your heartache?"

"I'm ashamed of something I did back home, and afraid it's

going to come out, sooner or later. Then everyone will hate me."

"That's good." His tone said he meant, her problem was worthy of misery. "Are you a dangerous criminal? A pervert?"

"No. So, what about you?"

"I'm a pervert. A feh. Isn't that enough? Worse than a dangerous criminal, eh? What do you think?"

"I… I don't know. I mean, no! Not even close. But you have Cap'n Frogbelly. Or are you guys not getting along?"

"Frogbelly. What a name. It was funny at first. Now I'm sick of it. Did you know he used to own a transportation company? He had a fleet of caravans, not this motley — but well-maintained, mahm! — bunch of antiques."

"What happened?"

"What do you think?" Tad asked.

"One of his competitors threatened to set him up on perversion charges, so he had to flee. The government confiscated the business. The competitor bought the fleet at auction."

"That's it, more or less. Except the competitor settled for forcing him to sell out. Said competitor being my father."

"Oh, no."

"He blamed… Carl. That's his real name. He blamed Carl for quote corrupting his son unquote and made out that Carl seduced me when I was still a minor — a lie — to stick it to Carl and keep me out of jail."

He fell silent, then continued more grimly. "You know, if Carl dropped me for that little prick Panno he'd be way better off. He'd be free."

So that was the thing between Tad and Panno the Pouty. "Is he interested in Panno?" Solyra asked.

"He says he's not. But give it time… I love Carl, and I ruined his life. He thinks the same — that he ruined my life, no matter how many times I tell him that I never, ever want to go home."

"That's good," Solyra said, and they both laughed. "What's your real name, then?"

"Teyod."

"Would it be dangerous if we call you by your real names? I've always felt embarrassed calling the cap'n Frogbelly. It doesn't seem respectful."

"No, don't do that. The last thing I need is for my parents to somehow find us and send a message: come home, all is forgiven, as long as you promise not to be a pervert anymore." He sighed. "I shouldn't have told you, really."

"Don't worry. Your secret's safe with me."

"I'd say the same, but I don't know your secret. Child abuse? Home-wrecking?"

"No, nothing like that. Not girl stuff. Just business machinations. Lying and cheating. Bringing a good man down. All that. See? I'm a soulless merchant through and through."

"Really." Pause. "Hey, I was just kidding."

"I know."

"Don't cry. It totally messes me up."

Solyra sniffed back her tears. "You men are all alike."

"Close enough, anyway."

They began to walk back toward the encampment — and then broke into a run, screaming: "Fire! Fire!"

OUT OF THE ASHES

DESPITE THE CHAOS, A BUCKET brigade of half-naked crew and passengers quickly formed a line from the river to the smoking cargo wagon, and steam soon joined the billows of smoke.

Terring, in the wagon that was burning, was about to pull loose a bale of smoldering rugs when Solyra suddenly climbed up.

"Get back!" Terring yelled. He tossed the rugs clear, his eyes watering from the smoke.

"The fulgus can't get hot!" she cried. "We have to get them out."

"Get back, I'm on it!"

Terring had just taken hold of another bale, scorching his hand on the rope, when Jerzy started screaming. His clothes were in flames. A bucket of water dowsed him, and Terring lowered him out of the wagon into Brid's arms. Peg hurried up and they half-carried, half-walked him to her wagon.

The fire was nearly out. Terring had cleared the fulgus and Zago was poised to sprinkle them when a strange sound froze them. Terring stood bewildered listening.

A music that had no tune, and yet carried every tune under heaven.

Jerzy's groans pulled Terring out of whatever trance had fallen over him. "Let's get on with this," he said.

Zago sprinkled the fulgus, Terring playing water bearer, while Brid, Tindy, Dan and Robet worked on in a reeking cloud of steam and smoke to rake wads of still smoldering wool out of the wagon. Tad, Frogbelly, Onyx and Ebony managed to round up the animals that had pulled their stakes and bolted.

"I can take it from here," Zago said. Terring jumped down from the wagon and went to Jerzy.

The hostler lay groaning on a hastily made pallet. Peg and Baloos had cut off his clothes and the burns gleamed with ointment in the lamp that Gobi held up.

"Anything I can do, Peg?" Terring asked.

"Help lift him into my wagon," she said.

After Jerzy was settled on one of the sleeping platforms in Peg's wagon, Terring was about to take the kids for a walk — anything to distract them from their own horrible memories of fire — when he heard Solyra at the foot of the wagon.

"Zago? Let's talk."

Zago froze for a moment, unwrapping a sodden bale of rugs. Then he pretended he hadn't heard her.

"Zago!" she called again. Brid said something to him, and pointed toward Solyra. He nodded and jumped from the wagon, a very unconvincing nonchalance on his face.

Baloos and Jaleen had taken Erin and Raal in hand, making a show of calming Snowball, who wasn't daunted in the least. Terring rubbed his stubbled chin, looked toward where Solyra and Zago had gone. They were out of earshot, but Terring didn't need to hear in order to know that she wasn't just asking him how the fulgus were doing. Her face, in the light of the lamp between them, was furious.

"Are you and Diaa Bihst now, is that it?" he heard her demand as he approached them.

"No! No. Don't blame them." The lamplight revealed the defiance that crept into Zago's face. "They teach reverence for life. Any kind of life! Not just people."

"Oh, I see," Solyra said. "Yes, I've noticed that you've been taking a bite less meat with your supper."

"You don't understand!"

Terring didn't either, but something made Solyra's voice tremble with rage. "What's going on?" he asked. Neither even glanced at him.

"I understand more than you think," she growled at Zago. "Those pamphlets you're so fond of quoting were written by a hack."

"How do you know?" Zago demanded.

"Because I hired him! Take some outdated fulgu science, put it together with some Bihst crap, and — behold! The divine spark within fulgus is born. Throw in a couple of lunatics and students, and you've got the fulgu rights movement, tailor-made to make the life of my competitor, zizero Terring, miserable."

Zago gaped, his eyes round. "I can't believe…"

"You better believe it." She gestured toward Terring. "He does, I assure you."

But Terring himself, in fact, could hardly believe it. He could hardly believe any of this. He could barely sort out what to deal with first.

She turned on Diaa, who had crept up. "I suggest you hop on the next caravan going east. In fact, I'll pay for you to go by coach, that's how fast I want to put the miles between us."

Terring reeled with everything from the fire, to the strange trance that music had set on him, to the accusation Solyra seemed to be making — that Zago and Diaa had deliberately fired the wagon. He gripped hard the cord of control within himself. When he spoke again, his voice came out harsh but at least not in a yell.

"This is what we will tell our companions. You, Zago, and

you, Diaa, were smoking in the wagon and it got out of control. No confessions. You'll settle for that amount of idiocy. Don't you dare blab anything else! Understood?"

Zago and Diaa nodded.

"I'm sorry," Terring said, "I didn't hear that."

"Yes, sir," Diaa said, and Zago, "Yes, zizero."

"What did you say?" Terring asked, glaring at Zago.

Zago gulped. "We'll tell everyone that we were smoking in the wagon and it got out of control."

Diaa echoed him. Their tearfulness evoked not a drop of pity from Terring. He only hoped they could actually keep to the story. But then, they wouldn't want it known that they'd deliberately set the fire to rescue a bunch of rocks.

"Diaa, do you believe that nonsense about fulgus being alive?" Terring asked.

"I don't know," Diaa whispered.

"You heard them," Zago said. "You hear their song."

"By heaven," Terring fumed, "you've...."

Solyra put a hand on his arm. "Never mind that for now," she said. To Zago and Diaa, "You two go and help at the wagons. And what will you say to your companions whose belongings and cargo you've damaged, and whose friend you may have disfigured and crippled, and is crying in agony?"

Diaa gulped, but a few sobs escaped, and maybe a few drops of pity watered Terring's heart. "We were smoking and it got out of hand," Diaa said. Solyra made Zago repeat it, and they left.

As much as the deception stuck in Terring's craw, he hoped Zago and Diaa would stick with the story. The last thing they needed at this point in a long, hard journey was an irreparable rift.

He turned to Solyra. "Are you really sending her back?"

"Do you want to keep her?" she asked back.

"For earth's sake."

"Never mind. It's not my business what goes on between you two."

"Nothing goes on between us."

"It's not my business," she repeated. "And of course I'm not sending her back. It's not her fault anyway. Not really."

She turned her face away but not before Terring saw tears track over her soot-smudged cheeks. He dabbed them away with his bandanna.

"It's not your fault, either, Solyra."

"It is. And now poor Jerzy…. Peg will never speak to me again."

"Nonsense."

"I never should have let Zago take time off to attend those cursed fulgu rights meetings."

To his own amazement, Terring felt a laugh in his belly. "You encouraged him with that nonsense?"

"I thought he'd do a better job… As a fulgu keeper."

"You silly little pussycat."

"I am not a pussycat." But a smile trembled on her lips.

"You can't deny you're silly."

She gave a tremulous laugh even as two big, fat tears rolled down her cheeks. He longed to kiss them away. But an unsteady love affair was another thing they didn't need. And he'd seen the flinch she tried to hide, when he touched her face.

>> <<

TERRING FIGURED THE DAMAGE WOULD have been worse had he and Frogbelly not mandated fire drills. Still, worthless as Baloos and Jaleen's rugs were, they were all the couple had, and now another bale was destroyed. The rest of the crew's little trade concerns — silks, raw wool, dyes, toys, gems — had fortunately been in the other wagons. Unfortunately, not all the supplies were, and the roadhouses, with their comfortable array of dry goods, had disappeared after the Plid crossing. Some lean days stretched between here and the next caravansary.

Add some days, too, for an unscheduled layover. Peg didn't want Jerzy jolted by any movement, and the rest of the crew had to repair the burned wagon and finish salvaging the cargo. Frogbelly's first order of the day, though, was to call Terring Fulgus — minus the fulgus — to a conference, out of earshot of camp. Tad spread some of Baloos's scorched blankets on the river bank. It was the last gesture of courtesy offered by Frogbelly Freight.

Frogbelly didn't raise his voice as he spoke, but his face, flat and hard and flushed, spoke as loud as a yell.

"Zago, the fire was your first strike so I won't hold it against you too much, though believe me, I'm keeping track. As for you—" he pointed at Diaa "—one more piece of trouble, and you're out. Doesn't matter where we are, you mess up again and you're on your tail with your baggage and a day of food and water."

Terring knew that it was vital to keep out of Frogbelly's way when it came to running the caravan. Still, only knowledge of the fire's real cause kept Terring from ripping into the man.

It didn't keep Diaa quiet, though. A ridge of hair bristled from her forehead to the nape of her neck and her lips drew back. "You don' like me 'cause o' what I am."

"That's right," Frogbelly answered. "I don't like plain, unvarnished trouble and that's what you—"

"You won't kick anyone off this caravan," Solyra broke in. "No, sir, you won't."

Frogbelly's face flushed deeper red, and Terring drew a breath to speak, but Solyra shot him a look, shoved her trembling hands under her apron and pushed on.

"Yes," she said, "Diaa and Zago were foolish and wrong to let the fire happen. But the business with Bo — which must be the other piece of trouble you're referring to — wasn't Diaa's fault. That was your fault, if fault must be found. You hired the bum, right? So knock it off with threatening my Diaa. She pulls her weight around here and then some."

"All right," Frogbelly said. "I'll knock it off with her and take it up with you — and with Terring, my so-called security officer, who seems more intent on watching me than…." He paused, apparently to rein himself in.

"You friggin' right I'm watching you, Cap'n," Terring said. "And you know why."

The color that dropped out of Frogbelly's face seemed to rush directly into Tad's.

Solyra put a hand to Terring's arm and squeezed it hard. Painfully hard. "I know why, too, and you can knock that off, partner. Now, gentlemen, let us resolve the matter at hand. We have work to do."

Frogbelly pulled himself together with a visible effort, while Terring, with what must have been an equally visible effort, attempted to digest or at least swallow down yet another secret Solyra had not seen fit to divulge to her "partner."

"No one told me your cargo is hazardous," Frogbelly said. "Then last night Robet told me you two were wild about what might happen if your cartons of fulgus caught. So tell me yourselves, if you please, Zago, since you seem to have an intimate knowledge of them, what would have happened if the fire hadn't been put out when it was?"

Zago shrugged rather than answering. He was scared witless, Terring realized. Then he burst out, "They're alive!"

Frogbelly looked disgusted. Tad turned to Terring.

"Are they hazardous?" he demanded. "That's a yes or no question."

Terring gulped down another gutful of rage to answer in the calmest tone he could muster. "There's not a yes or no answer to that. If pod fulgus are activated, they give off energy."

Frogbelly didn't go for a calm tone, forced or not. "If they're activated they give off energy. I take that as, yes, they're hazardous! That they might have exploded last night! And Solyra talked me into putting them all in one wagon. The same wagon your employees used as a smoking lounge."

Solyra opened her mouth to answer—but Terring cut in.

"Cap'n, I will monitor the fulgus from here out and furnish you a status report every day. Zago will tend them under my personal supervision. I'll pay extra to bunk in the wagon with them. I apologize for the security slip."

"I'm sorry," Zago mumbled.

"I'm sorry, too," Diaa said, her voice edged with a whine.

"Consider extending apologies to each member of the caravan," Frogbelly said. "For myself, apologies accepted, providing there's nothing else up your sleeve that will endanger my caravan or passengers."

"There's nothing else," Terring said. "At least on my side."

Tad swelled up like a game cock. It was Frogbelly's turn, this time, to cast oil on the waters, which he did by lacing his fingers through Tad's.

"As far as compensation for our shipmates..." Frogbelly trailed off. "We'll have to work that out."

Terring supposed he should be grateful that Frogbelly didn't make more of a flap, though that was probably due to his idea that Terring was a blackmailer lying in wait.

"I'm sure we can come up with a fair arrangement," Terring said.

"Right," Frogbelly said. "Well, you just stick to your end of things."

"That cargo is my last chance in the business," Terring said. "I can't afford to let it be damaged or compromised."

"See that you don't." Frogbelly and Tad left.

"Thank you for stickin' up for me, Solyra," Diaa said.

Terring wasn't the only one tamping down his emotions. Solyra's smile to Diaa was painfully forced.

"Zago, what's the condition of the fulgus?" Terring asked. "You said last night they were safe."

Zago drew a deep breath. "Well, I'm pretty sure none of them opened—"

"What do you mean, pretty sure?"

"They could be just cracked by a hair, but they don't… They don't sound like they're open."

Zago said the last a little defensively, expecting ridicule, probably, but the memory flashed on Terring of that music that had entranced him, even in those desperate moments. He'd gone back to the lockers after the fire was out and hadn't heard anything. "What do they sound like? Now, I mean."

"They're a little stirred up."

Terring drew a breath to curse, but Solyra put a hand on his arm. They seemed to be taking turns keeping each other from blowing their lids off. "What do we need to do?" she asked.

"They should be submerged in water overnight at least every other day, preferably every day."

"That'll be a hell of a trick when we're in the mountains."

"It will indeed," Figgo said. He had been completely silent and, as usual, unreadable throughout the conference. He was silent again now, but no one spoke. Everyone knew he wasn't done talking.

The sun, about halfway up the sky, flashed on his goggles as he raised his face to follow a trio of water birds coming in, wings creaking, to land with a splash on the thin, brown river. Brid and Robet had wanted to snare some of the birds, but Peg forbade it: she'd seen nestlings paddling around in the water.

Figgo adjusted his goggles. "The people on this journey crave a new start in a foreign land," he said. "I am going back to my homeland in order to gather my kinfolk and take them back east to a new life. At least, those who survived the army of criminals called the Death Bringers."

The stories of the Death Bringers described such cruelty, many people back east simply didn't believe them. Terring had seen; he believed.

"They burned barns," Figgo continued, "hacked apart fruit orchards, leveled workshops and stores and homes. They desecrated our land and emptied our wells and the canals that watered our fields. To rebuild what is needed to live would take more people than the Zhengahk has, for the Death-bringers also killed and killed and killed. Many villages no longer even exist. For the scattered survivors, poverty is the best they can hope for."

Though his face was as inscrutable as ever, he couldn't push from his voice traces of overwhelming grief. Usually, his control made it easy to forget how young he was. About Zago's age. He'd been barely more than a child when horror raked his homeland.

"Zizero Terring's previous fulgu business would have given us the means to go to a better life," Figgo continued, "but unfortunately it was forced into bankruptcy. Now Terring has promised we can start again. If Terring Fulgus succeeds, some of my people may have another chance, though it will be in exile. Better exile, though, than starvation and disease.

"The Bihsts know the conditions, yet they elect to push on. I'm sorry to say that they, too, will flee the Zhengahk with the rest of us, once they have tried to live in it. So, Zago, if you value life and have a compassionate heart, please weigh your unfounded belief in fulgu sentience against the reality of the humans and their companions withering to death in what is now called the Taglimagan, the Waste Land."

He stood; Terring signaled Zago and Diaa to walk him back to the camp. Terring couldn't help thinking that this cursed meeting was like a nesting doll, getting smaller and smaller as people left, yet with a new surprise at every depth.

"What about Frogbelly?" he asked Solyra.

"What about him?"

Terring contained himself. "What do you know about him that I don't know?"

She frowned at him. "What everyone knows."

"Everyone except me."

She stared at him, and a sort of pitying look came over her face. She spoke very gently. "There are men, Terring, who love other men. They're called fehs."

How did she do it? One moment, Terring was ready to jump up and down and scream from pure fury, the next, he could barely stop from laughing out loud. It was like his great-aunt, who could always tickle him out of a pout.

He assumed a puzzled look. "Of course there are. I love other men. I love Figgo. Jerzy. The other lads."

Her smile grew fixed and pink crept into her cheeks. "I mean, they sleep with each other."

"Right. Tent mates. Just like me and Figgo and you and Peg." It was a true wonder that he could keep a straight face when she looked so utterly earnest.

"Not like that," she said. "Like...like a husband and a wife. You know."

"No, I don't know, Solyra. I've never been married."

Her cheeks darkened to red — then he caught her hand as she made to swat him.

"You 'lumph skull!" she cried. But she was laughing.

He folded her hand between his. He wanted to say, my silly pussycat. He wanted to kiss her hand. He wanted to kiss much more than her hand. He settled for relishing her smile. But then he remembered the point, which was that she knew something he didn't know about Frogbelly.

"Solyra, I don't give a stoat's butt about Tad and Frogbelly being man and wife, fehs, or whatever you want to call it. And yes, Norvadale has morality laws against fehs. But no one enforces them. Our Cap'n didn't leave Norvadale just to love freely. He's on the run from something. What kind of name is Frogbelly? Come on. And I caught him pilfering a wanted poster from a mailbag, back at the Oaks Wayside."

She looked away, and slowly pulled her hand from his. "You've got nothing to worry about with Frogbelly. He's a good man whose only crime is to love."

Maybe she was right. Certainly she wasn't going to say more. And Frogbelly had shown only integrity. So far. But

Terring wasn't about to stop watching Frogbelly, and it was just as well that Frogbelly knew as much.

>> <<

WHEN THE CARAVAN ROLLED ON, Jerzy rode on a hammock in Peg's wagon. Brid cut a window into each side of the wagon and covered them with bombazine to keep the flies out but allow a cross-breeze. By the end of a week, under Peg's constant coddling care, assisted by Solyra, new skin began to cover the worst of the burns.

"Gar, Darklocks, I don't know what I'd do without you," Peg whispered to her, as they gently daubed his burns in weak salt water.

You'd be a lot better off, Solyra thought.

"Aiee...." Jerzy groaned.

"I'm sorry," Solyra said.

"'S'all right." He tried to smile, gave up and closed his eyes, then bit his lip and fell silent again.

On Figgo's advice, Jerzy's friends had nobly raided a ground bee's nest for honey. Peg spread the honey over the still-raw skin, then with Brid and Robet holding Jerzy up, Solyra and she re-wrapped him as tightly as they could, quickly passing the roll of linen bandage back and forth.

"Th'art doin' great, Jerz," Robet boomed as they eased him down. He seemed to think Jerzy's ears had been affected by the burn.

Brid punched Robet in the arm. "Pipe down, man. People will think there's an buffalumph in here."

"Aye, th'alt mend, Jerz," Robet said, only moderately lower. "Assuming th'important parts be aye accounted for and in good repair."

Jerzy laughed. "Buffoons. Shaddup and get out. Let the ladies tend me."

Brid and Robet snorted and guffawed as they left, but under Peg's evil eye they didn't dare make the obvious jokes.

"Peg," Jerzy said.

"Hm?" Peg leaned over him, but he didn't say anything. He just looked at her.

Peg blushed from the edge of her wig down to the collar of her shirt. She began to move away, but Jerzy caught her by the arm.

"Let me look at the face of my sweet angel." There was no mistaking the tenderness in his voice.

Solyra slipped out, clattered around with the pots and pans, waved Frogbelly away from the wagon, and pounced when Peg came out.

"Well?"

Peg smiled, but she wouldn't talk until the meal was made. Then she and Solyra took their plates and cups and a blanket and went to sit on the grass. The early flowers had withered, but spring's freshness lingered.

"Tell," Solyra demanded.

Peg looked fondly at her. "This is your first smile for at least a week."

"Don't try to sidetrack."

Peg laughed. She looked beautiful when she laughed, clumsy wig, knobbly nose and all. "Gar, Darklocks, do you know, he told me he's had an eye on me for a long time but was afraid to come near. He didn't think I wanted or needed a man at all. Which spirit he likes. He said, 'I like a woman who can think for herself.' Then... we kissed. We kissed each other!"

"Was all in good repair?"

"Smarty-pants!" Peg grabbed off her wig and swatted Solyra with it. "The man's an invalid, for all love." She settled her wig back on, then said with paradoxical primness, "Yes. Not that we made much use of the equipment at hand. Jerzy wants us to be married first. All proper he is."

"Be careful, Peg," Solyra said unthinking. "Gar, what a thing to say. What a wet-blanket I am."

"No, Darklocks, I know what you're saying. But Jerzy is an honest man. I've never seen ought to prove otherwise."

"I'm so happy for you, Peg. This is the best thing that's come along in an age." She held up her tin cup. "Here's to love, to you and Jerzy."

They clinked cups, and finished their dinner.

"Does it hurt, Solyra?" Peg asked suddenly.

Solyra was glad she'd been looking down, so Peg wouldn't see her astonishment, that her wise and all-knowing friend was a virgin. The question brought its own kind of pain, too. It had hurt — but that was with Dahn.

"It might hurt a little," she said, "but with love, it won't matter." A pitiful answer. "And then you get used to it. I mean, it grows more pleasant as time goes on." The more she said, the more pitiful it got.

Peg wisely changed the subject. Sort of. "Now, in the time-honored tradition of the newly besotted, I'll interfere with your relationships."

"Hopeless all around. Don't waste your effort." She agreed with Terring that cleansing confessions weren't the order of the day. Even so, she chafed between feeling deceptive and being glad she had reason to keep her secrets.

"Well, I would say you've been a little harsh with Zago and Diaa," Peg said, "given that the fire was an accident. A stupid accident, but still. Except that Diaa stole your man, and that was no accident at all. Still — don't be mad at me for saying so — you did let him go mighty easy."

"Who?" Solyra asked.

Peg gave a gloating laugh. "Oh-ho! So that's how it is. Can't decide, eh?"

"That's not it," Solyra snapped. "That's not how it is with Zago or Terring. Assuming that's who you're talking about."

"Question is, who are *you* talking about?"

Solyra wasn't sure herself. Had she betrayed Zago by

distancing herself? Or had he betrayed her by taking up with Diaa? And had Diaa betrayed her by taking up with Zago?

And what about...? But Terring didn't count.

"I'm a fool about love," Solyra said. "I don't know what I feel."

"Maybe you need to figure it out. And I was referring to Zago. Or at least I thought I was."

"One unassailable fact is that Zago's my employee. Regrettable as that's been lately."

"That can make things sticky. Still, if you love him....Jerzy said it took all his guts to say anything to me, and not just because I'm a devil with a wrought iron skillet. He was afraid of how it'll play out around here, with the crew. Now he doesn't care — well, he doesn't care as much. That first night, when he was in so much pain, he thought he might die. He said it let him know what makes life worth living. Said he's already wasted too much time keeping his feelings to himself."

The two women drifted into their own thoughts, Peg no doubt thinking about Jerzy, Solyra thinking about Zago. She didn't resent Peg's saying she'd let him go mighty easy. It was true: she'd wanted him to drift away. Now she wasn't so sure. Had she let him go out of just plain fear? Was she avoiding her own feelings?

She didn't know the answers. She didn't need to.

She knew missed Zago. She missed his damp body pressed to hers, his hand lazily stroking her hair, his light sweet kisses on her breasts, her neck.

She wanted him back.

CRYSTAL BEADS

"Diaa's jealous of us," Zago said.

Solyra nestled against him, on a blanket at the edge of a flat, shallow river. "No offense," she said, "but Diaa let you go easily enough."

It was true. Solyra hadn't seen any signs of a breakup fight. The fire seemed to have put distance between the two of them.

"Well, sure."

Solyra turned to look at him. "What do you mean, well, sure?"

He smiled shiftily. "I guess she wasn't very attached to me."

"I guess not. Maybe it's hard to have a real relationship on a trip like this."

"Terring isn't over the moon about us either."

"Why should Terring care?"

Zago's smile took on a certain male smugness. "I beat him out, didn't I?"

Solyra had to laugh. "No contest there, lover boy." She meant that Terring wasn't even in the contest, but Zago didn't take it that way: his smile grew yet more smug.

"I guess not everyone's got my little ways."

"You and your little ways."

Zago kissed her hair and by gentle degrees he laid her down again.

His hands were skilled, Solyra knew, and his heart sensitive and kind. The rigors of the road had not diminished his energy, either. Solyra only wished she were more appreciative. She was fond of Zago and wanted him to be happy, to find joy in her body and his own. That was enough for her, but not for him.

He lay on his side with a sigh, his hand on her belly. "Little ways or not, I still haven't learned your secrets, Solyra. But one of these days, I will. And then I'll make you happy."

Why? She had an impulse to demand. Why isn't what we just did good enough? "You already make me happy." She couldn't help but hear the petulance in her voice.

He looked at her with the smile of a man of the world to a child. It was a reversal of their usual roles. "You don't know what happy is."

And Diaa does? But that wasn't a question to ask aloud.

Besides, the morning was too sweet to lose in sulks, the air dewy and soft on her skin. Like Zago, she thought, but without the demands.

The Bihst gong rang, signaling the end of the morning service and the start of breakfast. Solyra sat up and brushed the sand off herself and shook out her underwear. "My happiness will just have to wait," she said. "I need to get back and help Peg."

"I thought you had breakfast off."

"I do, but we have to start lunch early."

"Right. The big welcome feast." They pulled their clothes back into order, then returned to camp.

Last night, Terring had learned from the soldiers patrolling this stretch of road that another caravan traveled a half-day behind, and Frogbelly had decided to wait for them. He didn't really want to, Tad told Solyra. Sheff, the other caravan captain, wasn't known for running a tight outfit and was sure to mooch supplies. Still, this far west, the courtesy of the road dictated joining up, and the soldiers appreciated anything that made their job easier, including combined caravan groups.

As Zago and Solyra came up from the road, a dust cloud heralded Sheff's outfit. By the time Solyra got to the kitchen, she could make out the crowd of animals and wagons.

Peg glared at it, hands on her hips. "Gar. Sheff would kick up his beasts to get here for lunch. Then he'll hold us up daw-dling all the way to the Ihm." She prodded the corn pudding, then covered it again and took it off the fire to finish cooking in its iron oven. She chuckled and added, "The Bihsts are bat-tening down the hatches. Sheff has a reputation for carrying liquor and sex-workers out west."

"The Bihsts have the right idea." Solyra wasn't quite jok-ing. She didn't despise sex-workers. If anything, she pitied them, after the glimpses she'd had into their lives through her husband. That didn't mean she enjoyed their company, though.

"I wish we could have kept ahead," Peg said, "and so does my Jerzy. Booze and loose women are fine on land—" as the caravaners referred to stationary life "—but they can wreak havoc in a caravan. And we haven't had either for a while. The boys are all pent up. Well, not to worry. Even if our lads get a bit distracted, they'll hold onto their duty. And we've been through worse, haven't we, Darklocks?"

"That we have."

Sheff's caravan arrived a little before midday. They'd left Yarf City the week before, and though endless grassland stretched around them, the road had not yet subdued them. Nor had they run out of cheap perfume. The cloying smell evoked unpleasant memories, as did the rouged cheeks and blood-red lips. The men grew boisterous and boastful in a way all too familiar. After one of Sheff's officers patted her bot-tom, Solyra decided she wouldn't go near any of them again for anything.

Figgo retreated to join the Bihsts; Terring stayed at table

with the rest of the party. Zago was at table, too, drinking, but not making merry. The booze seemed to have killed his cavalier attitude toward Diaa. He glowered at her and the man who had an arm draped over her shoulder. Glowered to the accompaniment of a banjo, a panpipe, and a singer with garish red hair. For now, the lady warbled of love under the willows. It was only a matter of time before the songs went bawdy.

"I'd join the Bihsts," Solyra said to Peg as they swilled the pots with sandy river water. "Except I'd rather listen to drunk idiots than sit with Figgo."

"Never mind old Figgo, Darklocks. We'll have our own private party." Peg half-lifted a flat bottle from her apron pocket. "Sheff's way of saying thank you."

Peg's wagon made a pleasant hideaway with its two screened windows. The juice from a few precious limes and some sugar made the stinky weird yellowish booze almost palatable. In fact, two cocktails later, the stuff was downright tasty.

"We better cork this," Peg said.

"I s'pose yer right." Solyra burped, then put a hand over her mouth.

"If you're going to be sick, don't do it in here."

"No, but I need to pee."

"You know where to find the pot."

"I also need more air, or I will be sick."

"We'll go together."

Even as the shadows lengthened, the larger party showed no signs of winding down. Frogbelly, Tad and Jerzy, along with a few soldiers, kept apart, in case things started get out of hand, but staggering around drunk, alone, wasn't a good idea. Solyra was glad Peg was with her.

"I feel better already," Solyra said on the way back from the women's privy. Then she stopped. "Peg, I hate to ask, but can I put my jewels in your cabinet? It's just one bag, and it's locked up, but I just don't like it being with the wagons."

One of Peg's boundaries was that she wouldn't let her

pharmacy become a safe deposit for the caravan. Until now, Solyra hadn't taken advantage of her status as bunkmate to push her; she hadn't felt a need.

"Sure," Peg said. "It's not a bad idea."

They detoured to the wagon where the valuables were stashed in a locked box under the driver's seat.

"Wait here," Peg said. "You're in no shape to climb up with all the drinking you've done."

Peg was hardly in shape to climb either. It took her a few tries to get up to the driver's box, and then the lock was stuck.

While Peg cursed and fumbled, Solyra looked along the line of wagons. Sheff's train had more wagons than Frogbelly's, but his were mostly smaller passenger coaches, several of which had windows with shutters. A slam came from one of the most gaudily painted wagons, followed by a woman squawking, a man yelling, then laughter.

"What happened?" Peg called down.

"A shutter came loose on a boody wagon. Sounds like someone was caught in the act."

Peg guffawed. "Not one of our angels, of course."

"Never." It hadn't sounded like Terring, at least.

"A blue leather pouch, you said?" Peg asked over the side.

"That's it. And would you get Diaa's pouch, too? It's brown. Should be with mine." Diaa's pouch might hold trinkets, or just a few coins, but she'd be upset if it were pilfered.

"Sure thing." A few moments later, Peg held them over the edge. "Can you catch?"

Solyra pulled out her apron to make a pouch, and Peg threw them in. Solyra pocketed her pouch, idly squeezed Diaa's pouch. It bulged with round, hard lumps. Solyra squeezed it again. Faceted lumps.

Almost of their own will, as Peg cursed her way through locking the box, Solyra's hands drew the bag open and shifted the cloth that wrapped its contents. She slanted the pouch to the late afternoon sun and looked inside.

Crystal beads glinted and sparked.

The drink vapors evaporated. Solyra drew the pouch closed, pulling the toggle beads tight. As Peg began climbing down the wheel, Solyra slipped the pouch in her pocket.

"Peg, I need to tell Diaa I've got her pouch. Would you take my stuff?"

"Sure." Peg jumped to the ground and looked toward the party. "Not even sunset yet, and the sexworkers have already rolled up the drunks. I guess it's just as well you're sleeping in my wagon again, now that Jerzy's back to bunking with the boys."

Normally, Solyra wouldn't have lost such a prime chance to tease Peg, but she just said, "Thanks," and strode toward the plank tables.

She hardly knew what she would say to Diaa. You stole my crystal beads. Or: You looted my frock, then handed it back to me and expected me to be grateful. Or just: You thieving bitch!

It wasn't hard to get Diaa away from the party. The man she'd been carousing with had his head on the table, a pool of drool seeping from his snoring mouth. Zago was gone. Diaa didn't seem very drunk, though it was hard to tell with her.

They went to the river, toward where Solyra and Zago had dallied that morning. The sun's angle transformed the water from a flat brown serpentine to a sparkling ribbon.

Once out of sight of the caravan, on the beach under the river bank, Solyra pulled Diaa's pouch from her pocket. "What's this about?" She tossed it to her.

Diaa stared down at it, her mouth open, then looked back at Solyra. "What are you doing taking—"

"Taking your things? I think that's my question, not yours."

"I wasn't stealing 'em. I was gonna give 'em back."

"Oh, and then you changed your mind?"

Diaa threw the pouch back at her with a snarl. "Yes, I changed my mind," she growled. "Cause you stole something of mine." Her eyes narrowed and she hissed, her crest bristling.

"You stole my man! You threw him away and then you took him back just to spite me."

"You have nothing to do with Zago and me." Solyra picked the pouch up from where it had fallen on the beach. "Or with my beads."

"You never loved him at all. You just used him." Diaa growled softly again. "You know what he told me?"

Solyra knew that whatever Zago had told Diaa, she didn't want to hear it. She should walk away right now. But her feet seemed to have grown roots into the sandy river bed.

"He told me he feels sorry for you." Diaa panted slightly, her fangs glistening. "He told me you don't never like it, no matter how hard he tries. And he don't like doing it with you, either. Not really. You make him feel mean and dirty. He says when he does it with you it's like he's hurting a woman. But he can't say nothing. And he can't be with me anymore. Because you're the boss." She spat out the last word.

"You're a liar." Solyra's voice kept steady, amazingly steady, considering her entire body juddered as if she had a fever. Her hairnet, already loosened, dropped at her feet and her hair tumbled down. She thought she could even hear the beads clinking within the pouch that dangled from her hand. She wadded it up. "Still, you can keep the beads. After all, you did 'fix' my frock, didn't you." Squinting into the sun, she tossed the pouch back at Diaa.

Diaa clutched it to herself and doubled over, as if it were a brick hitting her stomach. Then she burst into tears.

"I was gonna make a dress for you!" she sobbed. "A beautiful dress. Back in the good ole days. I thought you and Zago loved each other, and we were all friends, and I was gonna make you a weddin' dress with beads and lace and all kind o' prettiness. But you never loved him at all. You passed him to me, and then jus' when I'm loving him, you took him back. You might as well have left me by the side of the road. You ain't no kind of friend. You don't love no one. You only love your money. And your cursed beads!" She threw the pouch at Solyra as hard as she could.

It flew open.

Solyra lifted her head to stare at the crystals arcing in the sun, like droplets from a pure, clean waterfall. They seemed to move slowly enough to count, even in their hundreds, a shower of rainbow sparks thrown by the slanting sun. She held her hands out from her side as they sprinkled her, as if she were relishing a rain storm, even as she sank to her knees in the cool, damp sand. Diaa's feet swished away through the grass.

Panpipes played in the distance. An evening breeze soughed in the cottonwoods, where little birds sang. Solyra's hair stirred and some of the beads sprinkled from it onto the damp sand, where they lay like fragments of ice that, impossibly, refused to thaw in the warm sun.

A shadow fell over the sand and she looked up.

Who else, but Terring. She could make out only his silhouette as he stood gazing down at her. Probably smiling at a good old-fashioned cat fight.

He scrambled down the bank and helped her to her feet. He wasn't smiling. He was solemn, and gentle. The scents of liquor, grass, and clean mud, wove around him. Silently, without touching her skin, he picked the beads from her hair and clothes and from the sand, and put them in the pouch.

Then he knelt at her feet. He put one arm around her legs, the other around her hips, embracing her, his head pressed to her belly. It was as if he were holding her down to the earth, and it made the rest of her—from her belly to her breasts to her head, feel as if she were flying up. She lifted her arms and closed her eyes, and tipped her face blindly to the sky.

Slam! A woman screeching, men whooping. Solyra dropped her arms with a laugh and gave Terring a hand up.

SHORN

"Your hair!" Peg shrieked.

"Oh, Solyra," Zago sighed.

Terring just stared, frowning.

Solyra shrugged. "It was too hot and too much trouble."

Despite her nonchalance, Solyra had to resist the urge to put her hands to her head — her close-cropped head. Her hair, in four braids, lay coiled in the cotton bag she had slung over her shoulder, the root ends tied together with red ribbon and the tips with blue.

"I think it looks nice," Diaa said stoutly. Not an hour after their fight, she'd apologized and swore by her life that what she'd said about Zago was spiteful lies. Solyra accepted Diaa's apologies and gave her own. And didn't believe that what Diaa said about Zago was lies. They hugged and to everyone's obvious relief came back from their talk holding hands.

"I'm glad someone likes it," Solyra said with a forced smile.

"It does, really," Zago added feebly. "Look nice, I mean. It just surprised us."

"At least it won't take her forever to wash her hair," Frogbelly commented, and Tad guffawed, "Ever the romantic."

"Short hair is indeed very convenient," Figgo said, "and I am certain it becomes Solyra."

Everyone gaped at him, including Terring, until Peg grumbled, "Well, I don't know."

Solyra didn't know either, but Figgo's stiff, awkward compliment touched her. She skewered a puffy marshmallow confection, one of the many oddities in Sheff's cargo, and sat at the fire to toast it. As she turned the skewer, she pretended to be absorbed in browning the marshmallow just right, but she felt Terring shooting her short glances as if he couldn't stand to look longer.

Solyra couldn't begin to guess if he had overheard her fight with Diaa over the beads. She decided he hadn't. It was just too humiliating to believe otherwise. In any case, he didn't allude to it. Neither of them spoke of it, or of the change in their relationship. Maybe Terring didn't understand it any more than she did. They were kinder to each other, at least.

But whether or not he had actually overheard the fight, Diaa's words hung between them in Solyra's mind.

Solyra knew Diaa hadn't just spit out lies to hurt her. How many times had Zago said things like, Did I hurt you? Relax, I won't bite. I'm sorry. How many times had he said *that?* I'm sorry.

Maybe it didn't matter. The now dead affair with Zago had only brought the truth to light. The truth being, she was incapable of true intimacy. Frigid, Dahn used to say. Terring probably sensed it in some way. He was watching her, but he hadn't made an approach.

Then again, he might have thought that she and Zago were still together. They hadn't made a public break, and for all his rough-cut manners, Terring kept to a male code of honor.

Meanwhile, poor Zago, baffled and hurt, must have wondered where he went wrong, what with her making excuses, avoiding him. She would have been happy if he'd gone back to Diaa, but anything she did to encourage that would be seen as the boss lady passing him down. At least Diaa hadn't drowned her sorrows with Sheff's crew, much to the disappointment of certain of them who'd hoped to enjoy the favors of an exotic species of woman. She stayed close to Frogbelly's caravan, occupying herself with tending the animals.

Solyra examined the golden-brown marshmallows. "Perfect," she said. She gingerly nibbled on one, burned her tongue, and blew on the molten treat to cool it. The monotonous singsong of the Bihst evening prayer drifted to the fireside.

The hack Solyra hired for the fulgu rights nonsense had told her that the Bihst religion was "obscure and hazy," perfect fodder for the movement. The little she'd read herself of their philosophy had come off as dreary. According to the literature, some of them never married, choosing never even to have sex in their whole lives. She guessed that Gobi might be such a one.

Yet if the Bihsts themselves were anything to go by, the religion must have been more cheery than it seemed. In every way, they'd shown themselves to be good companions, pulling their weight without complaining and never missing a chance to help their caravan mates. Baloos and Jaleen had thrown themselves full-heartedly into parenting Raal and Erin. Their care showed in Erin's slowly blossoming confidence, and Raal was finally starting to take part in the horseplay with the others. After Sheff's caravan joined theirs, the Bihsts kept mostly to their own group, but they treated everyone respectfully, including Sheff's less savory passengers.

Solyra stacked a half-dozen marshmallows on her skewer and put them over the fire.

"Binging, huh?" Zago said with a knowing look. She'd told him, truthfully, that she was in her courses. At least they'd already established that she didn't like to make love during that time, especially away from hot baths.

"No, it's a bribe. I'm going to ask Gobi if he'll make me some hair nets."

"What do you need hair nets for?" Terring demanded. "You don't have any hair left." He sounded annoyed, just as Peg had, as if Solyra had damaged his own property when she cut her hair off.

"It'll grow back, and when it does, I want nets." She added to Peg, "And you can't have them for your fruit."

"Best fruit nets I've ever had," Peg said complacently. "Prettiest, too. But I swear I won't touch these if it'll keep the hair on your head." She frowned and added petulantly, "Honestly, Solyra."

"Gobi did a good job on the horse tack," Frogbelly said, tactfully changing the subject. "I just wish he worked with leather. I'm not used to wool halters. Though it seems just as strong."

"I like the wool tack better," Diaa said, "It's softer." A discussion about the merits of different kinds of tack and halters was launched.

Solyra checked her marshmallows and went to the Bihst group. They had stopped singing, and sat in a silent circle on a floor of rugs. At the center was the little statue of the laughing fat man, surrounded by a braid of fresh grass. A lamp hung from a pole stuck in the ground.

Solyra's parents hadn't raised her to follow any religion, though their busy port town offered meetings of all varieties, from word worshipers to tree huggers to Bihsts. Dahn had insisted their wedding take place in a temple where they apparently didn't worship anything at all.

Solyra attended the Bihsts' dance and flexion exercises almost daily, but she'd never yet attended one of their prayer services, beyond general blessings on the food or their animals, and the prayers for Jerzy. During those, Gobi chanted and everyone else just sat or stood around.

Now, the Bihsts communed wordlessly with the statue, sitting cross-legged, eyes half open, faces expressionless, inward.

Solyra was about to sneak away when Gobi, without looking away from the statue, gestured her to join them.

Solyra sat a little behind him and Baloos and stared at the statue. The silence went on longer than usual, or at least it felt that way. Solyra's thoughts swelled into an almighty chatter, then quieted, as if they got tired of themselves, but whatever mystic secrets the Bihsts heard, all she heard were the sounds of the world: the prairie hen that Brid had captured clucking to her peeping chicks; little rustles of snakes or lizards in the grass, a woman's laugh, the huff of a horse. She saw only the pleasantly colored if low-quality floor of various rugs, and the statue.

Solyra tried to maintain the solemn mien of the Bihsts, but finally she couldn't help smiling. However profound their philosophy, the statue looked like a fat man in diapers who was laughing so hard, he'd fallen on his behind. If this was their god, no wonder they were so cheerful.

Softly, Gobi said something, a word, and the circle slowly stirred back to life. A few jokes were made about stiff knees. Erin flapped her foot, giggling that it had fallen asleep. They didn't ignore Solyra. They took her in as if she joined them every evening to worship the laughing fat man.

Gobi wrapped the statue in a square of silk, then stuffed it and his ceremonial wig into the cabinet and closed it. Other than the wig, he'd conducted the service in his usual fireside outfit, a tunic and pants of drab homespun. The road had transformed his tubbiness into stockiness.

Solyra proffered the skewer. "I brought some toasted marshmallows for you, but I reckon they're cold and tough." Their etiquette was to denigrate the food they made while offering the skewer first to Gobi. He would wave it away until she insisted. On the third offer, he took a marshmallow and passed the skewer on, thanking her and laughing as the still-warm, gooey inside oozed over his hands.

After some polite chitchat and a round of tea, Solyra took

the severed braids and knit netting out of her bag. "I was wondering if you could make a wig using this hair and netting."

She addressed the group generally, but Gobi wiped his hands on a wet rag, then took the hair and netting from her. He handed the netting back to Solyra after just a glance. "That's no good for a wig, but no worry. I have some to use." He ran his hand down of the braids. "You tied the red string at the root?"

"That's right." Peg had griped that her wig was rough and easily tangled because the individual hairs didn't lie in the same direction.

"You want it for Peg's wedding, yes?"

"Is that possible?"

"No problem."

Gobi was one of those people who seemed to look right into a person. It didn't feel invasive, but as he gazed at her, Solyra occupied herself with cleaning the skewer with a handful of sand. She didn't want anyone getting a peek at her tarnished spirit.

"Can I pay you anything?" she asked, looking up again.

"No, that's all right." He murmured something else, something religious, Solyra guessed.

"Well. Thanks very much." She would pay him somehow; she'd just have to be crafty about it.

Solyra got the sash for Peg's wedding dress out of her baggage and brought it back to the campfire. Work on the dress could hardly be secret, and Peg had kicked and fussed that it was too much; she could wear her plain old clothes; Jerzy would be. Of course, that wasn't true. Jerzy's chums were making him a wedding suit: Terring carving elaborate bone buttons at the fireside, Robet working a multi-colored sash. Nothing under the enormous sky could stop Peg's friends from outdoing them.

Onyx and Ebony had managed to barter a couple of yards of their knit lace for a torn dark red silk dress and jewel-blue petticoat from one of the sexworkers, and together with Solyra and Diaa, had remade the dress as a caftan and the petticoat as an underdress. The colors were so far from Peg's usual drab browns and grays, she looked a different person, for the try-ons. The cut was modest but the wide blue sash accentuated Peg's slender waist, one of her star attributes.

The crowning touch, literally, was to be the wig. Once the idea of using her own hair came to Solyra she hadn't hesitated to lop it off. Only after the braids were in the bag had she worried about how Peg would take it.

Solyra settled on her rug at the campfire, lay the sash over her lap, threaded her needle, then got out the fringe she'd made of the crystal beads Terring had salvaged.

"Oh, no you don't." Peg said.

"Oh, yes, I do."

"No." Peg put her hand on Solyra's. "I mean it." She leaned over and kissed Solyra's cheek. Tears sprang to her eyes and she whispered, "I know what the hair is about. It's enough. Too much. I couldn't stop you with that, but this... No. I refuse, honey."

"It's just a little fringe." But Solyra felt selfishly relieved, and not just because Peg knew about the wig. For all that the beads had put her through, she was ridiculously attached to them. They were like a part of her.

"You need to keep something for yourself," Terring said. It was as if he'd read her thoughts. Solyra busied herself with folding the fringe around the card.

"Oh, don't worry," she said lightly, "I do plenty of that." Her eyes happened to meet Zago's; then they both looked away from each other.

>> <<

PEG MADE A RADIANT BRIDE, and Terring had to say Jerzy looked pretty respectable himself, in the suit got up for him by the crew. Frogbelly acted as Peg's father, Solyra was her attendant, and Jerzy's best buddy Robet stood by him. Gobi performed the ceremony, Erin threw flower petals in the air, and everyone cheered and ululated Diaa-style, then turned to the feast that had been three days in the making.

Terring, though, couldn't keep his eyes off a low, distant cloud of dust. It wasn't like the wall of haze from sky to earth that heralded a dust storm. Nor was it the spinning, freakish whirls that sprang up even on still days.

Terring took Figgo aside. "Would you listen?"

Figgo knew what he meant. They walked away from the noise of the party and Figgo lay down, his ear pressed to the earth. He stood again. "It is buffalumphs."

Terring cursed. Chances were, the animals were heading to the river — heading this way. He went to Frogbelly. "Call off the party, Cap'n."

Frogbelly didn't ask questions. In minutes, the merriment dwindled to silence. Terring got the buffalumph skull from the big wagon and held it in his hands as he spoke.

"A herd of buffalumphs is coming this way." A woman cackled and was shushed. "Trying to flee them would be futile. It would even be dangerous, since noise and movement agitate them. So we'll have to sit tight. And be calm. We'll be all right as long as we don't attract their attention or upset them in any way."

Terring split crew and passengers into two groups. One group would cover with cloth or mud anything bright or reflective. The other, larger group was set to digging out a shelter under the river bank. Once everyone got working, he called together Frogbelly, Tad, Jerzy, Baloos, Onyx and Ebony, and a couple of Sheff's sturdier and more sober crew members.

"If they come toward the caravan, we'll have to try to herd them away. The shelter can only take so much weight." No one looked at Terring as he spoke. They seemed as unable as he was to look away from the growing dust cloud. Terring thought he glimpsed the gleams of tusks. "Hopefully we won't have to do that. I don't think they'll come this way. The bank is high here, and they don't like to jump."

Terring gathered the rest of the caravan people. "Sheff's passengers will be under their own officers." He spoke as quietly as he could. "Frogbellies follow orders from Peg and Solyra. They know what to do. Anyone who doesn't follow orders endangers all of us. So do what they say. And if they tell you to go into the shelter, get in there fast, stay put, and keep absolutely quiet."

Terring, Frogbelly, Tad, and Sheff checked and rechecked the wagons to make sure everything was as dull as it could be. Jerzy's crew saddled the fastest horses, with rags tied around every bit of metal on their tack. Terring only wished that Sheff's passengers were more reliable, and more sober.

He was leading his horse to the side away from the shelter when Solyra came to his side. She'd worked hard all afternoon with not a word of complaint. She'd encouraged and calmed the others as needed. He was proud of her.

"Do you think you'll have to go?" she asked.

He looked away from her, toward the herd. He could distinguish the largest animals, now: a bull with four horns, a cow. Each would weigh as much as the big wagon loaded. A sense of mortal danger sliced into him. He didn't think he was afraid for himself. But Solyra's question, her eyes looking into his, her hand on his chest, and her soft, grass-fragrant hair surely made him want to live. "I hope not."

She heaved a sigh, looked at the herd, back at him. "Zago put the fulgus at the end of the bank, in the water."

"Not in the shelter."

"No. But if the herd runs over the bank at the shelter...."

"Shhh. We'll be all right." He smoothed back a strand of her mud-streaked hair. "I don't know what we would have done without you today."

She gave a laugh, then lowered her head and rested her

brow on his chest. Of one accord, they embraced each other, then without another word went to their stations.

By dusk, the ground rumbled audibly, and the setting sun glinted on the proboscis horns of the bulls and cows. Peg and Gobi ordered everyone to the edge of the shelter, but since it was wet and chill, they didn't yet go in.

Peg and her helpers served a cold dinner. Everyone ate without looking away from the buffalumphs, as if they could deflect the herd with their eyes.

"Yes," Gobi said. "They're turning away. Going down river. See, the lead cows? They follow them." The news rippled down the line like a sigh of relief.

Then, in the quiet, the panel on the boody wagon slammed down.

Solyra and Peg hardly needed Terring's order to push the people into the shelter. Everyone saw the buffalumphs raise their huge heads. Terring and his fellow herders jumped on their horses and rode out. The buffalumphs turned and began moving, moving more quickly than anyone would think such lumbering beasts could.

>> <<

IN THE SANDY DAMPNESS UNDER the river bank, raw fear filled Solyra from her hair to her toes. Still, she managed to count heads and ensure everyone had made it into the shelter, and Peg and Sheff's crew leaders did the same. The cool dimness filled with stifled cries.

Then their voices were swallowed by a literally earth-shaking rumble.

Solyra opened her mouth to scream, and dirt filled her mouth. Choking, she reached for Diaa and Zago like a mother reaching for her children. Jaleen and the other Bihsts encircled Erin and Raal, and Figgo, too. Gobi's lips moved not in panic but in prayer. The calm courage that emanated from him let Solyra breath again.

Peg suddenly crawled away, toward where the fulgu lockers were stashed — toward where a hoof had broken through the bank.

"Peg!" Solyra screamed. She might as well have been voiceless under the thundering hooves. She lunged away from Zago and Diaa, and scrambled on her hands and knees after Peg. She seized her ankle. "Stop, Peg! No—"

A white flash.

Then nothing.

—

SOLYRA'S EYES WERE OPEN. BUT she couldn't see.

"Help." Her scream came out as a croak, but someone heard her. Someone with rough, calloused hands took her flailing hands and held them down.

"No, you can't touch your eyes."

Someone else held her legs, to stop their mindless, kicking panic.

"Sh, sh, sh, it's all right. You'll be all right."

Zago kissed her forehead. A cool, damp cloth dabbed her face.

Solyra shuddered as she stopped struggling. She remembered: the buffalumphs turning, the scramble into the shelter, the stampede. Peg trying to save the lockers.

"Peg," she whispered.

Silence.

"Peg." It came out a little louder that time. "What happened to Peg?"

"She's…." Zago broke into sobs.

"No, no," Solyra groaned. Then she screamed hoarsely as the tears burned her eyes.

Someone else told her to close her eyes. She hadn't known they were still open. The lids scraped her eyeballs, and cool packs were laid over them.

"Terring?"

"He's with the animals." It was Diaa.

Voices came and went.

"It's temporary," a man said. Solyra didn't know the voice. "Your sight should be back by morning." Pause. "It's about midnight now."

Before Solyra could speak again, Frogbelly took her hands. She could feel the still-healing rope-burn she'd rubbed ointment into a few days ago.

"Tell me what happened," she said.

"Can I?" Frogbelly asked.

"Yes, tell me."

But he had been asking someone else. The physician from Sheff's caravan. That was the man who spoke to her. She couldn't make out his answer. He must have given permission, though.

"We succeeded in diverting most of the herd down river," Frogbelly said. "It's where they wanted to go. But about a hundred of them broke off and ran over the shelter. One must have hit an earthpig burrow, poked a hole in a crate. Zago said…"

Whatever Zago said, Frogbelly decided not to get into it, but Zago filled in, his voice thick with grief. "It was the locker that was in the fire. The fulgus in that corner were partly activated."

Frogbelly continued, "Two of the fulgus blew up. You and Peg caught the main of it." His voice broke and his hand tightened. "Peg was killed."

Solyra lay panting, not kicking and screaming and crying. Frogbelly wept, almost silently, then continued. "Your eyes got burned and you took a blow to the head from flying debris."

"Is everyone else all right?" She could hardly get the question out.

"Terring's shoulder was dislocated, but we reset it. He's with Jerzy's crew....." Frogbelly's voice broke again.

"Jerzy?" she whispered.

"He's ... being tended to. His horse stumbled and he got dragged."

"Don't tell him about Peg," Solyra said right away.

"Nobody's gonna tell. He's out of it anyway." A pause. "He'll be gone before morning."

"I'm sorry, cap'n," Solyra whispered.

He patted her hand and she felt his lips touch her forehead. "Everyone else is all right."

Gobi sat by her but only for the brief periods he could spare from Jerzy. It was Diaa who nursed her through the long night. The blindness was like a bond not only over her eyes, but over her whole spirit. To weep was so painful that she simply couldn't let tears flow. Seizures of dizziness took her now and then and she vomited into whatever Diaa put under her mouth. Diaa and she talked at times, mostly they were silent. Diaa slept, the touch of her hand slackening. Solyra thought maybe she slept herself a few times.

The air changed. The breeze of dawn carried the song of the Bihsts. She followed the gentle singsong; she let her mind and all its sorrow ride on it. It was a sweet respite from grief and pain.

She had been gazing at a square of white on blue for a while before she realized — she could see! The white was an awning; she was lying in its shelter on a pallet in a wagon bed. Birds sang from a blue sky.

A man's quiet sobs. Another. Diaa's keening wail. Jerzy had passed.

THE DEEP

FROGBELLY HAD PLANNED TO STAY in the capitol city, but decided instead to go on to Harraz, a scrappy, sprawling caravansary at the foot of the Apfas. No one protested. The treats they'd been looking forward to — shopping in real stores, sleeping in real beds, eating fancy food — held no relish.

Solyra didn't even want to get out of bed each morning, but she did, once her sight came fully back. She worked with the rest of the crew doctoring the animals and repairing the wagons and harness — for sale, since only pack animals could make through the rough, narrow mountain passes. Solyra had offered the balloon up for sale, and Tad would have taken her up on it, but after a long, heated discussion with Terring, the balloon was kept packed.

Until they got cash from the sale of the animals and equipage, they couldn't finish provisioning for the next leg of the trip, and since repacking the freight was a specialty that only Frogbelly, Tad, Brid, Onyx, and Ebony possessed, the rest of the crew had some afternoons free.

Terring and Figgo spent their time off visiting Terring's old friends in the area. The Bihsts made a pilgrimage to an ancient commune. Solyra would have spent the enforced idleness wallowing in her thin bed with its rough blankets, but Diaa didn't let her. While the rest of the crew caroused or visited or prayed, Diaa dragged Solyra on sightseeing excursions.

They wandered dim, fragrant and incomprehensible temples and dusty museums. In a library, they perused exactly the kinds of books and magazines Solyra had prayed for: information on fulgu cultivation. But she couldn't concentrate, and the simplest concepts evaded her.

It was all only pretty sights and so much paper. Nothing blotted out the image pasted over Solyra's inner vision: two graves, side by side, piled with rocks and marked only by a stunted shrub and some colorful rags decorated with prayers and pictures of horses who would, the Bihsts said, transport Jerzy's and Peg's spirits to a paradise. Hopefully, there they could at last make love. The knowledge that Peg had died a virgin, her one true love unconsummated, stabbed Solyra to the heart.

Diaa kept up a constant, cheerful chatter, and for her sake, Solyra tried to respond. Diaa was in mourning, too, after all. She and Jerzy had become good friends, and everyone had loved Peg.

One morning, though, Diaa's enthusiasm wasn't contrived.

"Get up, get up." She pulled the blankets off Solyra and grabbed her hands. "Frogbelly says we have the whole day off and we're going exploring."

Solyra stifled a moan and sat up. "So where is it today, my scenic tour guide?"

"It's a surprise. Wait till you see," she gloated. "And wear your trousers and a tunic and vest. It'll be colder than you think."

Solyra doubted that any place approached even lukewarm under the blistering sun of the Ihm. Still, she dressed as directed. They were about to leave the room, when an impulse took her. She pulled Diaa back. "Sit down, Diaa. I want to tell you something."

The beds were only about an arm's length apart, and when they sat facing each other they were knee to knee.

"Diaa, do you love Zago?"

They hadn't touched that topic since their drunken blow-out on the riverbank. Diaa looked down, then nodded.

"And he loves you?" Solyra asked.

Diaa shrugged, still not looking up. "I don't know." Solyra saw tears fall on her hands. "He don't talk to me anymore. I thought maybe when we rested here he would explore with me. But he spends all his free time here with people who worship rocks. Maybe he don't want to be my friend because it would tread on you."

"It wouldn't tread on me for Zago to be your boyfriend. Diaa, I'm very fond of Zago, but I don't love him in that way. He's not mine to give... I don't want you to take it that way." She shook her head. "We've been through too much together for me to donkey-poop around. I just want to say, Zago and I... We haven't been together lately. And it won't hurt me if you and he take up with each other again. That's all."

Which was donkey poop. They hadn't made love since Peg's and Jerzy's deaths, but Solyra had taken for granted that they would resume when they emerged from mourning. Losing him for good would hurt. Still, what she said was true in essence.

Diaa looked in her face, her eyes still wet. She didn't say anything, just took Solyra's hands and squeezed them, then jumped up.

"Enough of this girly weepy stuff," she said. "We're gonna be late."

"Since when do you worry about that?" But she forced herself to get up with almost as much spring as Diaa.

The Bihsts, except for Panno, were visiting another commune, and the hostler crew seemed unable to tear themselves away from the carnival grounds, but the exploration party was bigger than Solyra expected. Terring and Figgo, Zago, Frogbelly and Tad, and Panno waited for them, along with a local guide, Shirra.

They rode donkeys into the scrubby, arid landscape. Shirra pointed out various rock formations with names like Gold Tit and Bearded Hollow. "Bunch of hard-up miners mapped this place," she said. Traces of older habitations crumbled on the walls of some of the cliffs, but the original people, Shirra said, had long since disappeared or merged peacefully with pioneers from back east. Their previous guide had given a different story, that the merging hadn't been so peaceful, but Panno was the only one to take it up with Shirra. She gave noncommittal answers. Though she was a native of the Ihm, the topic didn't seem to interest her, or she might have wanted to avoid offending her customers from back east.

They stopped at late morning. Solyra thought they were taking a break, but after settling the animals in a simple shed, Shirra took them to an rough opening in the ground. It looked like a giant badger hole.

"You're kidding, right?" Tad asked.

"Kidding what?" Diaa demanded. "Don't tell me you're afraid to go in there." The guide, uncoiling a rope ladder, glanced at them but kept out of it.

Panno gave a "tsh!" and Tad threw him a dirty look.

Frogbelly patted his belly and looked at the hole, as if measuring the fit. "Shirra, what's inside?"

"A wondrous cavern," she said in her usual flat tone. "With lamps."

"A wondrous cavern with lamps," Tad echoed. "Well, you all enjoy it. I'll wait here in the wondrous outdoors. With sun."

"What's a cavern?" Solyra asked.

"It's a big, dark hole in the ground," Tad said.

Panno muttered something, of which Solyra caught the word "coward."

Tad turned on him fast, but Frogbelly was faster. He grabbed Tad's arm and took him apart. They talked and Frogbelly tipped Tad's chin up and gave him a quick, light kiss on the lips.

Shirra caught it and quickly looked away, her mouth puckered as if she'd bitten into something rotten. Solyra quelled the urge to shove her into the hole. Maybe she would have felt the same as Shirra, not so long ago. But she resented the guide's disdain for the two men who had pulled her and her companions through so much hardship and heartache.

Panno turned away from it, too, but for different reasons. Everyone in the caravan had figured that Panno was mad-jealous of Tad. The comically improbable touch was that Frogbelly himself seemed utterly unaware of the young man's infatuation.

Shirra hooked the ladder on a sturdy ledge and descended, lighting a few lamps hung on the wall. Tad managed to descend, goaded by Panno and coaxed by Frogbelly.

For her part, Solyra was excited. She'd heard of caves in the sides of mountains, but never of a cavern below ground. The lamps allowed them to see their feet, but didn't spoil the velvety, cool, wet rock-smelling darkness that lay beyond the lantern's circle.

"Wait," Tad said when they were all on the ladder like drops of water on a double string. "Pardon my curiosity, but what if someone just throws down the ladder as a sick joke?"

Shirra pointed to metal rivets pounded into the wall. "We can get out that way. It's just a little harder, that's all. And once we get down in the cavern proper, there are pegs in the ground that we can follow if we lose light. It's perfectly safe."

"I'm glad somebody asked," Zago said to Tad. But Solyra was certain Zago had no fear of this mineral realm.

Once they reached the floor, about thirty foot-lengths down, Shirra held up her lamp, and they all murmured in astonishment, even Tad.

Dripping stones roofed an earthen chamber, as if the

ceiling had begun to melt, then mysteriously froze again. Other stones rose up from the floor in peaks and chunks. Where the lamplight touched, the formations glittered as if made of crystal and mud.

"I thought it would be like a great big… well, a great big hole," Tad said.

Diaa giggled. "Me, too."

"Amazing," Terring said. Figgo listened, turning his head, but he kept his hands clasped together, like a child in a glassware shop. If he was frightened, he would never let on.

They continued down the sloping floor of the chamber and through tubular passages, guided by Shirra's lamp. Most of the time they went stooped over. The ceilings bristled with spearlike formations, many hanging down to Solyra's shoulders. Shirra pointed out various features with names as ridiculous as the outside rock formations, though at least not all centered on female anatomy: the Great Organ—not male, but the musical instrument, Mother's Lace Curtains, Pool of Wisdom, etc.

Solyra stopped listening and let herself get lost in the strangeness of it. Shirra lit other lanterns to illuminate new sections. Sometimes the sloping walls looked like sideways beds of cauliflower. Other times, columns made gleaming clusters. And Diaa had been right about wearing her vest. The burning noon above them was a world apart from the cool deep.

"It looks like your beads," Zago murmured—they'd all dropped their voices. He pointed to a range of white icicle-like formations.

"It does," Solyra whispered back. "I should have brought them along, so they could meet their cousins." She touched the rough formation, and her hands came away damp and slightly gritty.

They continued to another chamber. Terring paused several times pretending to examine a formation but really, Solyra guessed, to stretch his back. Frogbelly had understated the injuries Terring got in the buffalumph stampede. Besides his dislocated shoulder, his back had been wrenched. Solyra had offered to make hot packs for it, but Figgo told her he would take care of it. Like a guard dog, he let no one near Terring. Or rather, he didn't let *her* near. She never got a word with Terring, without Figgo hovering nearby. On one hand, she didn't care. On the other hand, it was annoying and hurtful.

Tad made no bones about being oppressed by the cavern, though when anyone offered to go back he refused.

Finally, a spacious chamber opened around them. Terring straightened immediately, putting a hand to his back. Tad looked relieved and stretched his arms up, as if to prove to himself that at last there was plenty of room to breathe.

"How about I blow out the lamp for a few minutes?" Shirra looked at Zago as she asked.

Solyra wanted her to blow out the lamp, but for Tad's sake she was about to say no, when Figgo said, "Go ahead." A huff of breath and the light went out.

The darkness was utterly complete. Solyra put her hand to her face and didn't see a thing. She knew intuitively her eyes would never grow accustomed to it, for there was absolutely no light for them to grasp. Yet this dark didn't suffocate like the blindness from the fulgu flash. It held Solyra as if she were nestled deep in an earthen womb, the mineral smell all around. She could smell her companions, too, the sour and musky fragrance of their flesh and Figgo's rosewater. They were so familiar, so dear. They were her family. She felt utterly safe with them.

The thought brought her a joy so intense, she let out a little sobbing whimper. But Tad's breath quickened, and Diaa whispered, "Let's light the lamp again."

For some reason, the sudden brightness made Solyra and Diaa giggle. Terring's gaze lingered on Solyra's face, then without a word, he gently pressed his bandanna to her cheeks. She hadn't realized they were wet with tears.

They emerged into the other world, a day of sun and dry air. As they headed back to Harraz, Shirra described the nature of the cavern, its age and mineral content, its estimated size, the strange reptiles hiding in the depths, eyeless in their endless night, the bats that covered the walls in what she called "chimneys," outlets to the above-ground world. She spoke to the group, mostly, but she watched Zago.

He had looked dazed when the lamp was relit, and he literally had trouble emerging from the cavern, his legs and arms trembling with whatever mystery had clasped him there. Under the bright sun he lingered in his own dream. Shirra was telling of the children who had first discovered the cavern opening when Zago broke in, speaking aloud but almost to himself.

"It was like going inside the song," he said. "But the source was deep. So deep."

Shirra said quickly, "Stay here with us, Master, and we'll give you a house and everything you need to live."

Solyra opened her mouth to protest, stopped herself. Diaa gave a little growl, but otherwise she, too, kept quiet. Shirra was offering Zago a kind of priesthood, and neither of them could deny it for him.

But Zago shook his head and, for the first time since leaving the cavern, his gaze lost its softness. He sat up and looked around as if awakening from a dream. "No. No, thanks." He smiled at Shirra. "I'm honored. But I have commitments."

Shirra bowed her head, then picked up the story of the cavern's discovery as if it had never been interrupted.

When the group stopped to rest and water the animals, Diaa and Zago went upstream together to fill the canteens. They came back holding hands.

That night, Solyra had the room to herself. She'd expected Diaa's and Zago's intimacy to be a blow, but it wasn't. Maybe the cavern had rearranged things, in a healing way. Although she dreaded losing forever Zago's sweet kisses and his warm, damp embraces, she knew she'd done something right and good, when she'd talked to Diaa this morning.

Yet sadness and something like fear uncoiled in her. Even in the fold of her chosen family, she was truly alone. She lay in bed, staring into the dark and feeling hollow. The fantasy of she and her mother and father living in a cottage on the ocean—fussing over the decorations, collecting shells on the beach, sitting on a veranda listening to the waves—didn't soothe her as it usually did.

She'd given up on fantasies of having her own children after a couple of years of marriage, figuring she couldn't have them. Then Dahn revealed that he'd had himself altered so that he couldn't sire children. In one of his unpredictable and devastatingly honest moments, he'd asked, "You wouldn't want another of me running around, would you?" Zago, too, was incapable of siring children. Just as he'd said, the books in the Ihm libraries confirmed that fulgu keepers were sterile. Diaa was glad. As much as she enjoyed frolicking with Erin and Raal, she had no interest in being a mother herself. For Solyra, it was just as well, too. She was in no position to have children, and Zago wasn't the man for her. But later, when she settled down....

If she had chosen Terring over Dahn, that summer when they were courting her, how different her life would be.

Dahn had been so gentlemanly, all manners and grace. It would be nice to say, she'd sensed something untrue in him, but she hadn't had a twinge. To her, Dahn had been a dashing man with pale hair and smiling dark eyes, not quite young, but not old, either, wealthy and mannered.

What had he seen in her? A shy, virginal girl — "I could smell it on you," he said later — whose parents were too low on the social scale to hear the gossip about him, too humble not to be thrilled that he courted their daughter, too insignificant ever to lay anything against him, no matter what he did.

Some whispers must have come to them. A week before

the wedding, they sat Solyra down and questioned her about whether she was sure she wanted to marry Dahn. Did he smoke much? Drink? Did she ever notice anything peculiar about him? As if she would know what they were trying to learn from her, their well-sheltered daughter. Now she couldn't help but see they'd been clearing their consciences, basically getting her permission to give her to a man of dubious character.

She was almost relieved when a knock pulled her from her thoughts.

"Solyra?" It was Tad. Something must be wrong.

"Come in."

Tad opened the door. "Pack your things and meet us in the stables. Dress for riding. Hurry." He was gone before she had a chance to ask questions.

She didn't need to ask, though. The Collectors had caught up with her. And even if Frogbelly was willing to go on the run for her, she wasn't willing. She'd have to give herself up.

COLLECTORS

IN A HURRIED, PRIVATE CONFERENCE, Frogbelly confessed to Terring why he was on the run. His so-called crimes were no more than Solyra had said, and Terring didn't consider men loving each other criminal. Unfortunately, Tad's parents didn't feel that way. Still, Terring wasn't about to jump caravan, even if he could afford to. Which he couldn't. He didn't like Frogbelly as a friend, but had grown a stubborn loyalty to the man and the crew.

As they joined the others in the barn, he couldn't help hoping the Bihsts would drop out. Even in a group, traveling through the mountains was dangerous, and rumor had it that some of the surviving Death Bringers had holed up in the more remote passes to prey on travelers. Bihsts wouldn't be much use in a fight. Neither would Figgo, for that matter. Nor Solyra, though Zago, for all his mush about fulgus, had become adept with bow and arrow.

Terring was just securing the fulgu lockers when Solyra hurried up to Frogbelly.

"Stop, Cap'n! I'll turn myself in. You shouldn't have to be running for me."

Before Terring had a chance to demand what in blazes she was talking about, Frogbelly answered with a grim smile. "You're not the only one who's wanted here." He raised his voice slightly. "Gather in, everyone, and listen up."

Once everyone circled him, their faces attentive, he fell silent, rubbing his chin. Tad put an arm around him and stared at the gathering as if defying anyone to call Frogbelly on the fact that he seemed to be losing his nerve.

Terring hardly listened. He knew what Frogbelly's problem was. Finally. What he didn't know was, what Solyra was "wanted" for.

Frogbelly took a breath, and staring somewhere behind his caravan group, he spoke. "As some of you know, Tad and I left Springfill under a cloud. Because we're Fehs."

He paused as if to allow his audience to digest a startling truth — he and Tad were Fehs! As if everyone didn't already know!

"Mister Korsten — that's Tad's father — threatened to charge me for—for perversion. Corrupting his son."

He was impassive, but his face flushed. "It turns out the cloud is darker than we thought," he continued. "Korsten actually submitted the charges to the authorities. Where we're from, that's a capital crime, so I'm wanted dead or alive. Trying to prove the fact that Tad was of age when we met…. Well, against a man like Mister Korsten, the odds are not in our favor. Tad, at least, is wanted alive. Mister Korsten laid on a huge reward for his safe return. To make the pot sweeter, Solyra here has creditors offering a reward for her. And Zago. Their reward alone wouldn't justify the cost of extradition, but a posse of Collectors got wind of Tad and me and are planning to ambush us on our way out of town. My guess is that Bo somehow learned Tad's and my real names."

Some of the caravan people murmured, but Frogbelly continued over them.

"Fortunately, my friends here at Harraz led the Collectors

to believe we're leaving the day after tomorrow. The Collectors will see through that quickly enough, but hopefully we'll get a head start."

He drew another big breath. "In short, Tad and I are making a run for it. Once we reach the Zhengahk, we're home free. There are no laws there against people like us. Solyra and Zago — like I said, I doubt anyone will bother you. It's me and Tad they want. The posse is a tough bunch, top of the line, and they're after a fat purse. We know of some secret passes in the Apfas that might throw them off our scent. Or we might be forced into a showdown. So there it is. You can come with us, or you can go your own way from here with no hard feelings whatsoever."

After a short silence, everyone just went to their animals and busied themselves with adjusting tack and fastening on saddlebags.

"All right," Frogbelly said quietly.

Figgo signaled to Terring and Solyra, and they went outside the gate to speak in private.

"I warned you not to trust that woman."

"That woman" didn't speak, but Terring could hear her breathe. He could see her pulse thudding in her neck, and her body trembling. Terring drew a deep breath himself, let it out slowly. No point ripping Figgo's head off, though the man should have known better than to utter anything resembling "I told you so" at this moment.

"What's the story, Solyra?" Terring asked in the calmest voice he could muster. "Are the fulgus yours or not?"

But he'd guessed the answer: Not. Why else would creditors pursue her? Surely not for that slum pile she'd lived in back in Norvadale.

Solyra swallowed. "They're mine."

"Yours in spirit? Or legally."

She was silent, then said, "We can dissolve the business if you want."

Terring refrained from exploding. He even managed not to tear his hair out by the roots. "That's very nice of you, Solyra. And I'm sure all those equally nice border agents on the way here will lose the logs that recorded Terring Fulgus crossed here with stolen fulgus."

"You didn't know," she said.

"No fooling!"

"And — and the fulgus are still in my name."

"Technically, true," Terring bit out. "Though that fine distinction may not keep me out of jail. Not to mention the quaint concept of being an honest man."

She didn't speak, just swallowed again.

He stared past her into the dark. Signing his name to stolen goods was bad enough. But what made his stomach churn was being deceived.

By her.

Again.

Again!

Never mind. Time to evict his balls from his brain, figure out how to deal with this mess.

He could simply turn himself in. It would be messy, it would be humiliating, but he knew, without a doubt, that his family would bail him out.

He also knew, without a doubt, that Solyra would do time.

"We'll just carry on," he said.

>> <<

BY DAWN THE CARAVAN HAD left behind the foothills, with their terraced orchards and burgeoning fields of squash and pumpkins, to climb among aspens and pine. In late morning, they entered one of Frogbelly's secret passes, a narrow fold of rock threaded with not much more than a footpath.

The main road, so Terring had been told, was smoother and wider, with stupendous views and a breeze. The pass trapped the air, damp and hot, and mosquitoes feasted on every inch of available flesh.

Most of the time they traveled single file, walking to spare the animals. The bony rocks of the uneven mountain trail weren't easy on the feet, and Terring's back hurt badly, the injury he'd taken during the stampede coming back with a vengeance. But even if he'd been a whiner, the fortitude of his companions, including young Erin, would have shamed him silent.

At dusk, he got through setting up camp, but could only pick at the boiled rabbit and greens they had for dinner. He dreaded the sleepless night that lay ahead, and dreaded the long day that lay beyond. More than the pain, he feared being crippled up, a burden to the caravan.

"That's it," Solyra said suddenly. "You're getting a massage twice a day." The command carried every bit of bossiness she'd have learned from business life, along with the touch-ups from Peg.

"Yes," Figgo said. "That is correct."

Everyone stared at the spectacle of Figgo and Solyra, agreeing.

"Take off your shirt," Solyra ordered Terring, "and lie on your stomach." She added to the rest of the caravan, "For earth's sake, this isn't a carny show."

Terring stripped and laid himself down without a word, cautious as an old man. Figgo, like a faithful hound, stationed himself at Terring's head. Solyra rubbed sunflower oil on her hands and straddled Terring without putting her weight on him, paused, then eased down to lightly rest on his upper thighs. Had it not been for the pain....

He heard her rubbing her hands together again. She had just put them on his shoulders when Figgo said, "Begin at the small of the back. Work toward the heart."

Solyra paused, then did as he said. While Terring pondered the unintended double meaning of Solyra working toward his heart, Figgo continued to instruct her. Between the two of them, the locked up muscles relaxed. Bones seemingly upside down slipped into place. The rest of the caravan lost interest and went about the business of settling in for the night.

The feeling of Solyra's hands went from not unpleasant to pleasant to … extra pleasant as her touch gentled from earnest kneading to strokes. Long, luxurious strokes.

"That's enough," Figgo said.

He spoke quietly, but his voice carried a harshness. Terring was half-tempted to tell Figgo, she didn't need to seduce him to cheat him. But really, he didn't want to. And he didn't want her to move off him. But she did, and covered him not with a rough wool blanket, but with her own quilt, worn soft.

Terring feigned sleep. Diaa and Brid and Robet, picketed the horses and mules, discussing which animals were getting along, which had bickered today. Tad and Frogbelly murmured over a map, Onyx's knitting needles clicked softly. Zago sang his lullaby to the fulgus.

The truth was, he was in love with her. Or he'd never stopped loving her. There was simply no getting around it. No matter what she did to him, he just didn't seem capable of hurting her.

Not true.

He realized, all at once, what he'd done when he'd sold his fulgus to another broker. She'd taken out a loan with her house and its contents as security. The contents, including the fulgus.

It would be easy to let the blame rest on her. She'd taken a foolish risk. She's counted her fulgus before they ripened. Just like anyone in the business. Just as he had, when he raised a frame on the Zhengahk, years ago.

Still, she could have done the right thing. Instead, she fled with property that belonged to the bank. And never told him, even as she signed the contract that bound together their fortunes.

The quilt smelled of her. Not a feminine flowery perfume,

but her sweat, her scent. Her hair, part of it buried now beneath the prairie grass, with Peg and Jerzy.

The quiet bustle of the caravan had gone to cricket song and the gentle sigh of the dying fire. She spoke, in barely more than a whisper. "Why don't you massage him, Figgo? You know how."

Figgo didn't answer.

"You're a physician, aren't you?" she persisted. "You know all about aches and ailments. You helped Peg—"

"I have no healing touch."

A log slipped, crackled, subsided.

"All touch is healing," Solyra said finally. "All ... benevolent touch. And you know so much." She was right. Figgo had described the lay of every muscle and bone on Terring's back as clearly as if he'd had an anatomy book printed in his mind.

"I do not have the healing touch," he repeated. "And without that, knowledge is nothing." He took a deep breath — and didn't let it out as a sigh.

"We will do body work on zizero Terring twice daily," he continued. "And if the Bihsts will kindly take over your cooking duties, I will use that time and every other moment we have to teach you the rudiments of healing."

"Shhh'u'wah," Solyra murmured, Zhi'nging'ha! for thank you.

"Shhh'u'wah here, too," Terring said.

>> <<

AT DUSK, TWO DAYS INTO the Apfas, they entered a village tucked into a crevasse so steep and sharp, the buildings clung to the sides, flanking a thin river and its pebbly beaches. The rush of water gusted coolness.

Canoes, some with bundles of firewood in them, bobbed at the river banks. On the slopes behind the buildings rose emerald terraces of greens. Saplings, probably fruit trees, their trunks ringed with burlap against deer and rabbits, mounted the crevasse sides. Everything looked new — with not a soul in sight. Solyra guessed the elaborate wooden screens covering the windows of the stone houses hid watchers.

Frogbelly ordered a halt. "Wait here, and for the love of heaven, don't make a move for your weapons. Don't even reach for a canteen."

He dismounted, then removed his weapon belt, which held two daggers, a working knife and a sword, and laid it on the road. Then he just stood there, his hands a little away from his body, until at some unknown signal, he went to a blue-doored house. The door opened; he disappeared inside.

Toggly shifted and whickered and, at Solyra's whisper, grew still again. The chill dusk was touching darkness when the door burst open. A man bustled out, with Frogbelly behind. "I oughta brain you, Carl," the man said, but Frogbelly grinned.

"Everyone at ease," he yelled. "You can dismount. Bring your bedrolls and personals; Cyon's folks will take care of the rest."

Men and women emerged from different buildings to take the animals. Whatever negotiating Frogbelly — or Carl — had done, the people clearly weren't trustful. Normally, curious children, not adults, greeted travelers. Then she realized that the women were men. The village was a male Liberty.

A young man led the Frogbellies into the blue-doored building, taking them through a foyer crowded with spears, swords, bows, and clubs, then upstairs to a long, uncarpeted room furnished with rows of string beds. "Back stairs go to the privies," he said cheerfully, "and you're welcome to all the hot water you can heat." Solyra put her saddlebags at the foot of a bed, then headed out to check on Toggly.

The stables, nearly at the other end of the village, were more well-maintained than the guest quarters, fragrant with fresh hay, clean leather, and newly milled pine. Toggly and she kissed and nuzzled each other, and Toggly nosed out from Solyra's pocket a stub of carrot she'd saved from this morning.

The mare's coat was well brushed, but Solyra ran her hands over her anyway, with special care on her legs, and checked her hooves. She marveled over how second nature this had become for her. As routine as applying cold creme to her face and neck every night, back home. It had been a long time, since she'd had cold creme.

Diaa came out of the stall where her pony was and they met Zago at the door.

"Freight's in the dorm," he said quietly.

"I wish I were," Solyra said, "but I've been called on to make dinner."

"We'll help," Diaa said.

"No, Diaa, why don't you take a nap?"

"What's the point?" Diaa giggled. "No place to have fun around here. Frogbelly told us so."

Onyx and Ebony were already plucking birds in the kitchen, their large hands covering nearly half a bird per pluck. The fowl were a mix of tough looking chickens and scrawny game birds, but the potatoes were freshly dug, the carrots crisp and bright, and the peas tender and sweet. Diaa and Zago got to work rinsing a mountain of salad greens, and Solyra, Erin, Baloos and Jaleen began mixing the crust for a couple dozen pies. Soon the huge kettle sizzled fragrant with butter and veggies frying.

Solyra was calculating how much flour it would take to thicken the broth when a chubby man came to the door, surveyed the kitchen with pursed lips, then turned on his heel and left. It must have been "his" kitchen. He couldn't resist coming back and adding a few fistfuls of his own herbs to the pie filling bubbling on the stovetop, then taking over.

Solyra didn't mind a bit, nor did anyone who ate the pies at the trestle tables set up in the great room. The meal passed mostly in silence — if the munching and slurping of several dozen people could be called silence. They drank watery barley ale.

The place felt different from anywhere Solyra had been. There was a roughness in manner, and a gentleness; a lack of tension together with the paradoxical certainty that an argument could easily escalate into a fist fight. Frogbelly and Tad were both hearty and a little uneasy.

Solyra rose to help clean up, but Frogbelly waved her, Terring, Baloos and Jaleen over to where he and Tad sat with the man whom they'd first seen.

"This is Cyon Liberty, the governor here," Frogbelly said. "Solyra and Baloos and Jaleen are chiefs of my caravan. Terring's security. Solyra's a Liberty, too, in the Zhengahk. She and Terring are looking to raise a fulgu frame on her property. Baloos and his folks are Bihst missionaries."

"Panno your boy?" Cyon asked Baloos.

"Yes, he's ours." Baloos looked around to where Panno was clearing a table and as if he'd been tapped on the shoulder, Panno looked around at him, looked at Cyon, then went back to his work.

"He asked if he could stay here," Cyon said.

Baloos nodded. "He told us." He took Jaleen's hand. "He's a man, so it's up to him."

"Is he a hard worker?" Cyon asked.

"Oh, yes," Jaleen said. "He pulls his weight." Her eyes suddenly filled with tears, which she quickly dabbed away. "If this is where he wants to be.... We want him to be happy."

"Does he get along with people?"

"Pretty well," Baloos said. "He's a bit of a loner but not antisocial."

Tad gave a slight grimace but didn't contradict Baloos.

Cyon took it in, then nodded. "I'll call some of the guys together and we can interview him tomorrow, if he's serious. Maybe you two can be there."

"Just let us know when and where."

"Will do," Cyon said. "Now. Your posse of Collectors was sighted on the Mohig Pass."

"Great," Tad said. "Just great."

"You knew we couldn't shake them," Frogbelly said.

"Yeah, but I hoped we'd get a little more of a lead."

"Well, you didn't," Cyon cut in. "There's about a dozen of them, armed to the teeth, and with dogs. We know these ones. Nasty and mean and good at what they do, dogs and all. They took a couple of ours before we armed up. They won't dare come here, but once you're on the Mohig—"

"The only way out of here," Frogbelly put in.

"Right. Once you're on the Mohig Pass, they'll be waiting for you. If you need ammo, we've got it to spare, and we've got manned posts as far as Buzzard Peak, but from there, you're on your own."

Baloos cleared his throat. "I guess it's obvious to everyone by now, we won't bear weapons."

"So," Tad said, "that makes nine nonfighters for eight of us to defend, not to mention the cargo. Unless you know how to fight?" he asked Solyra.

Solyra shook her head.

"Well, hopefully we can pick off some Collectors in the next couple of days," Cyon said. "Us criminal types could do with a little practice in…" He left the rest unsaid, maybe for the sake of the Bihsts.

"So you're gonna make 'em meaner?" Tad asked.

Cyon gave a grim laugh. "They don't need to be peppered with bolts to get any meaner. They're just as mean as they can be already. I think they're more than a bit troll. In fact, I'm pretty sure they're left-over Death Bringers."

Death-bringers. The bandit army that had razed the Zhengahk.

"I thought they were defeated," Jaleen said.

"Defeated, but not exterminated," Terring said. "The battle of Hawk Gulch finished off most of them, and the Zhengahk Guard did their best to root out the rest. Still, some managed to retreat to the mountains. Most of them came from here, originally."

"And we're working on cleaning out the rest," Cyon said, "with the cooperation of the Zhengahk Guard. But this pack won't go down without a fight. A vicious fight. Especially since a lovely Collection agency back east provided them with arms and supplies and the promise of a big fat reward."

>> <<

THEY SPENT THE LAST EVENING at Cyon Liberty packing the animals and rechecking their weapons, then devoured a feast that Cyon's kitchen crew prepared.

Solyra was grateful for a night off. Terring's battle drills over the last three days had tightened up every muscle of her body and stuffed her head with military tactics. She did feel a little less frightened and a lot more useful, even if daunted at being made "captain of the noncombatants."

After clearing the plates, most of the crew played cards. Solyra drank a cup of herb tisane with Frogbelly and Tad.

"As you've probably gathered by now," said Frogbelly, "Tad and I plan to settle in the Zhengahk. Question is, can we find work out there? I had a transportation company back east."

All pretense at being an illiterate captain one step up from a muleskinner had been dropped back at Harraz. He'd even visited a barber there, and replaced the saggy shorts and grimy pullover with clean trousers and a flannel shirt.

"If things work out for me," Solyra said after he described his company, "they will for you." She couldn't imagine not hiring him, especially since he had experience with balloon transport.

Frogbelly grinned. "I was hoping you'd say that."

Solyra grinned, too; she'd bagged a transportation manager complete with references. "Can I start calling you two Carl and Teyod?"

"Why not?" Carl slapped his stomach. "The ole frog belly

is half melted off already. The rest'll probably be gone by the time we get to our new life."

"If we get to our new life. And call me Tad; I've gotten used to it."

After a little more chat, he and Carl went to join a card game at another table. Terring and Figgo joined Solyra.

"Good news," Solyra said, "Carl has agreed to be our transportation manager at the field. He used to own a transportation company, mostly local but some over the road. They hauled everything from bricks to lumber to porcelain to chickens."

"You did not consider consulting your partner?" Figgo asked.

Solyra was deflated. "I'm sorry. I should have."

"Yes, you should have," Terring said. "Did you actually hire him as a manager?"

"No, but… He can handle transport balloons. He should have some kind of position."

"That is beside the point," Figgo said. "You should have consulted with us. What if the job has already been offered to one of zizero Terring's crew?"

"Without consulting me?" Solyra asked.

"Yes," Terring said. "Hiring labor is my lookout."

"You don't like Carl," Solyra said. "Or Tad."

"Like or dislike is, again, beside the point," Figgo said.

"What matters," Terring said, "is that our labor force works smoothly."

"Zizera Solyra, you have no inkling of the social structure and customs in the Zhengahk," Figgo said. "Zizero Terring does."

They were both making the same point, and they were right, but Solyra felt pecked at. Whenever she discussed business with Terring alone, they were of one mind, completing each other's thoughts, building on each other's ideas. Whenever Figgo jumped in, they bickered.

Solyra nodded and said with forced equanimity, "I'll tell

186 >< KEATES NELSON

Carl he must apply just like any other employee, or bid as a contractor. I'm sure he'll understand, given that he's run his own business."

"And next time—" Figgo began.

"Let it go," Terring said.

Figgo nodded with equanimity probably even more forced than Solyra's.

"I'm getting a refill," Terring said, lifting his cup. "Anyone else?"

"Thanks," Solyra said.

The moment he left the table, Solyra wished she'd offered to get the tea instead. She had a feeling Figgo was going to speak his mind. She wasn't wrong.

"You are not equal partners with zizero Terring," Figgo said. "You are an investor; he is the executive."

Solyra fought against answering, and lost. "The contract that you drew up, that Terring and I signed, does not specify any such thing, zizero Figgo. You should shake that thought right out of your mind."

"In essence, that is the way it is. You know nothing about the venture into which you are flying. Without the expertise of zizero Terring, you would have only a piece of land and some fulgus. If that much. For all we know, no viable fulgus survived Zago's folly."

"That remains to be seen, doesn't it?"

"It does indeed." He was silent, then, as if he just couldn't hold it in, "If only I had been able to steer zizero Terring from entering into a partnership with a woman like you."

Solyra felt a chill at his words, a woman like you. But she was being paranoid. It wouldn't take more than her affair with Zago to fix her in Figgo's mind as a loose woman. And surely Figgo was referring to the "stolen" fulgus. And her machinations against Terring Fulgus.

It seemed a century ago, but really it was only a season. And while her business had been wrecked in just a day, Terring's business had gone down in a long, bruising fight. Her string of triumphs had been a series of disasters for Terring and for Figgo.

"Don't trouble yourself, zizero Figgo," she said in the most confident and soothing voice she could muster. "Our business will be a success."

Behind her, she heard Tad and Panno. She couldn't make out the words, though their voices were raised.

"A success!" Figgo didn't raise his voice. On the contrary, it dropped to hardly more than a whisper. "Your keeper has destroyed who knows how many of his charges, not to mention the precious cargo of our companions. Your aide is a promiscuous woman who has instigated one catastrophe after another. Where is the success? We have less now than what we started with, and we have not even arrived at the field."

Solyra had hit herself so many times with that stick, it just didn't hurt anymore. "Zizero Figgo, if you want to crumple me, you'll have to be more creative. But leave our employees out of it. And may I say that I'm saddened by your contempt for Zago and Diaa? I only hope you continue to be so skillfully two-faced. Diaa especially considers you a friend and mentor."

Solyra leaned toward him. "In other words, Figgo, leave them out of it. Just you and me. Single combat." She leaned back again. "Though, honestly, I have nothing against you."

Satisfying as it would have been to get up and leave on that note, it was yet more satisfying to watch him digest her words. He could keep a nonchalant expression, but he couldn't stop the blood from creeping up his neck. Not only that, but struggle as he might, he couldn't resist the bait. Solyra reckoned she couldn't have come up with a more tempting worm if she'd tried.

"Why should you have anything against me?" Figgo demanded. "I have never done wrong to you or your associates."

If he was honest, rather than correct, he would have said

only, "I have never done wrong." Surely that was how he saw himself: never doing wrong.

Solyra was just about to tell him so, when Figgo cried, "Stop them!"

Solyra turned just in time to see Terring quickly put down the mugs he had looped through his fingers and grab Panno. But Panno wrenched loose and lunged toward Tad.

It was over in moments. Panno never had a chance, though Tad didn't hurt him, maybe out of deference to Baloos. Tad merely clipped Panno on the shoulder, tripped him, then stood a-straddle over him, twisting his wrists behind his back.

"Let him go, Tad," Baloos said.

Tad obeyed, backing off as Panno sprang up. With Baloos's gentle hands holding him, Panno didn't engage again physically. His anger wasn't spent, though.

"If it weren't for you," he spat at Tad, "Carl would be free. You're killing him!"

Tad's face flushed dark, and Solyra guessed not just from rage: He agreed with Panno. She wished she could comfort him, but this was for the boys to work out. Including Carl, who hurried up.

"What's going on?" he asked.

Panno turned to him, sudden tears in his eyes. "The Collectors'll kill you, Froggie! Let Tad go home to mama, and we'll stay here. Together."

Carl looked incredulous. "Panno, you're... You're dreaming. Tad's my life. We're together forever. That's all there is to it."

Panno drew a breath to answer, just as Cyon clapped his shoulder. "You want to stay here, kiddo, it's time to stop being a fool. Right now."

In a long silence Panno digested both Carl's and Cyon's words. Finally, he straightened his clothes and nodded. "Yeah, I want to stay here." He tried for tough, but his voice trembled and tears spilled down his face. He left as quickly as he could without tossing away the scraps of his dignity by running.

Carl shook his head and slapped his stomach. "The caravan adventure diet must be working. I never thought two young bucks would fight over me."

Tad just stared at him, a smile touching his face. "Together forever." He grabbed Carl in a hug and the two men stood embraced like two trees grown into one.

Solyra sat again, but her smile faded at Figgo's stiff, dour face. Terring rejoined them, with the mugs. He looked from Solyra to Figgo and back. "Everything all right?"

Intuitively, Solyra knew that Terring's wrath for her and Figgo's quarrel would fall on Figgo, not on her. And at some obscure urge to protect Figgo, she smiled and said evenly, "Everything's all right."

Or maybe she was just sticking to her own rules: single combat.

BATTLE

"WE'LL MAKE OUR WAY BACK to the main road," Terring said as they lined up to leave Buzzard Peak, the last outpost of Cyon Feh. "Then we can travel in a bunch rather than single-file."

He'd even thought of trying to leave by balloon, one of his more ridiculous inspirations. Or desperate inspirations. Leading a group of mostly nonfighters through this danger had kept him awake, nights, his back knotting as if cringing at what lay ahead.

He just prayed they could make good time. Once they were over the mountains and into the Zhengahk, the Guard there would ally with them.

"No point in trying to get through on the sly, anyway," Carl said, "given that the Collectors are already on our trail—minus three that Cyon's boys killed off."

"Didn't get any of the dogs, more's the shame," Tad said.

Queenie lifted a lip and growled, as if to say, "Leave that to me." But even with the spiked collar she so proudly sported, Terring couldn't see her taking on a gang of mastiffs. Unlike her master, she'd gotten fatter on the journey.

"You protect the noncoms, Queenie," Terring said, giving

her a scratch behind the ears. Queenie looked up at Carl and, at his nod, plopped down at Solyra's feet.

Every evening, Terring visited paradise as she worked on his back. The rest of the time, they were polite and distant. Outwardly, at least. Inwardly, Terring was torn in two. He didn't know if he could ever trust her, and trust in his mind was the mainstay of a marriage — yes, preposterously, he wanted to marry her. And even if the betrayals of their past were erased, she refused him. Not in words. It just seemed that whenever they drew close to each other, a fresh betrayal drove them apart.

As captain of the noncombatants, though, she was all he could ask for. She looked after everyone, had done so even before Peg's death, checking daily and nightly on people and animals. Terring didn't know how, but she'd made them a sort of family, just as Carl had formed them into a smoothly working crew. Terring hoped he'd formed them into a fighting and defending unit.

They reached the main road without incident and ate lunch at a big shelter strewn with garbage, with the adjoining hillside as an open, communal toilet. Neither waste nor trash was fresh; Brid figured that the last visitors to the shelter had stopped there several weeks ago.

While Carl and Terring debated sleeping there, Diaa gave a short yowl and came rustling back up the hill she'd been exploring, hair bristling in a ridge and fangs bared.

"Bones," she half-growled, half-whined. "A big heap of bones."

"Human bones?" Terring asked.

Diaa nodded. "And maybe some trolls," she whispered. Terring remembered Diaa saying something about having lived at a trollhouse, and insisting she wasn't one, as if it wasn't obvious. "They're old, but...."

Figgo finished her sentence. "The bones were gnawed..." He swallowed and continued. "Gnawed by humans and trolls."

No one wanted to stay in a Death-bringer shelter, even long-abandoned, or near the bones, old as they were, and after Gobi sang over the remains they pressed on.

Only a few hours past the shelter, though, they were forced to stop. First Erin, then Diaa, then the rest of them, began vomiting. Diarrhea set in. Not wanting to attract attention with a fire, they'd taken a chance on a stream by the road and now they were paying for it. Terring fetched water, and Solyra boiled it with salted beef, smoke or no smoke, though her belly must have been as knotted as his.

Everyone made themselves tend their duties. They had no choice but to rub down the animals and herd them to a little pasture, and to stand sentry.

The Bihsts carried on with their evening worship, faithful as the sun, not of the laughing fat man, but of the bare-chested woman holding a flower. Terring hoped that, whoever their goddess was, she would keep the Collectors at bay. They'd hardly need dogs to follow the stench of the caravan, nor weapons to collect a bounty.

Morning found the caravan alive, at least, though weak, exhausted and emptied out. Solyra boiled up more broth, and they wearily packed up and moved on. No one rode.

Midmorning, Figgo signaled a halt. Everyone watched, dead silent, as he turned his head this way and that, listening. When Queenie whined, Carl commanded her to be quiet.

"The dogs," Figgo said.

They moved on, faster, but the Collectors moved faster still. By noon, Diaa said she could hear the dogs, and too soon, everyone else could. Even from the distance, the yammering and barking cut through the patter of aspen leaves. The bird chatter had ceased.

"How long do you think before they catch up?" Terring asked Figgo.

Figgo turned his head to catch the direction. "If the terrain is much the same for the whole way, we have the afternoon, maybe early evening."

Five hours.

"We need to get to the next road level," Terring said. "With any luck, the map is right and a shelter will be up there. You fortify, and Robet, Brid and I will try and divert them." Diaa stepped forward, but Terring shook his head. "Not you, Diaa, the dogs will catch your scent too easily."

"I'll go," Tad said.

"No, no, you stay with us," Carl said quickly.

Tad opened his mouth to protest, then clamped it shut and stared away over the valley.

"Why shouldn't he?" Brid asked.

Terring answered. "As long as Tad's with the caravan, the Collectors won't make an all-out attack. They don't want to lose their reward."

>> <<

THE SHELTER STOOD ALONGSIDE THE road, as promised by the map, and its stone walls and slate roof looked sturdy. First order was routine: take care of the animals. After they were unburdened and unsaddled, Raal, Erin, Gobi and Queenie brought them to a rundown corral around the bend. Solyra felt a pang as she watched the animals go. They were as much a part of the family as the human contingent.

As Tad stacked the fulgu lockers in a corner of the shelter, he asked the inevitable: "Why not use the fulgus for weapons?"

Solyra put a hand on Zago's shoulder, to staunch his indignation. "Because they'd kill us before they kill the enemy."

"Still," Tad persisted, "as a last resort."

Figgo spoke this time. "We will not need a last resort. Our captains Terring and Solyra will ensure our safety. And with my own experience in military operations, and zizero Baloos's engineering expertise, we will make a tidy fortification. But we must get to it right away."

Gratitude flooded Solyra, not just for the confidence in herself, which she needed, but for the heartening effect of Figgo's words on the group. They set to work with a will.

They wedged crisscrossed branches and loose rocks into the shelter's unglazed windows, and filled every available vessel with water. They even emptied some of the food into linen wraps to make more water vessels available. They dug in as if for a siege. But things would likely be decided one way or another before another day dawned.

The distant baying of the dogs kept Solyra's nerves taut, but the work of making the shelter as safe as possible for her companions braced her mind to a clear, almost acute calmness.

She sent a crew up to check on the animals. She took reports from the scouts. She made sure everyone ate and rested. She and Erin and Raal tore underwear into bandages.

Onyx and Ebony felled and dragged scrubby trees across the road and bolstered them with boulders. The hillside was similarly barricaded. They left what Figgo called a trick gate, which would allow Terring, Brid and Robet to get back inside, but whose main purpose was to draw the enemy. If the Collectors took the bait, they would be funneled toward where more Frogbellies, pitifully few, hid behind the barrier.

Solyra could distinguish between the deep rough dogs' voices now. One dog was louder than the rest, its bark piercing. Another's bark was somehow more savage, while another gave out a constant roaring bay…

Everyone had stopped talking to listen.

"How many are there, do you think?" Raal whispered.

"About ten," Jaleen said briskly, "and it's time to get back to work."

Solyra shook herself. "Let's roll the bandages."

Nothing could stop them from listening as they worked though, and calculating how far the Collectors were.

The fighters took their positions. Baloos went out to check the barricades. Solyra and Gobi rechecked the medical supplies.

A silence fell, an eerie silence that stretched on and on — a man began screaming, screaming, pausing only to take breath, screaming. Erin shrank against Jaleen and burst into sobs. Queenie whimpered and might have howled had Baloos not put a hand on her head. It was almost worse when the screams ended.

"Who was it?" Raal gasped.

"Robet," Figgo answered. His face was gray, hard, blank.

Raal buried his head in his hands, and Erin sobbed into Jaleen's bosom. Robet had been a favorite with them, always ready with a game or prank. Solyra wondered if Brid had recognized his best friend's voice, if he'd witnessed his best friend's agony. She wondered if Terring had... Fear pressed her heart and squeezed her stomach.

The pack was muffled now. "They are on the road below us," Figgo said. "They are moving as a group and will reach the barricade in about ten minutes." He listened more, then added, "I think they are pursuing Terring and Brid."

Solyra stood, wondering if her legs would hold. They did. No choice. They had to. "Remember everyone: stay here until ordered otherwise." Her voice came breathless, rough.

"Leave a weapon," Figgo ordered. "Hand it to me."

Solyra didn't know how Figgo planned to defend the shelter, but she gave him her biggest kitchen knife. "It's very sharp," she warned.

"Good."

He suddenly looked very young, childlike. She always forgot that he was just a young man. Not a child, but younger than she.

"I'll send news back when I can." She turned before leaving. "Don't let Queenie loose."

Gobi and Solyra crept toward the barricade through the bushes at the roadside to keep hidden from any archers who might be on the lower road. The sun was behind the mountain, though dark hadn't yet fallen. Carl and Tad, at the barricade, didn't notice Gobi and Solyra's approach.

"No, I won't let you," Carl muttered. Solyra stopped and signaled Gobi; they unashamedly listened. "Tad, I'll die for you, gladly. But I won't live without you."

"I've got to," Tad said, between a sob and a growl. "I should have done it back at Harraz. I can't let the rest of you get killed. They're attacking. Let them take me, and then the rest of you will be free."

It was an undeniable truth, and Carl swore at it. Solyra had considered turning herself over, but the reward wouldn't have been enough to placate the Collectors.

Tad broke away from Carl as Terring and Brid dashed in the gate. Seeing them whole, Solyra had to blink away tears of relief.

"I'm turning myself in," Tad said before Carl caught up.

Terring quickly dismounted. "No, you're not. We need every fighting man we've got."

"If I—"

"No. To be honest, if I thought it would save the innocents we have in our protection, I'd say, go. Better yet, I'd rob us all to pay the reward. That's why I went to take a look at them. That might have worked with normal Collectors. But Cyon was right. These aren't normal men."

"Are they trolls?" Diaa asked.

"They're broken men. Death Bringers."

Solyra knew suddenly why Figgo had wanted the knife: not to kill the enemy, but to kill his companions. If it came to that, Solyra hoped he started with Erin…. She swallowed a shuddering sob.

"Now keep in mind," Terring said, "they're not counting on an element of surprise, nor have they sent scouts. We didn't give them a chance. They're going to stay mounted and go for an all-out assault. Expect them to come by the road. They might fan out when they find the barrier, but hopefully they'll aim for the gap. The dogs could go every which way. Now get to your positions."

Gobi put a hand on Solyra's shoulder. "Come, Solyra. To our post."

>><<

A CHILL CLARITY CREPT OVER Solyra as they went to the tumble of boulders that was the triage station. She'd thought she couldn't kill. Now she was sure she would if she had to. She would do whatever she had to do, to defend her friends.

The Collectors' dogs fell silent; the whole mountainside fell silent, as if the rocks themselves listened as hard as Solyra did for any hostile movement. As the deepening shadows of dusk mingled with the light of the rising full moon, the weapons glinted at the barrier. A nightbird called: the Frogbellies' warning.

Darkness sprang into chaos. Dogs roared and men shouted; weapons clashed; thwacks and thumps, screams, crunches.

The sounds sickened Solyra near to retching, even as she strained to see the battle down the road. Then Brid came running half-blinded by blood dripping into his eyes. Solyra didn't need to think. She doused the head wound with spirits and held it closed while Gobi neatly stitched it shut. The sweating skin was slippery, and Brid trembled, not with fear but with energy. Once the wound was closed, Gobi made Brid take three gulps of water — "One, two, three!" — before letting him dash back to the barrier.

Bodies scattered the ground. Collectors? Dogs, too, sprawled on the roadway. Solyra felt a stab of pity for them. Then she remembered Robet's fate, and her pity vanished. Gobi prayed steadily, softly.

Ebony came back, shoved a hand missing the ends of two fingers at Gobi.

"Hold her hand, tight," he ordered Solyra. He took the flat, blunt knife he'd put on the lantern's chimney and pressed it against the stumps of Ebony's fingers. Ebony jerked but Solyra steadied her, and she didn't pull away from the knife, even as the smell of charring flesh filled the air. Ebony grunted and bit her lip, that was all. Solyra panted until her own dizziness subsided.

"Drink," Gobi said. Ebony drained the canteen, nodded, took up her weapon and sprinted back to battle.

The moonlight allowed only glimpses of the fight. Solyra gasped as another dog scrambled over the barrier, gasped again when it was killed.

Then a shout: a horse jumped the barrier.

Solyra's mind burned clear. She waited. Everything slowed, the horse moving as if through cold molasses, the rider's black-toothed mouth writhing something, not words. A sickening stench came with him.

Solyra sprang out and grasped his leg hard with both hands.

In the stretched-out interval of time, she wondered that her fingers didn't sink into his flesh, as into rotten meat. Then she yanked him down with all her might.

He landed partly on her, partly on the road. She didn't even know if he still held his weapons, but she clawed and bit and punched at him. He screamed back, more than he ought, for all her ferocity. He must have broken a bone in his fall. Still, he managed to shove her off, and as Tad ran back he dove into the brush at the side of the road.

Solyra chased him with a savage, single-minded determination. He would not escape. She slid, nearly tumbled in a whirl of whipping branches, knots of scrub and sandy dirt, clumps of grass burning through her hands, dust, and she was on the lower road. Tad tore past her. He reached her quarry before she did. The rider stumbled a few steps — rather his body stumbled. His head bounced off the road. The body collapsed.

The night went silent.

Then voices called from the road. Not battle voices. Terring: "Catch the horse!" his voice as loud and clear as a sea captain's, and a horse whinnying. Erin crying "Grampa!" and Baloos answering.

"I'm going up, Solyra," Tad said. "Carl's hurt. I'll send someone to help." He thrashed back up the hill, saying to someone on the way, "She's all right."

And she was. Then she looked down.

At her feet, the moon full on him, lay Robet — his remains. The dogs had feasted on his face and belly.

Solyra wanted to vomit everything out of herself, from her toes to the tips of her hair.

Instead, she knelt beside Robet, stripping off her tunic and chemise. The tunic she draped over his body; she tucked the chemise over his face. She straightened his shredded and punctured legs and arms, and laid his weapons neatly beside him. She was combing his blood-clotted hair with her fingers when she heard, "Solyra," softly. She glanced up. Terring knelt beside her. She finished combing Robet's hair.

She and Terring rose, and Terring took off his shirt and gently pulled it over her head, dressing her as one might dress a child, or a doll.

The shirt reeked of sweat and blood. She pulled it out, looked at the blood spot, then at Terring again. Sweat soaked his face, and tears, too, fresh tracks in the grime and dust and spatters of blood.

"Not mine." He seemed unable to speak above a murmur; she couldn't speak at all. "Onyx will carry him to us." He held out his hand, and Solyra took it and let him help her back up the slope.

The upper road bustled with torchlight, smoke, voices. An incongruous memory arose: emerging from the underground cavern in the Ihm: crossing from a silent, mystical underworld into the world of life.

She got to work. Nearly everyone who'd fought had wounds, thankfully minor. Blood sheeted Carl's face, but Gobi assured her it was only a scalp cut.

The moment Carl stood from Gobi's suturing, Tad grabbed him in a clinch. The two men stood with their arms around each other, then broke apart and joined the others. Figgo had directed them to strip the bodies of the Collectors of any identifying jewelry or belongings, to hand over to the Zhengahk Guard. They also took money and weapons, and herded the animals together with their own.

Onyx returned with Robet's body wrapped and bound neatly in a tarp. The Collectors were dragged into a gully and covered in rocks, while Ebony, Brid and Tad slung Robet up in the tallest of the scrubby trees. Solyra assumed they would bury him the next day, but Tad said not. "His people get disposed of like that. Up in the trees. I guess they dry out or the birds take them."

A bonfire warmed and lit the shelter. The injuries tended and the worst of the gore and dirt and blood bathed off, Solyra and Jaleen made a hot meal, a combination victory and funeral feast. It started subdued, with Gobi chanting a prayer for the dead of both sides, but finally the battle had to be told. Each of the Frogbellies filled in what the other missed.

To Solyra, sitting with the Bihsts against the wall, it was a gruesome stew of blows and cuts, dismemberment, death. As Tad commended Zago for "cutting the guy in the red bandanna in two," Diaa purred, but Solyra put her head down and silently wept, mourning the gentle Zago that once was. When she raised her head, she met Terring's gaze across the fire. He looked as sad as she.

Eventually, the talk died down along with the fire. Ebony and Brid volunteered to stand watch. Two of the Collectors had escaped, but one of them was badly wounded and the other had carried him away on his horse, so they didn't expect trouble.

Solyra lay in the dark, listening to the breathing of her family, her companions. Gobi had left the statues set up, and a little oil lamp cast a glimmer on the half-naked goddess and her fat companion. Solyra thought she was the only one still awake when Terring got up and crept out of the shelter, murmuring the password to Brid.

When he came back in, his hands were looped with a little garland of wild flowers. He knelt before the shrine and put the flowers around the goddess's shoulders. When he caressed the statue with his rough hands, his thumbs brushing her breasts, Solyra shivered as if his hands touched her own body.

Then he came and lay behind her and curled his body to her back. And without a word she nestled into him.

She felt wide awake, as his lips touched her hair, and she felt as if she were floating. Her heart pounded and a warmth grew between her legs, like what she'd felt with Zago, but far more poignant, more penetrating. She felt Terring, hard against her buttocks and a little whimper escaped her throat, and Terring answered with a sigh. He held her tight; she pressed against him. She was completely filled with the wish, so imperative it was more need, to take off every stitch of her clothes, to be completely bare to him, to open herself to him, to bring him into her.

She couldn't, of course. Not with her companions so close around her, and poor Robet waiting for the birds to scatter his remains. But the simple fact that she felt such a desire flooded her eyes with tears of joy, even in her sadness.

SWEET & BITTER

AT THE FIRST BORDER MARKER of the Zhengahk, in the foothills of the Apfas, they cheered themselves hoarse and drank ale straight. Carl even let Tad waste a precious bolt by shooting in the air. Gobi blessed the border post while Erin, Raal, Tindy and Dan danced around it.

Carl proclaimed a day of rest, both a treat and a necessity for animals and people alike. Their pace through the Apfas, even after the battle, had been merciless.

They set up camp on a pine-rimmed meadow on the shore of a shining blue lake, the most beautiful place Solyra had ever seen. She almost wondered why she would leave such a place in favor of the arid land that lay only a week or so ahead—the vast property that everyone was now calling Solyra Liberty.

She was governor of a huge property. She was the Liberty.

Even this close, Solyra's future in the Zhengahk glimmered unreal, like a fantasy.

And maybe it was. Figgo had made clear, her position was largely ceremonial. The Zhengahk comprised independent Liberties tied together by trade agreements, mutual protection and a court of justice that had been organized after the war. Each Liberty was ruled by an elected council, and while council measures required the Liberty's seal, refusing to seal was very rare.

Figgo wasn't about to let Solyra think she had any power.

He kept his personal dislike out of his words, but it emanated silently from him, all the more since she and Terring now slept side by side. They were chaste, since only the scouts were allowed to step outside the group, but no one could miss the change in their relationship. Not that anyone made much of it. Their status as a couple was absorbed without a blink, as if everyone had merely been waiting for them to acknowledge it themselves. How Peg would have teased and crowed!

After the lakeside camp was set up, Carl and Tad insisted that Solyra and her kitchen helpers go for a swim in the lake. The others would start the meal.

The sensible part of Solyra said she should wash her clothes first, so she could hang them to dry as soon as possible. But she hadn't done more than rinse her face for days. She stripped to chemise and pantaloons and waded in the lake.

The pure, clean water, cool but not cold, laid balm on all her burns, bites, bruises, cuts, scratches and scrapes. She wouldn't have believed she could do so much damage to herself, and be so oblivious. Only when undressed had she seen the extent of it. She paddled slowly in the water, a little away from the others. Except for Terring, swimming toward her, intent as a beaver.

"I should splash you," she said, but she didn't. She put her arms out and he pulled her in, and they embraced in the water. Where they touched, their skin was hot, while the water eddied cool around them. Solyra's legs wrapped around Terring's waist without bothering to check with her mind. Terring's body, pressed against her, didn't ask questions.

"This is unprofessional," Terring said, but that didn't stop him from taking one arm from around her hips to caress her breast. Solyra's breath caught, and he grinned. "Let's go some-where private."

They swam to the warm, sunlit shallows of a little cove out of sight of the camp. In the privacy of their watery bower, they finished undressing. He bent his head to kiss her throat, and then he was inside her, their union like a molten core in the cool waters.

Solyra felt her body warm and expand, she felt his climax pulse through and through her. But when he withdrew, she was still wanting.

He kissed her face and lips, and hugged her tight. "It's been a long time for me, my pussycat," he whispered. "I'll finish you up next time." He grinned. "Just give me a few minutes."

She didn't protest it was enough, as she had so many times with Zago. For all the aching keenness in her body, she felt alive from the inside out, even beyond her skin, as if her body had joined the gem-blue lake and spicy-sweet pines and warm blue sky. "This is so nice," she said, "I'm not sure I want you to finish me up."

Terring's grin broadened. "Oh, I'll keep it going. I'll keep it going so long, you'll be begging me to stop."

The words snapped the spell. Solyra tried not to let it show, but Terring looked in her face, then gave her another kiss, a very gentle kiss. He wouldn't know how familiar his words were, that Dahn had said such things in an utterly different, twisted way. Yet Terring seemed to understand on some level, or at least he wasn't annoyed with her.

They drifted to an underwater rock. Terring sat and shifted Solyra so that she was sitting sideways on his thighs, one of his arms cuddling her to him, the other stroking her belly. She nestled her head on his shoulder.

"We'll take it slow and sweet…" He cupped her breast and lightly thumbed the nipple, and breathed in her ear, "Slow and sweet."

If Terring sensed that she wanted to weep, he didn't

question her, just kissed her hair and held her. Did he know that however hard he tried, she would never match his joy?

Yet she let her thighs fall apart when he murmured, "Now I'll stroke you inside," and she flinched only once when his hand softly lapped thrills all over her. His other hand supported her head so that her hair fanned in the water and her face basked in the sun, her thighs spread over his thighs, his rough hands softly undoing the secrets of her body.

She reached for him, but he took her hand and kissed it. "Float, my sweet girl, just float and I'll keep you safe."

Her mind and body scattered from each other. The wounds dealt by Dahn, and by Diaa and Zago, intended and innocent, stood like spectators, but at a remove. She wondered what would happen if she went limp, and she relaxed a little. Terring held her steady, though his fingers gave a sudden, harder thrust. She gasped, then let herself relax a little more and still Terring's body and fingers held her safe. She let herself go limp, or she would have, except her back arched and her skin thrummed and her heart beat hard.

Something rose over her. A tidal wave of terror and overwhelming grief. A cascade of sweet sensation.

She whimpered and the impulse to push away, to defend herself, to give a false laugh, came over her. But she let her arms drop, one behind him, one beside her; and she spread her thighs apart as wide as they would go. A keening sigh drifted from her, from deep inside, deeper than her throat or mouth or lungs.

Though Terring held her up, even as the wave lifted her, she felt as if she were falling. She surrendered herself with a sobbing moan.

Terring absorbed her moan, his mouth joined to hers, as if he were swept up into the same giant wave. A maelstrom of incoherent thought and emotion rushed through her mind. Then the wave crashed over her.

She was body, senses, all wrapped around his touch, and an exquisite current of energy bound them as one.

The water flushed warm with his fluids, and hers, mingling in the lake then dissipating.

When Terring kissed her face, it was almost like being brought back from a faint. Limp, Solyra moved her limbs to test them, to check if they still functioned. Her thoughts and emotions straggled back. She could hardly sort them out.

Wonder nearly submerged the fear of how much this man could hurt her.

Terring didn't ask her if she liked it, didn't ask how that had felt. He didn't comment at all, nor did he look smug — or just a little, in an endearing way. Mostly, he looked happy. They put on their bathing clothes again.

"Climb on my back and I'll ride you to shore."

"I hope I can stand once we're there."

They both laughed. By the time they were out of the cove, the distant sounds of the camp drifted back into their world, Diaa singing in her yowly, off-tune way, the kids splashing and laughing and yelling, Tad and Brid having one of their yodeling contests with Queenie joining in.

Solyra pushed off from Terring and swam by herself. The chill water streaming over her body invigorated and, putting aside the jumble of her mind, she felt almost normal when she got out. She quickly dried and finished dressing, glancing back toward the cove to reassure herself that no one could have seen or heard them. Still, as she went to take over bossing the meal, she was self-conscious, addled.

"All right, Tad," she said jauntily as she came up to the fire, "I'll take over now."

"No way," he said. "This is my show. But you can help. Rub the meat with the spice powder in the bowl there. And be sure to wash your hands really well when you're done. That stuff'll burn your eyes out."

Solyra glimpsed, out the corner of her eye, Figgo's knife

and the onions drop from his hands. He quickly bent and groped the ground, collected them and resumed his task.

They ate the grilled meat with the last of the corn grits and a cooked salad of onions and wild greens that the Bihsts had gathered. It wasn't much, spread out among them all, and they still posted sentries. But in spirit, the feast was a huge celebration threaded with a hint of melancholy.

The end of their long, arduous journey was in sight. They spent a barrel of ale reminiscing: the time the mule Dim kicked Baloos in the butt and nearly sent him over a cliff; the lucky day Brid caught a little flock of pheasants and Peg made them stuffed and roasted, with potatoes they'd bartered at a roadhouse for some of Onyx and Ebony's lace; the time Carl made Robet, Brid, Onyx and Ebony meticulously clean and polish every piece of tack in the outfit, in penance for getting them run out of a village for messing around with the maidens, or youths, in the twins's case.

They didn't talk about the fire, or the stampede, or the Collectors. They drank to Jerzy, Peg and Robet, and told some choice stories about them. Solyra had a flash of Peg in her wedding dress, wearing the "Darklocks" wig, and Jerzy so proud in his new suit, the ends of his mustache extravagantly puffed. Though her heart moved in her, she was able to savor the image for the first time since leaving their graves far behind under the endless prairie grass.

"Tad and I reckon we'll reach Solyra Liberty in a week or so," Carl said, "but we're sure to meet up with patrols before then."

"Once we do," Terring said, "word will spread fast that a Liberty governor is on her way. It's been decades since a new Liberty has come to the Zhengahk."

"How did the Zhengahk fall so far?" Tad asked. "I guess the question is really, where did the Death-bringers come from and how did they manage to wreak so much havoc?"

It was an area that Figgo had glossed, in his history lessons.

As he adjusted his goggles, they flickered in the firelight. The ale went around again, this time watered.

>><<

FIGGO DIDN'T SPEAK. HE SAT up, listening. Everyone else sat up and listened, too. All Solyra heard was the wind, and Raal and Erin playing with Snowball and Queenie.

"The children do not need to know this yet," Figgo murmured. The group relaxed.

Figgo fidgeted again with his goggles, then began.

"About four generations ago," Figgo said, "a famine spread over the Ihm. It was an unfortunate combination of a plant virus and poor husbandry of the land, and several harsh weather cycles. The drought affected the east as well."

"My grandma talked about that," Brid said. "She was a little girl. Her folks nearly went west over the Apfas. But the rains came just in time to save their farm."

"Many people indeed went west over the mountains," Figgo continued, "hoping for a release from starvation. But they were stopped on this side by the people of Zhengahk, my people. We wanted to keep our riches to ourselves. Riches we gained in part by exporting food. Our greed forced the refugees back into the mountains, where they…"

"The refugees were forced back into the mountains where they met with mountain trolls. They are like back east trolls, but more vicious, and more insatiable."

Diaa shuddered, and Zago put an arm around her.

"Those who were not murdered were…" Figgo listened again. Raal and Erin's laughter, Queenie's barks and playful whines, came like a distant dream, next to his words. "The people were raised as — as livestock — as beasts of burden and as meat. Yes. And since the mountain trolls had trouble bearing children, the captives were forced to breed. So, a new race came into being: the Death-bringers. The product of madness and lust and hard-heartedness.

"Before they descended on us we had changed our ways, but too late. After a long harsh war, they were defeated. But so were we. The land and our hearts are broken, ground into dust. The water has left us. The canals are dry, and the wells are meager."

The fire snapped in the long silence.

"But the canals are still there, right?" Zago asked. "And the soil."

Figgo turned his face not to Zago, but to Solyra. He all but said: Stop him. But she did not.

"So we raise the frame," Zago continued, "harvest it for ten years, fifteen at most. You go back east with your folks. Solyra and Terring go back east and fold their profits into a wholesale or retail operation. The field goes dark. You move on to the next field, or maybe not. Other technologies might displace fulgus by then, or maybe you'll find new fields in the Ihm."

Figgo listened with no change of expression, but even in the firelight, Solyra could see the flush creep up his neck.

"You know nothing of business—" he began.

"I know plenty!" Zago broke in. "I might seem like a goofball, but I've been in this business since I was a kid. I've read the same books you have; I've gone to the same lectures. And I've listened to you all making your plans, totting up harvests and accounts, telling each other stories about how wonderful it'll be to give people jobs — and pretending it's not all about getting a bag of gold you can bring back east. I'm sorry; I don't mean to be cruel. But in the end your people — your people, Figgo — will be left with a crashed frame, a dark field, and no money or jobs, because the fat cats will be snugged in back east." Tears sparkled in Zago's eyes. "A flood of exiles, human and fulgu, and the land is left hollow, its sacred lights extinguished."

Figgo stood abruptly. "Zizera Solyra, may I speak with you privately?" His voice was tight. He added to Terring, who also stood, "Privately, if you please."

Solyra made an "it's all right" gesture to Terring and walked with Figgo far enough away from the campfire for them not to be overheard. She didn't really want to talk to Figgo one-on-one. Terring's caresses had opened in her a joy whose depths she could hardly fathom, but they'd also left her tender and vulnerable. Not in shape for single combat with Figgo.

"You will regulate your employees," Figgo said without preamble. Solyra stopped herself from wiping away the flecks of saliva on her face. She'd never seen Figgo so angry: literally, spitting mad. And she knew she should humor him, just say: yes, you're right. But she was sick of Figgo's intimidation tactics.

"Zago has a right to speak his mind," she said. "And none of us can deny that other people will share his feelings. Surely you don't think that the people of Solyra Liberty will be silenced by your business concerns."

"Our business concerns, zizera."

"Yes, of course," she said, now as soothingly as she could.

"Yes, of course," he mimicked. "But the feelings of a few do not change the good of many. Nor do they change our charter. Our contract, zizera."

"No, but—"

"There are no buts to be considered." Figgo's voice had risen. He stopped, his chest rising and falling, and then went on in his usual level tone. "Whatever plans you may have with Zago, however you may have played on his sentimental delusions about fulgus, I'm watching you, zizera. Yes, this blind man sees, in his way."

A snake of fear slithered down her spine — but she'd resolved never again to let fear of a man freeze her. She swallowed, her throat dry. "Zizero Figgo, your implication is insulting and—"

"I call what I see. And what I see is a woman who ruined a man's hopes and dreams in a most callous and underhanded way."

"Terring and I have dealt with that," Solyra said as steadily as she could.

"Have you?" Again the snake slid down Solyra's spine. "Now deal with this, zizera. You and your employees will abide by the contract that you and zizero Terring signed and sealed in my presence. There will be no side agreements—"

"I don't—"

"Even if you know how to sweeten a deal." He turned and walked back to the fire, one hand a little in front of him.

>><<

SOLYRA WALKED IN ONE DIRECTION, then another. Her legs shook so hard, she wanted to collapse right onto the pine duff under her feet. Her blood pulsed in her throat and ears. Then she moved her feet toward the lake. She'd plunge in, and swim and swim and swim until she had no more strength to resist sinking under the chill water.

She was nearly at the beach when Brid stopped her. "Carl doesn't want anyone swimming at night. Maybe he's afraid of lake serpents..." He trailed off. "Solyra, what's wrong?"

Tad jogged up just then. He nodded at Brid and took Solyra's arm, walking her to where someone had dragged some logs to make an alcove at the edge of the woods overlooking the lake. Probably Zago and Diaa, Solyra thought with a detached affection, or Dan and Tindy.

"What's going on, Solyra?" Tad asked.

She didn't answer. Couldn't.

"Hey, talk to me," Tad said. "You're scaring me."

"Sorry," she whispered.

"What did that rat Figgo say?"

Even if you know how to sweeten a deal.

Tad didn't say more, but his quiet was open, listening. As Solyra's heart finally slowed, her thoughts came back. Numbness blanketed her emotions.

"Tad, I've told you about my husband."

"The mean-ass prick. Yeah."

Solyra drew a deep breath and stared at the lake. "We went to a convention in Booton, a business convention, sort of like a fulgu fair. With booths and displays and all. Workshops. There was even a model house... I'm babbling." She gulped in another breath and went on.

"Dahn had an important business deal that was hanging by a thread. So he wined and dined this man, the president of a company, a wholesale company. Dahn was angling for exclusive buying rights... We were — we were a retail outfit. So we needed good wholesale contacts. Good deals with wholesalers. Sorry. I'm babbling again." Shaking again, too, so hard her teeth chattered.

"It's okay, Solyra," Tad said. "I think I know where this is going."

"Right. That's right. You — you got it. He — Dahn, he, uh, he used me. He used me. He dressed me in this topless rig that was in fashion and we had this dinner and I got sort of drunk. And — and then we went back to our room and the man — and — and Dahn let him use me. But it wasn't, uh, it wasn't rape because I didn't fight, I'd agreed, you see. I agreed. To let them. I. Let them. Use me."

Solyra stared, frozen, shivering, at nothing, at the past.

"Can I hold you, Solyra? Would it help?"

Solyra burst into sobs, and she and Tad threw their arms around each other like children lost in the woods. She cried for a long time, then finally they drew apart and sat in silence.

It wasn't the first time she'd relived the memory of that night. She'd gone over it many times, in many different ways. For a long stretch, she'd fantasized. A bellboy had rescued her, just in time. She'd fought and escaped, and returned to her parents. It never happened at all. The other man proposed the deal and Dahn turned him down. Dahn dueled him. She'd killed the man; she'd killed Dahn; she'd killed them both.

She'd even fantasized that they really had forced her. That she hadn't agreed.

After Dahn died, she'd convinced herself that no one else would ever know, since the man had wife and children, and standing in the community. In fact, Dahn had used the incident as a tacit form of blackmail against him. Solyra thought she'd finally talked herself out of the terror of exposure and excruciating shame. Until Figgo got in his blow.

"He's just … abominable," Solyra said, mopping her face with a bandanna. "Figgo I mean."

"How does he come into this?"

"He and Terring were at that conference and—"

"Terring?" Tad tensed, as if about to dash to Terring and beat him to a pulp.

"No! It wasn't him. They didn't have anything to do with the 'deal,' except the man had been their customer. And Dahn rubbed it in. The next day at breakfast, he announced to Terring and Figgo that he'd snatched their account and smirked that we knew how to sweeten a deal. I don't think Terring got it, but apparently Figgo did. And tonight, he just sort of threatened to expose me. He said, our contract stands even if I 'know how to sweeten a deal.'"

"That is really and truly low."

"He thinks I'm trying to get the upper hand by seducing Terring."

"He's… He's not just blind in the eyes."

Solyra thought of Figgo's hands going limp when Tad had warned her about washing her hands after handling the pepper rub. She hoped for his sake he hadn't been blinded in such a way, that he'd gone blind gradually as some people did.

"There are circumstances that, well, bolster his case against me," Solyra said.

"So you're defending him?"

"No." She shook her head. "I don't know."

"So Terring is the good man you brought down?"

"Yes."

"Through nefarious business dealings, I take it."

"Correct."

"And Figgo is the loyal employee righteously defending said good man."

"Exactly."

"You know, I never liked Figgo," Tad said. "Now I can't stand him. For that matter, I don't care for Terring."

"Please. I don't want to start problems."

"Don't worry. I won't let it show. If there's one thing that Carl's ground into me day after day is that you can't be biased — at least outwardly — in a caravan."

"And don't tell anyone. Except Carl, of course."

"If anyone would be exposed by all this, it's Figgo, for his complete lack of human…. Never mind. It's your secret to reveal. But you know, if this whole thing came out, no one would hold it against you."

Solyra shrugged. "That I'm a whore?"

"You are not! Solyra, this caravan turns around you. Don't you realize that? Gobi said to me the other day, you're the tent pole of this outfit."

Solyra wiped her face and giggled. "I know I'm not buxom, but — a tent pole?"

Tad laughed. "His people are nomads. Tent poles are important to them."

"Can the tent pole rinse her face in the lake?"

"All right. We'll make an exception this once. But first, may I dispense a lame but heartfelt nugget of wisdom?"

"Definitely."

"Sometimes you have to forgive yourself, even if you haven't done anything wrong." He paused, then added, "I should know."

They stood and hugged. Tad went back to camp and Solyra waded in the lake, caftan knotted at her hips, and rinsed her face, then went slowly back to camp. Maybe the rest of them would overlook her past. Or maybe they would be disgusted. It didn't matter, in a way.

Carl and Tad would stick with her, and Zago and Diaa would, too. The Bihsts might disapprove of her conduct, but their kindness and equanimity always won out, whatever dramas played around them. The twins and Brid would most likely accept her past as just that: the past.

Which left Terring.

Oh, Figgo might have been blind in more than one way, but he knew how to fight. He couldn't have timed his revelation more skillfully. Had he calculated the exact moment when she couldn't bear Terring to know the worst about her? That would mean Figgo knew she...

She loved Terring.

Did she?

It made no difference. Figgo didn't know feelings. He just knew that she'd whored herself so her husband could steal an important account from Terring. That was how Figgo saw it. And he calculated that the threat of exposure was enough to cow her. Love had nothing to do with it, in his eyes. He didn't see love.

And he didn't need to. He had successfully brought her to bay. The irony was that it didn't give him anything that she hadn't already offered. It was like an echo of her first night with Dahn. A man forcing from her what she'd been willing to give. Then, it was her virginity. In this case, it was her wish to do her best by Terring.

Who was coming toward her, carrying a small lantern. He met her before she came into the circle around the fire. He held up the lantern and studied her in its light.

"What is it, Solyra? What did Figgo say? Or did Tad upset you?"

Solyra felt the beginnings of a false smile forming on her face. The words scrambled in her mind to form a false reassurance: Nothing much. Or try something more convincing, like:

He was just warning me not to try any tricks in the business, you know, like before.

Then something in her stood straight and tall.

Like a tent pole. A real smile touched her mouth. She wasn't ready to deal with the past coming down on her like a rock slide. But she wasn't going to go limp either, under Figgo's thumb. Figgo might have won this round, but the fight wasn't over. She needed time to regroup, though.

"Tad came to see if I was all right." She put a hand on Terring's chest. "Beyond that, I'm not ready to talk about it. Maybe Figgo is, or maybe not."

"He's not," Terring said flatly.

"Terring, can you let Figgo and I work it out between us?"

He slowly nodded.

"And you and I...." Solyra let her hand slide away. "We need to cool it. Until... I don't know." She swallowed, then took a deep breath. "Terring, I'm sorry I cheated you, back east. It was mean, but I swear I never meant to be cruel. That doesn't make it right, and I'm very sorry about it, Terring. I'm very sorry."

"Let's not keep that between us, Solyra." He kissed her forehead. "Let's make a new start, all right?"

"I want to. And I promise, from now on, I'll be honest with you. Just give me some time to sort myself out. I won't lie to you, Terring, but I.... I just can't be open with you. Not yet."

"Open or closed, I don't want to cool it with you."

The lantern reflected as two flames in his eyes. He put a hand to her neck, his thumb caressing her jaw. A delicious shiver went over Solyra.

"I don't want to cool it either," she whispered. "But it's for the best. Believe me."

"I can't believe that." He leaned to kiss her, but she stepped back.

The hurt that went through his eyes showed clear, even in the light of the small lantern.

THE VENGEFUL SON

THE WILD ANIMALS THINNED OUT, as did the vegetation, the further they went from the lake camp. Despite the sparseness of food and water, though, the area was well-patrolled, and Carl and Terring relaxed the guard, though they still kept pickets at camp and lookouts front and back as they rode.

On the third day from the lake, they reached one of the border markers of Solyra Liberty, a huge rock towering over a spring. Sweating but exhilarated, they still had three days journeying, but reaching the marker was an occasion to celebrate, all the more because this was the last water stop before the township of Solyra Liberty.

The celebration ended almost as soon as it began.

"The spring's not running," Carl said.

"You're joking," Tad answered. He held his canteen, freshly emptied into his mouth, suspended over his face.

"I wish he was," Terring said. "This is the rock, I'm sure." He glanced at the stunted juniper rooted in the rock. "And there's water somewhere in there that the tree's getting. But not us."

218 >< KEATES NELSON

Figgo turned from the group, as if to stare over the dry wastes.

He had not embraced the idea of returning to the Zhengahk—that was no secret. Still, Terring was surprised at how withdrawn Figgo had become since the lake camp. Then again, what was there to be surprised at? Even if everything seemed normal between them, Figgo surely sensed that Terring was boiling mad at him—especially since he wouldn't cough up whatever he'd said to make Solyra back off. Figgo wouldn't accept or reject his attempts at reconciliation. The only thing Terring could discern in this man he'd traveled with for so long was that Figgo had become yet more tightly wound within himself. It probably had little to do with their falling out, but Terring was sorry that Figgo's homecoming was such a trial.

"Well, since we're halfway to the town," Carl said, "no point heading back to the lake for water."

"Wouldn't it be dandy if we died of thirst after all this," Tad grumbled. "And who's to say the town isn't dried up."

"We won't die," Terring said. "And the patrol would have warned us if the town was dry. We'll just have to be careful the rest of the way."

They went back and rechecked the amount of water left and debated on how to proceed. Terring thought they should split the party, sending some on to the township while the others stayed in the shade of the rock. Carl wanted to wait for a patrol. Tad wanted to push on.

Then Figgo turned with a jerk toward the spring. Everyone fell silent. Except for Zago and Diaa, splashing their hands in the basin.

"It couldn't be," Carl said as they headed back over to the rock. "I looked…." He trailed off, his hands on his hips, staring at the spring-hollowed rock basin. Water flowed gently into it.

"Beautiful, fresh water," Diaa purred. She dipped her hands in the water and smoothed it over her hair.

"Cap'n, you looked thoroughly for water, did you not?" Figgo's voice was tight.

"That basin was dry as a bone."

"That's right," Brid said.

"It must have been blocked," Carl said. "Though something should have seeped out. Not to complain. Let's fill up, folks."

The flow of the water was thin but steady. Everyone took a turn at filling the water vessels. Terring waited his turn in the shade of the twisted juniper that, despite its dwarfish size, exuded a sense of having been rooted for centuries.

In the near distance, jagged rocks slanted up from the sandy ground. Tough, thorny plants littered the gritty ground; one of the donkeys was already limping.

Most overwhelming was the quietude. Only the slightest flickers of sand revealed tiny reptiles or insects. The sun moved in silence over the hot earth, with equally silent raptors gliding high up in the sky that was a more brilliant blue than the clearest autumn day back east. Even the crew had fallen silent. The only sound was water trickling and metal cups dipping into the pool.

Terring fetched a deep sigh. He'd seen terrible—horrible—things in this land, during the war against the Death Bringers. When not consumed by military concerns, he'd suffered excruciating loneliness. Yet the place sent a well-being through his very muscles, down to his bones. He was home. This was home.

He took his turn filling a pair of skins, then made his way back to the pack animals. He was heading back to the spring to fill his own canteen when everyone turned at the sound of horse hooves. Carl, Tad, and the twins scrambled for their weapons. It was only a lone horseman approached, but Terring dropped the buckets and ran for his crossbow.

The approaching horse was caked with sweat and dust, its flanks spurred bloody. A scarf swathed the rider's face. He rode up to the camp, one hand raised, the other on the reins. "I have a message for Zago!" he yelled hoarsely. "Which one is he?"

"No!" Terring shouted — even as Zago ran forward.

>> <<

SOLYRA DIDN'T UNDERSTAND WHY TERRING snapped a bolt to his crossbow; why Tad sprang forward with his machete—

"Here's from my father!" the horseman screamed.

Diaa's cry filled the sky.

The horseman jerked, startled, even as he loosed an arrow from his bow.

As Zago twisted and stumbled to his knees, then fell in the dirt, Terring dropped his crossbow and dragged the shooter from his horse. The animal pranced and would have run, dragging its rider, had Brid not grabbed the bridle and freed the shooter's foot from the stirrup. Amidst the shouting, Diaa's growl rose sharper, though Jaleen tried to calm her.

Solyra found herself on her knees beside Zago. She barked out instructions: Cut off his shirt, keep him still, cover him with a blanket; they'd have to move him into the shade of the rock; no, Gobi and Baloos were setting up a canopy. The shooter lay tied hand and foot.

Zago breathed roughly; she couldn't tell if it was pain or if his lung was hit. She dabbed at the wound and desperately tried to decide whether to extract the arrow or leave it.

Figgo knelt next to her. "Describe it to me."

Solyra answered in a voice far more steady than she felt. "The arrow impaled him, on his right side." She carefully felt the wound, and tried to ignore Zago's soft cry. "I think it might have gone between his ribs. I can't tell if it hit his lungs or if it's just in the flesh." Zago had bulked up, since they'd left Norvadale; he had muscles now. For some reason, that thought nearly threw Solyra into a fit of tears. She swallowed hard. "Both lungs are inflating."

"Let me feel," Figgo said. "Guide me."

Solyra took his hand and put it lightly on the arrow. "This is the shaft," she said.

He nodded, then carefully moved his fingers to Zago's side. "Hold him still," he said. Tad sat on Zago's legs; Frogbelly and Brid pinned his shoulders. Figgo probed the wound, his face impassive as Zago writhed and whimpered. At last, Figgo finished his examination by lightly patting Zago's shoulder and saying quietly, "I am sorry I hurt you. It was necessary."

"All right," Zago panted.

"The arrow nicked your lung and may have chipped a rib. I did not feel any bone pieces, but they could be under the arrow. You do not seem to be suffering internal bleeding, except under the skin. I mean, your lung is not bleeding into itself. That is very good, very lucky. I think the best treatment is to cut into your side and remove the arrow sideways. It will make a bigger flesh wound, but pulling it out may cause more damage to the lung. This way we can make sure no fragments are in the wound."

"Hack away, doc," Zago said with a weak smile.

Figgo said what Solyra both dreaded and expected. "Solyra will be the surgeon. I will direct, and Jaleen will be surgeon's mate. Be calm, Zago. Have confidence."

Onyx and Ebony made a shelter walled with rug bales and roofed and floored with tarpaulins, and put Zago on a pallet. Absorbed as Solyra was in preparing the surgical instruments, she barely noticed what the others were doing, until she glanced around and saw they were occupied with making camp. She heard Terring say the prisoner was the surviving Collector from the mountain battle. His father must have been the one Zago boasted of cutting in two.

Gobi and the other Bihsts chanted a medicine song. It made a soothing backdrop, but Diaa's growl, which had never subsided, rose into a high-pitched snarl, then fell into a sobbing growl again. Solyra put down the needle she was threading. "I'll be right back." She hurried to Diaa.

Onyx held Diaa by the arms as she stared at the prisoner. Her lips were drawn back and her brow furrowed. Her hair stood up in a ridge. A chill covered Solyra.

"Diaa," she said.

Diaa didn't take her eyes from the prisoner, who glared back, part defiant, part terrified.

"Diaa!"

Diaa jerked her face toward Solyra.

"I need help," Solyra said. "So stop being crazy. Pull yourself together and come with me."

A long shudder went over Diaa and her growl broke into a little cry as she turned away from the prisoner and came to Solyra.

"I meant it when I said I need you to help," Solyra said, smoothing Diaa's hair. "Do you feel up for it?"

"I don't know how." Diaa's half-whisper echoed the wild notes of her fury, shading to despair.

"Keep Zago as calm and comfortable as possible. Get him to suck on the rag dipped in the tea Gobi made, wipe his face, rub his feet. If Jaleen or I need something, you fetch it."

"I'll do it. Solyra, thank you for…for calling me back." The ridge still bristled in her hair, but it was subsiding.

Over the cliffs on the western horizon, a line of thunderclouds cast a weird spell on the light. "We better start," Solyra said. "I don't want a storm breaking out in the middle of this."

"It will not come." It was Figgo. "The rain does not come to my country anymore."

"Let's start," Solyra said quietly.

"Wait," Zago whispered. "Gobi."

Jaleen quickly fetched Gobi.

"Gobi," Zago said, "tell the man…" Zago took a breath, a short breath. "That I'm sorry. For killing his father. I'm sorry." Tears squeezed from his eyes: remorse or pain, Solyra didn't know.

"I will tell him," Gobi said. "We will sing for everyone."

Zago nodded and his eyes sank closed.

The operation seemed to stretch into an eternity, yet once the preparations were complete, the surgery itself went quickly. Solyra was used to handling Figgo's instruments, though until now the only surgeries she'd performed had been fixing wounds from the road and after the battle and removing porcupine quills from Queenie's nose.

For all their enmity, she and Figgo, with Jaleen's and Diaa's help, worked together as if literally of one mind. Solyra was dimly aware that others gathered by ones and twos as an audience to the surgical theater.

She finally finished the stitches and dropped the bloody needle and thread stump onto the platter that Jaleen held. She feared for Zago, who had lapsed into a stuporous doze. Yet she had to admit she'd actually enjoyed the surgery in a somber way: the total absorption demanded, and the feeling of complete unity with Figgo and Jaleen and Diaa, and, morbid as it was, the craft of using the instruments on flesh.

Figgo rinsed his hands again in liquor and thoroughly examined the wound by touch. "Good, that is very good. You will do fine, Zago."

Onyx and Ebony carefully moved Zago to a different shelter, this one on the sandy and soft ground near the spring, free of the irksome groundthorns, and soothing with the delicate trickle of the spring. Erin and Gobi took over watching him.

Clouds still towered over the distant cliffs but hadn't stretched over the sky. The first stars pierced the dusk.

Diaa picked at her dinner, managed to get some down, then went back to Zago. Two patrollers came. To everyone's relief, they took custody of the prisoner and left immediately to fetch a horse litter for Zago.

After the evening service, the Frogbellies clustered around the fire, while a deep chill dropped along with the dark. Figgo gestured Solyra and Jaleen aside, and Terring came with them.

Figgo asked quietly, "Zizeri Solyra and Jaleen, you followed my every direction, yes?"

"Jaleen and I followed your directions exactly, zizero Figgo," Solyra said.

"Yes, indeed," Jaleen confirmed.

"And you are sure nothing was left in the wound? No cloth or sand or splinters?"

"I inspected it as well as I could," Solyra said, and Jaleen added, "So did I."

"I don't doubt you. Nevertheless, I was not entirely truthful to zizero Zago when I said that he will do fine. Even with the best precautions, operating in the open air lends itself to infection, and undoubtedly there is contamination from the arrow itself. Fecal matter, applied deliberately. If only..." Solyra was sure he was going to say, if only he could see, but he continued, "It might have been better to leave the wound open to heal, but in this dusty environment and with the bleeding, maybe not. Either way, there was no good choice."

"We had to close the wound," Solyra said. "It couldn't have stayed open, not with the lung exposed as it was."

Figgo was silent, pensive. Terring took Solyra's hand. It was their first intentional physical contact since the lake. Even through her fatigue, the touch sent through Solyra a current like the hum of a fulgu.

Figgo's silence became a perceiving rather than pensive silence. When he turned his face toward Solyra again and spoke, his voice had hardened. But Solyra refused to draw her hand from Terring's — and Terring did not let her go.

"The faster we get Zago to shelter, the better," Figgo said. "Meanwhile, someone must watch over him all the time. If he grows restless, he must be restrained. We cannot let him tear open the sutures. Gobi is making a broth that combats fever and dehydration, and Zago must take in as much of that as he can hold. That is all we can do, besides keep the wound clean and the dressings fresh."

It struck Solyra that of all the people in the caravan, Zago most threatened Figgo's plans. Still, she had not even the slightest fear that Figgo would sabotage Zago's treatment.

For all their care, the dreaded infection set in within hours. Zago alternated between sweating and shivering. When he wasn't feebly calling for "mommy," he mumbled over and over the same string of nonsense words: pooby nooby scooby looby.... His skin was like dingy chalk, and his red-rimmed eyes fluttered part-open, part-closed, as if he hadn't the strength to hold them one way or the other. Diaa's eyes, too, grew red-rimmed. She tended Zago with a steady competence that did her proud. Solyra covered her own fear that Zago was dying.

The double whistle of the pickets' password woke her from a fitful sleep. She stumbled out of her tent and into the gray whisper of dawn, wearing only her chemise and bloomers, then quickly retreated. The patrol wasn't part of the semi-nudist colony the caravan had become.

She came out, dressed, to see seven patrollers, little more than silhouettes in the cloud-striped first light. A litter was fastened onto the back of a horse. She hurried to the medicine tent to prepare Zago for transport.

Diaa drowsed there, Zago's hand in hers. When Solyra touched her shoulder, she started and hissed, blinking her red, swollen eyes.

"Diaa, the patrol's here to take Zago to the town. We need to change his bandages a last time and help Gobi."

To Solyra's surprise, Diaa didn't ask to go along. But she quickly learned why, when Diaa bent to kiss Zago's damp forehead. "I'll take care of pooby, scooby, nooby..."

Solyra had the presence of mind to count the words in the long string of nonsense. Ninety-seven words, for ninety-seven fulgus in the lockers. Zago had named every one of them, and Diaa remembered every one of their names.

Diaa and Solyra unwound the bandage, swabbed the wound, and redressed it. As soon as they finished, two patrollers, a man and a woman, ushered them out of the tent and eased Zago onto a stretcher. Solyra and Diaa followed them to the litter, which looked like a wicker boat afloat on a horse's back.

"He won't die, will he, Solyra?" Diaa whispered.

"Of course not," Solyra said. "He'll have a few rough days, but he's a healthy man. He'll make it through." She prayed she wasn't lying.

They watched in silence as the twins lifted Zago onto the litter, wincing when he groaned at the inevitable jostling. Three of the patrollers and Gobi set off immediately with their load.

Solyra was about to go and help settle the animals of the other patrollers when Terring snagged her.

"Come to the fireside." He took her arms and looked in her face. "Come as Solyra Liberty." He grinned as Solyra's eyes widened, then gave her chin a gentle swipe with his shirt cuff. "You might want to wash your face first."

>> <<

SOLYRA DECIDED TO WEAR HER blue frock coat, though she had to unload nearly an entire pack to get it. Really, she should have discarded it months ago. It was the bulkiest thing in her luggage, and she hadn't worn it since meeting Lady Liberty. Yet she was glad she still had it. Putting it on worked the old magic of boosting her confidence. Even in the dim light, it was impossibly bright next to her stained trousers and faded thin shirt. Finally she dared a look in the hand-mirror that had somehow survived the trek, crouching close to the little lantern hanging by the barrel.

Though she'd worn her wide-brimmed hat most of the time, her face was tanned dark and her cheeks and lips burned scarlet. Her eyes were the same violet-blue as ever, but they looked out from her face differently, maybe because the austerity of the road had whittled the skin closer to the bone. "Tent pole," she whispered to her reflection."

She automatically went to get food for their guests, but

Jaleen smilingly turned her away. "Get to work, gov," she said. "We'll take care of refreshments."

Solyra drew a deep breath, smoothed her coat, and headed to the campfire. Her appearance differed from the way she used to look about as much as her mahogany conference table differed from a campfire with saddles for seats. Still, she set her face in the blandly placid expression that she'd always used for business deals.

The patrol commander and a civilian man sat with Terring, Tad and Carl. The rest of the Frogbellies and patrollers formed a circle around them. Figgo was absent.

As she approached, all of them stood and, to her embarrassment, bowed. Solyra's heart tripped into double-time, but she bowed back with what she hoped was gracious ease.

The civilian greeted her in Zhi'nging'ha!, then said, in slow, careful common language, "Solyra Liberty, I am Morssee, deputy governor." He was as wrinkled and weathered as an elder, but he held himself like a man of middle age.

"Well met, sir, and thank you very much for carrying our companion." She spoke in Zhi'nging'ha!, and he looked pleased. She sat; the rest of them sat. Her Zhi'nging'ha! would be a strain for them to understand and for her to speak, as would common language, so she reverted to Norvadale, with Tad translating. After the first greeting, any pomp was dropped. Such was the custom, Figgo had told them, and Solyra was glad of it.

Tindy and Dan brought trays holding cups of milky tea, and Raal and Erin served scraps of bread soaked with butter and toasted.

Morssee touched on the fulgu business only to recall that several employees of Liberty Solyra's late husband had visited the Liberty years before, and to suggest that once they reached the township, they might call a meeting of the Liberty's council in order to discuss it fully.

Nervous as Solyra was for her own sake, she couldn't shake

the feeling that she and her companions were building a rampart of silence around Figgo—and that no one, except maybe Terring, knew why. After the gourd made another round, she excused herself and headed toward the privy, then cut back to Figgo's tent, which happened to be out of sight of the campfire. Through the open flaps, she saw Figgo lying perfectly still. She knew he wasn't asleep.

"Figgo?" she whispered.

He didn't answer, but he certainly heard her.

Solyra squatted outside the tent. "Why are you hiding?"

"I am not hiding."

Solyra stayed. Finally, Figgo got up. He even let Solyra gently straighten and brush his clothes. However expressionless he kept his face, his breath came fast and the pulse in his neck pounded.

She took his arm and led him toward the fireside, then released him as they came close enough for him to continue on his own.

He hesitated, only a moment but long enough for Solyra to take in Morssee's startled dismay. A moment later, the patrol burst into ululations. Two of the patrol, a woman and a man, came and took Figgo's arms and almost carried him to a saddle, which, like Solyra's, they'd hastily covered with a sheepfleece.

As Solyra sat next to Terring, he took her hand and squeezed it. She leaned to him. For once, Figgo showed no umbrage. He wasn't paying attention to them. His lips trembled; maybe tears gathered behind his goggles.

Morssee hadn't joined the patrol's ululations, and he sipped his tea without taking his hard and impassive eyes from Figgo's face. However the patrollers felt about Figgo, Morssee wasn't of their mind.

The tea gourd, freshened with its straw polished, was passed to Figgo and he drank, a few drops spilling on his tunic.

In the silence, Solyra could hear the tiny plops.

Figgo passed the gourd on then folded his hands in his lap. They showed white-knuckled in the flickering firelight.

Solyra was the first to speak. "Would you tell us your story, zizero Figgo?"

Figgo took a deep breath, then nodded. "Yes, Solyra Liberty. I will tell my story."

FIGGO'S STORY

Dawn brightened the land, yet all was quiet. Only a few birds called. The animals whuffled and sighed, and the spring burbled.

Had Figgo been another kind of person, another kind of man, Terring would have put a hand to his shoulder, a steadying, reassuring hand. But for all the years they'd worked together, the many leagues they'd traveled side by side, even sharing a tent, Figgo managed to stay solitary. To touch him would be an invasion. Though Solyra had taken his arm to bring him to this meeting.

"I was a citizen of the Zhengahk," Figgo said in Zhi'ng-ing'ha!, "from a region not far from here, on the skirts of the Apfa Mountains." Tad translated in a murmur.

"You are still a citizen," Morssee said in Zhi'nging'ha! "You are ours." The words were not an embrace.

"Yes." Figgo bowed his head. "Our home was much like Solyra Liberty township. You'll see, Solyra, how it is—especially since your Liberty was unraided, untouched. The soft intertwine of the dwellings and studios, chambers cool yet light-filled. My family's compound had three courtyards. Our generations had spilled out of our house and into another and another. My parents were physicians, and I was educated to follow their path."

He stopped and listened as the wind sprang up, whistling fitfully over the rock. "The rain is falling somewhere." He turned his face up. "Can you smell its perfume?"

A sigh went around Morssee's group, and one murmured, "Water."

A woman patroller gave a rough laugh. "Rain falls. Somewhere else."

Figgo went on. "I was not much more than a boy at the coming of the Death-bringers, an army of criminals whose religion was to rape, and rob, and kill, and enslave."

The patrol murmured angrily.

"Like many others, my family was raped, robbed and killed. Except for some of us children. We were gathering soup nests in a cave when they struck. I saw the smoke rising and knew instantly what had happened. It was very difficult to hold back from trying to stop the raid, from running madly to the village. But I couldn't abandon the other children. As the oldest, it was up to me to bring them to safety.

"We managed to reach a Liberty army camp. The little ones were adopted by the soldiers, none forced to bear weapons. I would have been happy to take up arms. However, my skills as a physician, especially as a surgeon, were more valuable."

Terring kept his face even, as if he were not amazed to learn that Figgo had been part of the Liberty forces. He had not been sure, even, how long ago Figgo had gone blind, whether as a child or later. Now he knew — it was after the coming of the Death Bringers. He dreaded hearing more, but he listened in silence with the rest of the caravan and the patrol.

"For all of its valor and courage, defeat after defeat whittled our army away. The Death-Bringers' weapons were no more sophisticated than ours, but they used methods that we couldn't stoop to use: terror and extreme brutality. Their ranks

swelled with boys and girls whose lives they spared only to enslave them, to break them in as cruel soldiers, to maim their
spirits by forcing them to perpetrate unspeakable cruelties in
their turn. Even before I joined, the Liberty commanders had
come to the painful conclusion that they had not the force to
vanquish the Death-Bringers.

"Then, one sleepless night, I came up with a plan inspired
by the rumor that the Death-Bringers' commander had liver
disease. I confided my plan only to our chief, for its success
relied on complete and utter secrecy. After a long struggle with
his conscience, he agreed."

Figgo paused and drew a deep breath.

"I ran away from the Liberty army, into the arms of the
Death-bringers. I claimed to be homeless. This was entirely
plausible, and a few people from my village were slaves in the
ranks. They recognized me and backed my story.

"It took only a month or so for me to get where I wanted
to be: on the commander's staff. I did not get there to assas-
sinate him. Plenty of others were ready to take his place. In
fact, I treated his liver disease efficaciously. Fortunately, it was
winter, and the Death-bringers were resting up in the hills,
not campaigning. Otherwise... I don't know what I would have
done. As it was, I didn't have to kill. Directly. Once I had the
commander's attention and — and affection I carefully hinted
of a treasure hidden in a gulch."

"Hawk Gulch," a patroller said.

"Yes. The commander knew as well as I did that this gulch
was a highly risky position. What boots I licked, what ingra-
tiating words oozed from my mouth, to gain his trust. What
caresses and kisses I endured." Figgo shuddered. "Worst of all,
I had to listen to them...brag and laugh about what they did
to mothers and fathers, to children, to sisters and brothers and
cousins, to elders and babies. I pretended to understand that it
was the way of war. As if their perversions and chests of booty

made them the honorable warriors they boasted themselves to be."

Figgo started when one of the young men whacked the fire with a stick, sending up sparks. His commander spoke sharply to him. The young man dropped the stick, abashed. "I'm sorry."

Figgo nodded and gave a smile of sorts, but Terring could see that he'd been unnerved. Solyra touched him, just a light, brief touch of her palm on his shoulder, and he continued.

"Come spring," Figgo continued, "we swept into the region as a horde. I rode with the commander like a lapdog. His pet." His self-deprecating laugh touched Terring to the bone. "Any little settlement in our path, we decimated. I saw it all again, what happened in my village, happening over and over again."

Not blind yet.

"I knew it would be that way, but..." Figgo trailed off and sat in silence. He was perfectly still, as if ensorcelled, petrified. Or as if he were waiting for a blow.

"Go on," Morssee commanded.

Terring spoke first. "Is it understood that zizero Figgo acted for his people? That he — he tore apart his own heart to—"

Morssee cut in. "That is to be seen. Continue."

Figgo adjusted his goggles with a shaking hand. "I did not take part, pleading care of my so-called healing hands. Still, I gained a reputation for being hard, inscrutable. I was. Inscrutability was the only alternative to pretending to be merry, with the Death-bringers.

"One of the happiest days of my life was the one when I lured the commander and the army into Hawk Gulch. They looked forward to a big cave of booty, and that's what they found. Coins, trade goods, food — whatever treasures people could glean from their looted stores — all had been brought in as bait for the trap. My ruse might have gone undetected, had I not been betrayed. I think one of my own neighbors did it, and I might hate him for it, but there was too much fear, too much depravity to expect old loyalties to stand. It was a miracle that I went safely for that long.

"The betrayal came too late, at least, for the commander to retreat. He declared that he and his men would fill a lake of blood before they surrendered. And on the eve of battle, he had one last recreation. That was blinding me."

The patrol, and the caravan, too, murmured in dismay, though they must have guessed it was coming. Diaa gave a soft growling whimper in the back of her throat. Terring swallowed, but the lump stayed stuck in his throat.

"I do not know what they used," Figgo said. "Some liquid." He was silent, steadying himself, maybe.

Then he unbuckled the strap of his goggles and removed them.

Terring held his breath to stop from crying out at the scar-framed milky disfigurement that had been Figgo's eyes. Solyra couldn't hold back a sob, and Diaa gave a short, sharp keen. Gobi murmured a prayer, and Jaleen leaned on Baloos, bowed her head and silently cried. Thankfully, the children were sleeping.

Figgo covered his eyes again. "There is no need to mourn my sight, or to pity me. I was punished for my own treachery, but the reward was great. The Deathbringers filled their lake with their own blood."

Morssee's face remained hard, his eyes narrowed at Figgo.

"How did you escape?" he demanded.

"Some of the slave-soldiers of the Death-bringers considered me their liberator. They hid me, and nursed me through my injuries, then helped me get to Terring's ranch. They kept my secret, at least for a while. Terring adopted me as a brother, took me on as an aide, though I knew next to nothing about business. I could not bear to continue as a physician after what I'd done."

Diaa gave a soft trill, and Terring realized — as she must have — why Figgo had dedicated himself to her advancement, even if he didn't respect her. Terring had done the same for him.

"Terring gave me a reason to live again," Figgo said. "He gave me purpose. Terring gave me refuge, here in the Zhengahk and in Norvadale."

"And now you're home," Morssee said.

"My home is gone."

"Your home is here," Morssee retorted. "Take my word for it. It's all around you."

One of the more gentle-faced patrollers said, "You know, some say you're a hero. But some hate you. I'm just telling the truth."

"Yes," Figgo said.

"They talked about you for a long time at the grand council," Morssee said. "The army people said there was no other way. You gave us our last chance. The chief spoke passionately in your defense. But the villages that were sacked.... The people who lived through it saw you riding with the Death-bringers—"

"No one saw him do anything more than ride!" the woman cried.

Morssee held up a hand. "True. No one reliable, at least."

"I know I will have to stand trial," Figgo said. "I am prepared for that. And I understand you are obliged to—"

"May zizero Figgo stay in our custody?" Solyra cut in, thankfully before Figgo had a chance to offer himself up to the patrol. "You hardly know me, so my word means little more than what my title allows, but every one of my companions will attest that zizero Figgo traveled peacefully for many miles with us, with the intent to benefit his people. He's shown only honor in his dealings, and he's been a quiet and helpful companion. In our encounter with Death-bringers in the mountains, he did his best to comfort the young ones and he gave heart to those who fought. Without his help, our Zago would have perished of his wound."

Morssee looked in her eyes, then nodded. "We will escort you, Liberty, in any case."

Figgo murmured a thanks, then Terring took him back to their tent.

Terring could hardly take in the story he'd heard tonight. He'd guessed that Figgo had lost his sight to mishap or disease, or maybe to violence. But not in this fashion. He had not known the depth of Figgo's anguish. He had never seen the scars. Figgo always turned his back and covered his eyes with a bandage, when he removed the goggles. Terring found himself praying, inwardly, to the Bihst goddess, not in words but in feeling. A crushing guilt encircled his heart. He should have tried harder to understand his companion, to learn his story.

Figgo didn't need help settling in for the night, but Terring tucked him in as if he were a child. "I'll not desert you, Figgo."

Figgo didn't answer, then for the first time ever except when needing to be guided, he reached and touched Terring, a light touch on the shoulder. Just as Solyra had done to him.

When Terring came back out again, the rest of the gathering had broken up. Since they'd left the lake, Solyra slept with the Bihst group. But before she lay down, every night she made her own patrol, walking around the camp, checking the animals and people.

The caravan looked to Terring for safety. He knew weapons, fighting, tactics. Carl kept the caravan moving. But it was Solyra they relied on. She cared for each one of them. Just as Figgo said, her hands had healing in them. With grace, purpose, and care, she loved them, every single one, and it showed in every line of her.

But that kind of love, for all its beauty, was not the kind Terring wanted of her.

She stood now with Toggly, her head against the mare's neck. Starlight glimmered in her eyes as she gazed into the wilderness. Her hair stirred in the breeze that lightly swept the land.

She turned as he came to her.

"Terring, we'll make this business work. I vow."

He put his arm around her, and she leaned into him. He knew she was thinking of Figgo, whose passion for the success of the business was more painfully clear than ever. Figgo needed to redeem himself by helping his people to exile back east. And he needed to escape.

Figgo no longer saw the star-laden dark of night, or red rocks against the turquoise sky of day, the subtle purples and reds and yellows of the rocks and sand. Yet he would take in more deeply the subtle musky fragrance of the dry air, and hear the cries of life, all the more dramatic for their sparseness, and feel in his spirit the silent music that dwarfed the small business of the caravan. He'd called the smell of rain perfume.

Had he mourned in exile?

A surge of pity moved Terring, stronger than any he'd ever felt for Figgo's blindness. Figgo's family had been slaughtered, his village sacked. Zhengahk could hardly be much of a home to him. He was an exile in body and in spirit.

For Terring, uprooted from everything he used to call home, the Zhengahk gave him a sense of home he'd hardly known he lacked. Or maybe it was the feel of Solyra close to him.

Yet their only chance at surviving lay in leaving this place where rain was not life-giving moisture, but only a far-off fragrance.

>> <<

As the caravan approached the township, Solyra was filled with fear for Zago and Figgo, worry about whether she would be accepted as Liberty, anxiety about whether the people would accept Terring Fulgus. But all that couldn't dampen her anticipation. The day they were due to arrive, Solyra put on her frock coat and a riding skirt.

A crowd of cubes and domes and chimneys came into sight

under the face of a towering cliff. Walls surrounded what the cliff didn't guard. They weren't immense, but they'd been enough to deter the Death-bringers. A grove of cottonwoods and other trees stood at one end of the town.

By noon they arrived to the town gate. The sign that arched in metal filigree over it had been concealed from the distance by huge, old cottonwoods. As it came into view, Solyra's plans for a dignified demeanor were completely routed.

SOLYRA LIBERTY

Solyra gaped up at the words.

The wrought-metal sign had not been thrown together this week, or even this month. The vines twining up either side were too mature. Someone had imported the metal at considerable cost. That someone could be no one else but Dahn.

She'd come to bitterly disbelieve Dahn's promises that he would carry her out here, that he'd change his ways and make things better between them. Yet, he'd had this sign made.

He'd fantasized about coming through this gate together.

He might even have loved her after all, in his twisted way.

Someone said quietly, "Liberty?" and she pressed Toggly forward. The parade continued with Solyra in the lead. Auspicious drawings, freshly drawn with flour on the dusty ground, led through the gate and into the village: a joyous dog, a healing serpent, a peaceful rabbit, an abundant pig.

The drawings lifted her spirits, and so did the village's flow of domes and quarter-domes, arches, pine-mulched pathways, all in soft, earthy colors brightened by lines of colorful glazed tile. The source that watered the cottonwoods evidently gave only enough water to survive, and sturdy herbs, not flowers, filled the planters. In the center of the village, a dry fountain was ringed with silvery-green rosemary alternating with purple sage.

All dismounted in the little plaza, and a group of children came toward them, giggling and jostling. Solyra hung her hat on the saddlehorn, then squatted as a little girl of about eight, with enormous solemn eyes, held up to her a garland of bright cloth flowers. Solyra bent her head as the girl put the garland around her neck; she rose to see her companions wore similar garlands. The children burst into a song, in Zhi'nging'ha!:

"Welcome, welcome, Lady Governor dear, most honorable benefactor. Welcome cherished guests, welcome. Welcome, kindly beasts…" The song went on to extol their village, and the little girl and a boy took Solyra's hands and led her down the wide, dusty footpath that was the main thoroughfare. A group of young men and women led the animals away down a side street.

Most of the buildings were partly submerged in the ground and oriented, Tad explained, so the windows gathered light in winter and gave shade in summer. The red cliff loomed over one end of the town. In the distance, goats bleated and dogs barked. Neither saddle animals nor carts were visible on the main path.

The cheery children's chorus pointed out city hall, with double doors thrown wide to let out coolness and a fragrance of lamp oil, and the various businesses and temples, as well as the side streets, occupied by kin groups and communes.

By back east standards, the people who greeted Solyra were poor, and some were disfigured or maimed, but Solyra couldn't see them as sunk in the misery Figgo had portrayed. Their homes and businesses and the streets were neat and well-tended. Solyra wondered if they'd hidden the ravages of war for the day, if beggars had been ordered out of sight. But she didn't glimpse the kind of degradation that festered in the slums of Norvadale. The air breathed wholesome, with the normal smells of animals mingled with spice and food and the incense-like wood they burned for fuel.

The song and the children stopped before a group of adults dressed in richly embroidered caftans, some of which looked antique.

Solyra bowed to the children. "Shhh'u'wah." Her best Zhi'nging'ha! dissolved the children into giggles. They scattered like a flock of birds as an elderwoman came forward.

"Welcome, Solyra Liberty. I'm Isan, mayor of the town." She gestured to a compound whose entry was decorated with a venerable vine.

"Please enter your home," Isan said. "Dinner is cooking for you and your companions, and the bathing pool is ready. Your friend Zago is already settled in his bed."

Solyra couldn't have thought of any speech more welcoming than those simple words. "Shhh'u'wah." She kissed the mayor on both cheeks, and Isan smiled and squeezed Solyra's shoulders.

"We'll leave you now to rest and refresh yourselves. One of the children will fetch you to city hall when the day cools." She added, "Watch your step going in our buildings."

The door had a raised sill, presumably to keep out the street's dust, and mud if it ever rained. Solyra stepped over it, into the cool bright entry room. There, everyone took off their shoes, then continued inside to what was obviously a gathering room.

The furnishings were simple: a large table flanked by legged chests that doubled as benches; low couches arranged in a square, with a short table in the center. Rugs woven in various patterns and colors warmed the tile floor. A delicious aroma of corn pudding filled the air, along with the fragrance of the rosemary and lavender boughs that stood in thick, oddly shaped glass vases on a shelf over the fire.

Solyra had a conviction that the rugs had been given by various people from their own homes, like the herbs and the food and the vessels on the cast-iron stove in the kitchen corner. Hers was a potluck home.

She slowly turned around, hardly daring to believe....

She was home.

Young folks lugged in their baggage; Terring directed them

to bring the fulgu lockers to the pantry a few steps down from the kitchen.

Gobi came into the gathering room. "Zago is in one of the rooms on the back courtyard." He added quietly to Solyra and Diaa, "He should have only a few visitors for now." The two women followed him back along a curving passage.

The smell of sickness and pain met them even before they entered the room, the medicinal herbs only underlining it. Diaa stopped and choked back a sob, her hand pressing Solyra's arm. Then she straightened and went to the sick bed. Her face was anguished but her voice sweet, almost purring, as she took the rag from a bucket sitting by the bed, wrung it out, and dabbed it over Zago's forehead.

"I'm here now, darling. I'm here to watch over you..."

But Death's own shadow grayed Zago's face and hands.

Diaa rose from the bed side. "I'll get fresh water," she said quietly.

"And hot, too, please," Gobi said.

After she left, Solyra began to ask Gobi — but he stopped her with a shake of his head and a nod toward Zago. He meant Zago could hear them. Solyra doubted it, but she nodded and began to turn away, then stopped.

She knelt at the bedside and bent close to Zago's ear. "Zago, can you hear me?"

Whatever Gobi believed, Zago gave no sign of even knowing she was there. Still, she forced herself on before she could stop herself.

"Zago, if you live, I'll turn the fulgus over to you. You can free them. But if you die, by my eyes, I'll frame every single one of them. So if you care about your pooby nooby scoobies — live!"

She almost wished she could take it back, the moment she said it. But Zago probably hadn't heard.

Then his eyes fluttered.

Or she was imagining things.

FISTICUFFS

IN LATE SUMMER, FIGGO WAS exonerated by the Zhengahk court. No celebration marked his return to Solyra Liberty. Terring passed the word that he wished to resume his life quietly.

In their business offices, Solyra unpacked and filed stacks of documents, mostly from Terring's stores, on the new shelves that lined one of the adobe walls. She directed Terring and Tad as they pinned a topographical map on a wall. She scrounged up ink blocks, pens, paper and other supplies. She pushed around tables and chairs and lamps. She even brought rugs and fleeces from her home to cover the tiled floor.

Then she disappeared, pleading governor business. As if her vow to Zago whispered from her skin. As if they wouldn't find out, sooner or later.

After all, she could worry about her impulsive vow only so much. Liberty business, from council meetings to feasts held in her honor to laboring with Morssee over documents and files took most of her time.

Morssee had governed the Liberty honestly and competently, from what Solyra could judge. He was patient and thorough in teaching what she needed to know, and she believed he was sincere when he said he was happy that she would be taking on many of the duties he had been fulfilling.

Yet Solyra sensed resentment in him. She wondered if it was due to her protecting Figgo, and she considered asking him outright, but the time didn't seem ripe. They both had more pressing things to worry about.

The Liberty had not been physically destroyed by the War. But Solyra, new as she was, had to see it was dying. Dying of thirst. Even if the town and some fields around it had water enough for subsistence, the region was drought struck. The reserves in the huge stone granaries were dangerously low. If the harvest didn't yield more in a year or so, the people would be forced to eat the seed grain. And that would be the end of the Liberty. It was just as Figgo said. The fulgus were truly their only chance.

She dared not tell Zago, while he continued to hover between life and death, that she couldn't possibly keep the vow to liberate his fulgus. Figgo and Terring did fine without her, according to the reports Figgo sent. Carl was contracted for transportation. Terring had tracked down his former pod engineer. Baloos was in charge of the frame construction. Under his supervision, a crew was disassembling Terring's old frame to move to Solyra's field. Another crew was renovating an old compound to serve as the ranch house. The fulgus were moved from Solyra's root cellar to the root cellar at the Terring Fulgus office, and the twins hauled water for them. Terring found a keeper to tend them, though Diaa claimed the woman didn't have nearly Zago's sensitivity.

Solyra enjoyed the reports sent from the new ranch site. But what she really hoped for, in the mail, was news from back east. When she'd had arrived at the Liberty, one of the first things she did was send a message to her former clerk, Horace. As autumn touched the distant mountains with gold, a string of pack animals arrived carrying mail.

Solyra joined the excited crowd clustered around the

packages and letters heaped on a banquet table in the courtyard of the town hall. Her mail — the mail for the Liberty,
rather — was in its own pouch, which was handed to her first.

Solyra forced herself to walk, not run, back to her office.
She forced herself to riffle through the official packets. She
skimmed a letter from her creditors, surprisingly courteous
— but then she was free of their clutches. Only when she'd
cleared her desk did she open with trembling fingers the pack-
et with Horace's seal.

It held two letters: one from Horace himself and another,
still sealed, from the detectives she'd hired to search for her
parents. She dithered, opened Horace's first.

The contents of her house had been auctioned. Her staff
all had found new positions. The cook's son was in training as
a pastry cook. Solyra had to stop there and take a deep breath
against the rainy day memory of baking almond cookies with
the boy. Horace was managing a lucrative catering business,
but he claimed he missed serving her house. Solyra reread the
letter, folded it, then picked up the envelope from the detective
agency.

She opened the envelope and, with her eyes closed, drew
out and unfolded the report. She drew a deep breath and
opened her eyes.

They had not found her parents.

Solyra sagged over her desk. Hadn't she expected this? Yes,
but the truth still devastated. Every time.

"Liberty?" Gulin her secretary squatted by her chair, her
young face soft with sympathy. "Bad news?"

Solyra folded the papers, thankful that Gulin couldn't read
Norvadale language, and gave her a smile. "Not really, no." After all, the report hadn't said they were dead. Just missing.

Her mother and father were still missing.

"Gulin, would it be inconvenient if I took the rest of the
day off?"

As usual, it took Gulin a few moments to figure out Solyra's Zhi'nging'ha!. She shook her head. "Not at all, Liberty."

Solyra headed for a grove of cottonwoods that lay outside the village, alongside a wash. It was a popular swimming place, but with the children in school, the shallow flow was deserted. Solyra undressed, stretched luxuriantly and waded in, then flopped on her back, the sun spangling her face through the branches, the water laving her body, gently washing away her worries.

A splash interrupted her languid trance. She sat up in the water.

Terring paddled toward her. "Gotcha," he said, grinning like a dog with a fat stick in his teeth. He must have been lurking, waiting for his chance to catch her this one time when she was alone. And naked.

Solyra's mind raced with thoughts she couldn't even articulate as she sat up on the soft sandy bottom and watched him come near. He slowed and, instead of grabbing hold of her as he'd obviously intended to do, he knelt in the water.

"You look terrified." His smile lingered, but his face was more sad, or disappointed, than bemused.

Solyra forced a smile. Honesty. She'd promised him honesty. It was time to keep her promise. "I've been avoiding you."

Under the water, he took her hands and drew her close. "I will never hurt you, Solyra. I know I did, back in Norvadale. But I won't. Never again."

"You'll be mad when you hear what I've done."

He looked at her face — not in her eyes, except for the glimpses she allowed — and his eyes narrowed, but he smiled a little. "What have you done now, pussycat?"

Solyra licked her lips. "It's a long time ago." But not really. Only a couple of weeks, since she'd made the vow to Zago.

"Well, why not leave it there?"

She gave a nervous, short laugh. "Try telling Figgo that."

He kissed her hair. "Try telling me about it."

"Well. I — I…" Solyra licked her lips again. Terring could surely feel her heart pounding, see the pulse leaping in her neck. She was terrified, when it came down to it. She pushed away from him and swam backwards, evading his gaze. His arms trailed after her, but he didn't try to take her again.

"What is it, Solyra?" he asked gently.

"You remember that convention in Booton, when Dahn stole your deal?" Solyra resisted the urge to cover her breasts.

"Oh, yes." His eyes narrowed again. Of course he remembered. Dahn had stolen Terring Fulgus' most important customer.

Solyra let her feet down and discovered she could no longer touch bottom. She paddled, her feet scrabbling until they touched the sand again.

"The convention," she repeated. "Well, you remember what Figgo said at breakfast?" Wait — wasn't she supposed to be telling him about the vow to Zago?

Terring shook his head. "What he said about what?"

"About — about… No, I mean, Dahn said it. At the convention. Dahn said that thing about us knowing how to sweeten a deal."

Terring's face grew yet more guarded. And somehow Solyra had lost the shallows again and had to paddle forward. Her heart beat so hard, her whole body throbbed. "Well, I was the sugar. I—I sweetened the deal. You know?"

She could have choked on her own cloying smile. What effect it had on Terring, she didn't know. Because he turned and walked out of the water, put his clothes on and left.

She tried on the idea of drowning herself and settled for dunking her tear-burned face. How was it that she'd told the truth to Tad, but related the incident to Terring as if it were a nasty trick that she and Dahn had cooked up between them? She'd told the tale just as Dahn had: *You were in it just as much as I was, my hot, sweet, darling little whore.*

And Terring had broken his promise to her, just as she'd broken her promise to him.

Solyra had pulled herself from the water and was dressing when Diaa came tearing down the bank. Her face was radiant.

"Solyra! Zago's fever's broken! He'll live! Oh, thank you, Solyra, thank you, thank you! He told me your promise. You saved him! "

Solyra could have laughed. Or she could have cried. Instead, she hurriedly finished dressing and ran with Diaa back to the house.

Sure enough, Zago sat up in bed. He even had the strength to look smug as Diaa nestled purring beside him.

Terring stood near the window. He must have gotten the good news from Diaa and sent her to the river to find Solyra. His pasted-on smile completely disappeared when he turned to glare at Solyra. "Time for a little business conference," he said, "at the office."

>> <<

IN THE TIME IT TOOK to reach the office, a numb calm fell over Terring. It didn't matter what she promised Zago, he told himself. The contract wouldn't allow her to withdraw her fulgus. Would it? He wasn't even sure. He was too tossed around to think straight. But surely Figgo had nailed the fulgus to the business.

As for what she did, all those years ago — the past was done. Yet somehow it seemed fitting.

Figgo sat at one of the tables, with Tad beside him reading aloud a paper in a mix of Zhi'nging'ha! and Norvadale. He stopped mid-sentence as Terring threw himself in the chair near them.

"Do you know what she's done?"

Figgo raised his head and turned his face toward Solyra. He didn't bother to respond, any more than Terring waited for him to respond.

"She promised Zago he could have the fulgus. She said if he lived, he could have them. Diaa is all in a happy bubble over it. Well, I'm glad he's better, and I certainly don't begrudge Diaa her joy, but that's about as far as my noble spirit stretches."

Even Tad looked incredulous, but Figgo's face didn't change. "No problem," Figgo said calmly. "The fulgus are jointly held. Solyra's promise is worth nothing. It is too bad to make such a solemn vow, and then to break it, but it seems that Solyra holds her honor lightly."

"You can say that again." The shattering confession jolted again through Terring's mind. She'd whored herself, jauntily, for a business deal. She'd even smiled at the memory of it. Smiled at having broken him.

"What does that mean?" Tad demanded. "She holds her honor lightly."

"Never mind, Tad, just stay out of it," Solyra said.

"No. No, I won't. Hey, we're off the caravan now. Free to say how we really feel. So tell me, Figgo. Terring. What do you mean?"

Terring gave a humorless chuckle. "You don't want to know, my friend."

"Wrong on both counts. I'm not your friend, and I do want to know."

"Let's put it this way. She doesn't want you to know."

"Boys, stop it," Solyra said. "Break it up."

"See?" Terring said.

"Let's call it a question of honor," Tad said.

"Well, in the interest of gentlemanly honor," Terring said, "let's not discuss the lady's…doings."

"Ah. I get it. I see. I think I know what this is about. You son of a bitch!"

Tad hit so fast, Terring didn't even know it was coming until he was stumbling back with his right ear ringing. The next punch, to the gut, dropped Terring like a sack of dead fulgus.

He rolled over to his hands and knees, tried to stagger to

his feet, crawled a couple of paces, then wretched like a dog. He heard Tad growling, "Out of the way, Solyra."

"Now, Tad," she cooed. "Easy now, my brother. Come on. Let's go. Leave him. Let's go now, honey."

Terring managed to get on his feet. Against the rage pouring through him, he forced on himself the cold calm he'd relied on in far worse situations: riding through a sacked village, interviewing Redbeard's victim, sitting in a courtroom while Figgo's very soul was dismembered.

Tad faced him, fists clenched. Fine, except Solyra was ready to jump in front of him.

"You keep your mouth shut about whatever you think you know about honor," Tad says. "Same goes for you, Figgo."

"You can put your fists away, kid." Terring touched his cheek: already swollen. "We're not about to start a gossip fest. Though just for the record, you were the one pressing for details. As for keeping away from each other, I'm all for it. Just be sure to tell your uncle that I didn't break my contract with the pair of you. You threw down your hammer."

"Nonsense," Solyra said quickly. "We all need to cool off and regroup. Tad, please leave us to discuss this — this foolishness." She added quietly, looking in Tad's eyes. "Thanks for sticking up for me, but I'll be all right."

Tad's face was still tight and flushed, but he nodded and left.

Terring had never felt so shredded in his life. Losing a fight with a kid about half his size was the least of it. He'd been played for a fool, lied to — and come back for more. Again! He didn't trust himself even to look at Solyra. Instead, he turned to the map on the wall and stared at it.

All of it belonged to her: the fulgu field, the fulgus, the town, everything. Terring had fought for it, and come out with nothing but a dry ranch, a crashed fulgu frame, and a grove of dead peach trees. And a vivid set of nightmares. Now he was entangled with a business partner who betrayed him at every turn. And, as it turned out, he had betrayed Figgo, bringing him out here. The court had exonerated him, but not everyone else did. Terring saw the looks, heard the murmurs. Dragging his loyal friend out here, he'd dragged him into unimaginable shame and anguish. He certainly hadn't brought him to any kind of home.

"Gentlemen," Solyra said to Terring's back and, presumably, to Figgo's face, "I pray we will honor our contract with Carl's transportation business, rather than abide by a fisticuffs settlement. Especially since no one else around here is equipped to move the frames to our field." She sounded a sight steadier than Terring felt. "And I'll tell Zago that I made him a promise that I can't keep." She stopped. This time she didn't sound so steady. "Just let me wait until he's stronger. I'll talk to Gobi about the timing. Deal?"

Terring didn't answer. His jaw seemed welded in a clench. Figgo answered for him.

"Deal."

As if a deal with her would stick. But as Gobi would say, no choice.

>> <<

"You can't go back on your promise!" Diaa growled.

Solyra and she sat in the shallows of the cottonwood pool. Might as well consolidate the pain in one location, Solyra figured, though it was a shame to spoil such a lovely spot with one bad memory after another. At least the sun-warmed water unjangled her nerves a little.

"I don't have a choice," Solyra said. "When Gobi says it's all right, I'll tell Zago. And don't blame it on Terring and Figgo. It's not their fault I lied."

"You didn't lie. You made a sacred vow." Diaa dunked her head, as if to soak down the ridge that bristled along it, then came up again. "You can't break it."

"I tell you, Diaa, I have no choice."

"You do so. The fulgus are yours."

"They're contracted to the business."

"It don't matter!"

"It's not just my interests at stake, Diaa. What about you and Zago? And Carl and Tad? And all those people at the fulgu ranch, waiting for jobs?"

"No one wants that fulgu field, you know. Morssee's daughter told me so. You're taking those people from their other projects. Then once the frame is up, you have to let most of them go."

"I've heard the talk, Diaa. The flat truth is, without water, their projects aren't worth the sweat that's being poured into them. The Liberty needs money more than anything. Once the money starts coming in, they'll think differently."

"What will they do with money?" Diaa demanded. "There's nothing to buy around here. No food either. They'll move to the Ihm and be homesick forever. And this place will die."

An old book on the Zhengahk had been illustrated with etchings of rich, elaborately irrigated fields and orchards. No more. When Solyra rode into the countryside, she passed fallow fields, unkempt orchards and dysfunctional wind pumps. And she told herself: even if every field was fresh plowed, every fruit tree pruned and every wind pump turning, it would have made no difference. The abundant water that once blessed the valley crept along in little more than trickles. And the fulgu frame would not rob any viable farm labor.

Figgo was right. The only hope for the people of the Zhengahk was cash—and exile. For once the frame was played out, or if it crashed, everything was over for the people here. Solyra's people.

"Diaa, I can't break the contract. That's all there is to it. Beside, Zago is getting well, isn't he? So... what does it matter?" It was a tack that she'd promised herself not to take—another promise broken.

Diaa's brow furrowed, and she gave a light hiss, more

sorrowful than angry. "All of your lies and cheats swarm like shit-flies around you."

Solyra hid her face in the water, but Diaa must have glimpsed something in it. When Solyra came back up, she'd pulled her lips back over her teeth and her face had gentled. "I done my share of lying and cheating … and worse. You rescued me from that life. Now I have friends like Figgo and Gobi and Terring and all the Frogbellies. I learned a life I never dreamed of, back in that dirty troll house."

She took Solyra's hands, under the water. "I'm so happy now. It's like being in the middle of the big blue sky. To cheat is to pull clouds over yourself, nasty and dark. And this time, Solyra, you'll pull clouds over Zago, too." Diaa stroked her hands. "It's no good. The promise you made to Zago has more power than your contract."

Diaa released her, waded out of the water, got dressed and left.

Solyra paddled around aimlessly for a while. A cowardly part of her hoped that Diaa would break the news to Zago. The more insightful side of her knew that while the old Diaa might have blurted it out in fury, the new one would keep it to herself, to protect Zago's health, if for no other reason.

Despite everything, she was deeply moved by Diaa's words — at least the part about her life getting better — and she savored the flow of the water over her body, going in and out of the patches of sun and shade. She floated on her back, looking up into the clear blue sky of Diaa's bliss, and let herself go to it, let her mind follow a bird flying across, a little puff of a cloud traveling along, changing shape as it went. It was ridiculous, to feel so relaxed, when she really wanted to cry. Still, she couldn't deny the sense of well-being that sneaked through her.

Not that she wanted to. She needed all the well-being she could get.

>> <<

SOLYRA'S LIBERTY >< 253

THE COMPOUND GRANTED TO THE Bihsts was on a little square off the main street. Gobi sat on the bench beside the temple door. He looked up from the basket he was weaving and smiled. "Solyra, good to see you." His eyes, as usual, saw right through her, but he didn't ask what was wrong. He never did. He let people come along at their own pace.

"Gobi, do you mind if we go in?"

He put the basket aside, and Solyra picked it up and turned it in her hands, then put it to her face and breathed in its grassy dry smell.

"Mmmm. I can't wait till you get to hats."

"Next month, I think. A few more practice baskets."

Inside, he pointed to a stack by the door. "Take those home with you. I think a little lopsided won't matter for fire kindling."

She laughed. "Thanks, I will."

The temple was about as big as Solyra's main room and lit by a skylight and a few votives. The only furniture besides several cushions arranged on the thick rug was a long, low cabinet. The laughing fat man and half-naked woman sat on it, along with votive candles and the bowls of gems and flowers. An incense holder smoked spicy-sweet. All was quiet, with Baloos, Jaleen and the children out at the ranch.

Solyra and Gobi sat facing each other on two of the cushions.

"I… well, I got myself into a bit of a jam," Solyra said.

"I can guess. I was there when you did it. Nice jam, yes. Pickle jam, I think."

"Hot pepper pickle. And to make a long story short, I need to know when it's safe to tell Zago that I have to break my promise to him."

"Mm. Check with me in four days. He should be strong enough to take it by then."

They sat quietly for a while. Solyra was grateful for Gobi's straightforward answer, and grateful for his receptive silence.

Her gaze strayed to the female statue. With her tapered

waist and delicate breasts, a smile playing on her face, she was lovely. She was also an unpleasant reminder of the convention, where Dahn had bullied Solyra into going half-nude, to lure the "account" as Dahn called the customer. But the goddess's smile looked quietly joyous, rather than forced. And surely her fat companion wasn't about to pimp her...

"What does that statue mean?" she found herself asking.

"She is wisdom."

Solyra gave a laugh that came out scornful. "How does a half-naked woman represent wisdom?" She tried to make her question sound respectful, but again, scorn crept into her voice.

If Gobi noticed, he didn't show it. "The naked woman doesn't represent wisdom," he said. "The naked woman *is* wisdom. And love, too. And bliss, for men. Except for Tad. I think the fat man is Tad's bliss and love and wisdom. Or used to be. Now everyone skinny. Caravan adventure diet!"

He gave one of his hooting laughs, and Solyra couldn't help laughing with him, even as a teary feeling gathered deep inside of her. She gave a big sigh.

"Gobi, do you believe that the fulgus are sentient?"

"You asked me this same question before."

"I know."

"So, are they sentient?" Gobi repeated. "I don't think so. But does something live in them, like we do in our houses or tents? I don't know." He nodded toward the statue of the woman. "Maybe if I were her husband, I would know. But I'm only just courting her, and her best mysteries are still hidden from me. Zago hears the fulgus. I don't, but I'm a little deaf. You hear something, right? What do you think?"

"I'm...not sure. It's just a low hum. But the wind whistles and trees rustle. So what does a low hum mean? If I knew they were sentient, it might make sense to break the contract with Terring. But if they're not... It's not just that I would cheat myself. I would cheat Terring and my creditors, and Carl and Tad and you all..."

And her parents, if she ever found them.

"And Zago, too, and Diaa, even if they don't see it that way. Not to mention the entire Liberty."

After another calming silence, she continued. "I haven't told you about Tad and Terring getting into a fist fight."

"Everyone all right?"

"Terring didn't even land a blow. Tad knocked him around pretty smartly, but didn't hurt him much."

Dahn had dragged her to enough prizefights for her to know that Terring had gotten off relatively easy. Though the gut blow would leave an aching bruise for days.

"The fight between those two is a long time coming," Gobi said.

"I suppose. Anyway, I'm sticking with the contract. I've eaten too much flesh in my life to have scruples about the fulgus being alive, after all. I'll raise the fulgu frame and make a fortune, then I'll settle with my parents in a cottage by the ocean. If I can ever find them. I just wish I hadn't made that stupid promise to Zago."

"It was a generous gesture," Gobi said. "Don't regret it."

"And pickled hot peppers make a nice relish."

"Delicious," Gobi agreed.

A ROOT BEER WITH FIGGO

AFTER THE RED-LETTER, BLACK-EYE DAY, Terring Fulgus went on as if neither fight nor vow had happened. Despite the fact that Tad, and Carl, too, refused even to try to reconcile with Terring personally, they worked hard. Maybe because of what he'd been through at court, Figgo was subdued and Solyra didn't find working with him too bad. Or maybe he didn't care about personal feelings as long the business ran smoothly. He helped Carl and Tad restructure their procedures to comply with Zhengahk law. In return for Figgo's time, Tad built more shelving for the office and did copying.

Everyone was so polite and businesslike, it was as if nothing at all was amiss — except for the ice in Terring's eyes, the rare times he even looked at Solyra. He looked right through Tad. Thankfully, he left for the frame field on Day Three, as Solyra called the third day after the fight.

The worst ordeal, once Solyra didn't have to face Terring every day, was visiting Zago, having to smile through his physically feeble but emotionally robust anticipation of the liberation of the fulgus. He even wanted Gobi to preside at a ceremony. Gobi managed to sidestep him. Diaa, though she didn't perform the dubious mercy of disillusioning Zago, talked him out of making too much of it, on grounds that Terring and Figgo were really, really unhappy about it.

Solyra's favorite duty was her evening walk around town. People were friendly and mostly understood her broken Zhi'nging'ha!. The challenges they faced were daunting, yet Solyra would have found her position as Liberty satisfying, fulfilling — were it not for that lump of red-hot jam stuck in her craw. She wasn't sure, even, why she was taking it so hard. Somehow the vow had become balled up with everything else, as if all her lying and cheating rolled up into this one unkeepable promise. As if breaking it would brand her irredeemable.

>> <<

TERRING RODE DOWN THE FRAME line, heading back to the ranch house. A mile or so of posts already stood, each about chest high, and twenty-five foot-lengths apart, the empty cap-cages gleaming coppery new in the sun. A wagon passed, bearing the spools of wire netting that would be stretched taut between the posts. Once Solyra's pod fulgus were activated and installed in the cap-cages, the frame would resemble a very, very long fence with glowing postcaps. New fulgus would catch and mature in the netting. When Terring's own frame had been live, he'd never tired of the sight of it by night, especially as the child fulgus burgeoned, glowing more brightly than the parent fulgus.

Parent and child fulgus. Burgeoning. Just jargon. Zago's beliefs — as fostered by Solyra's idiotic pamphlets — were nonsense. Yet raw fulgus generated an almost mystical beauty.

The beauty ended at harvest. Once removed from the frame, the "shells" shut tight until they were activated to be installed in a building or device or, if of a pod variety, installed in another frame. An inactive fulgu was no more beautiful than an oyster pulled up from the ocean.

Solyra, an ocean child, had been amazed by the sweetness

of the lake water, at the resort where he'd courted her when he'd first returned from the Zhengahk. Before the war, before Dahn took her away. Like a happy fish, she'd swum and splashed and laughed, wearing a bathing costume that for all its outmoded modesty made Terring ache for her. The water had beaded like crystals on her eyelashes.

His every thought circled back to her.

"Zizero Terring." Carl caught up with him.

Carl hadn't said anything about the fight with Tad, but Tad must have told him, judging by Carl's unsmiling, cold courtesy toward his employer. Calling him zizero, after traveling through hell and high water together. Terring was dead weary of it, though he'd done his share to make the situation.

"The balloon looks to be in good shape, zizero. I'll test it tomorrow and then we can decide whether or not to make a road."

"Hopefully it'll work." A road would push installation back a month, putting them in thunderstorm season before the frame had a chance to stabilize.

Carl fell back and Terring rode on alone. When the frame was complete, Solyra, Zago, Tad, and the rest of the team would bring the fulgus. After all the preparation, installation would take only a day. It had to take only a day. Until all of them were installed, the frame was extremely unstable.

Terring had more news for Solyra, though, than the frame being complete. A letter from his brother had come in this week's mail bag. Recent innovations in fulgu products had made older brother see the light. He was willing to invest. And Terring was more than willing to accept, in large part because his brother would stay safely in Norvadale, while his money flowed to the Zhengahk.

Enough money to buy Solyra out, if she wanted.

She could pay her debts and return back east with enough profit to live on for years.

And she would be gone.

>> <<

THE DAY SOLYRA COULD LEVEL with Zago came almost as a relief. She was ready to get those red-hots down to her stomach, where they could form an indigestible molten lump. She took the morning off, and provisionally the afternoon, and went to face the music. Or rather, to face the hum, she thought grimly as she headed to her compound.

Zago wasn't in his room, nor were his slippers. Of course. The moment Gobi let him up, he would head for the offices, where they'd moved Nooby, Scooby, Gooby…

Figgo was out, but Solyra heard Diaa's and Zago's voices in the root cellar. Instead of going in, she sat at Terring's desk. From there she could see into the cellar where, in the dim lamp light, Zago stooped over the crates. His voice came as a crooning coo; it reminded Solyra of the way she herself spoke to the babies she cuddled in her walks around town.

As Solyra watched, as yet unseen, Diaa and he gave each other a light kiss. Zago touched her hair and murmured to her as tenderly as he did to the fulgus. They engaged in a long kiss, and Solyra quietly moved out of sight. The handle of the pump squeaked in the corner. She would have thought Diaa would know it was dry…

She rose to her feet as a trickle, then a gush of water sounded. And Onyx and Ebony had been hauling from the village tank all this time.

She sat again with a sigh, then idly picked up a bandanna that lay on the desk and pressed it to her face. It smelled of Terring.

When she'd finally let go of Zago as a lover, she'd been alone. Then Terring came along. An honorable man, handsome, well-spoken, kind — at least where kindness was deserved. The one she could have had, when she was eighteen, and again, not more than a few weeks ago. She'd lost him again.

If she could bring herself to tell him the truth, not just

about that night in Booton but about why she'd cheated him later.... How, after Dahn died, she was left alone, friendless, her parents gone, her confidence long-since stripped away....

Terring would never understand. She wasn't sure if she did. Her story read like a penny drama. Or just a bunch of lame excuses. Maybe it really did just come down to her own greed. Anyway, though she could easily throw away the few scraps of pride left to her, there was no point telling him whatever might be the truth. Nothing she had to say would thaw the ice in his eyes.

Diaa and Zago emerged from the cellar. Even before Zago spoke, she knew by their faces that Diaa must have told him.

"Is it true, Solyra?" he asked. "Are you thinking of taking back the fulgus?"

Solyra wished Diaa had left her at least the dignity of speaking for herself, but then, Diaa was the one who had been at his side, for his reunion with the fulgus.

"Yes, it's true, Zago. I'm framing the pod fulgus."

"But I'm alive, Solyra. Your promise healed me."

He looked so fragile and hopeful, as if she was going to tell him she was joking. Solyra forced herself to look in his eyes.

"Zago, I lied to you. That's all there is to it. If my lie healed you, I'd do it again and again. I know it wasn't right, and I won't insult you with excuses or persuasion. I just hope you can forgive me. And Diaa, if the forces that healed Zago feel cheated, let them take it out on me."

Solyra willed her own tears back with all her might. She just couldn't cry. It wouldn't be fair to him.

Zago didn't look angry. Worse, he looked crushed. He began to turn away, then faced her again, though now he didn't look in her eyes. "Will I be able to work on the framing? I know you'll have an podder there, but I'd still like to help. Make sure..." His voice trembled and he swallowed hard. "Make sure it goes all right."

"Of course you can be there, Zago. I promise. And this promise I'll keep."

Zago nodded and gave her a brief smile, then he and Diaa went back into the cellar.

She would keep the promise, too, ill-considered as it was. Installing the fulgus in the frame was a delicate business, and there was no telling what kind of emotional state Zago would be in.

Solyra glanced in the cellar, then looked away. Diaa held him as he sobbed over the fulgu crates.

>> <<

SOLYRA PLOPPED DOWN AT THE dining table at her house and raked her fingers through her hair. Everyone was gone; she was alone. She couldn't decide whether she wanted to take the opportunity to cry and wail, or to scream and throw things.

She was tired of being the target of everyone's anger. Tired of letting everyone down. Tired of taking the blame. Tired of being reviled.

Of course she wasn't reviled, blamed and hated by everyone. Still. She was tired of being a victim.

She gave a laugh at her maudlin self-pity and sat up again, then gasped. Figgo stood at the entrance of the dining room. "Figgo. You startled me."

"I beg your pardon."

"It's all right. Come in and take a seat. Can you...?"

"I can find the way." He came forward, his slender walking stick probing, then finding a chair. "It is very easy for me to get around here with my stick."

"I'll make us some beer." Solyra got two glasses from the sideboard, then stepped down into the coolness of the root cellar. As she got out a bottle of the fizzy spring water and the syrup jug, she wondered what in the world Figgo was doing here alone. Had something happened to Terring?

Her heart jumped like a frightened rabbit, then she put

her hand to her chest. "Silly," she whispered to herself. Figgo wouldn't sit around, calmly drinking root beer, if Terring was hurt. She came back to the table, poured a little syrup in the glasses, then lifted one to her face. She never could resist inhaling the sweet spiciness of the syrup before she poured in the fizzy water.

"It smells good," Figgo said.

Solyra opened her eyes.

Figgo wasn't calm, really. He sounded tense, though not in a way that portended bad news.

Solyra poured the soda in the glasses, stirred the drinks with a polished stick, then put a glass in front of Figgo, giving the table a little *thock*, so he'd find it. Then she sat and sipped her own beer and waited.

Figgo finally broke the silence. "It is unfortunate that Terring Fulgus has gotten off to such a bad start."

"Yes, I'm sorry." Solyra meant it, and at the same time, she didn't know if she cared. She was a crazy woman, ready to tear out her hair one minute, bland as an inert fulgu the next. "Figgo, rest assured, I just want to raise the fulgu frame. I have no intention of violating our contract in any way, as I just told poor Zago. I want Terring Fulgus to succeed. If we have a good harvest, maybe Terring will want to buy me out, who knows. Then I can move back east, try to find my parents and settle down. "

Even before Figgo asked, "Your parents are missing?" Solyra could have bitten off her tongue and spat it in the fireplace ashes. Still, she decided to give an honest answer, for a change.

"Yes," she managed to say, "my parents are missing."

"I am sorry, Solyra."

"I'd rather not talk about it."

He asked as if she hadn't said anything, "Are they back east, do you think?"

"I don't... I don't know. It's likely, though, yes. I had

detectives looking before... Well, when I still had money, but nothing's come of it."

"Perhaps I can help find them. Some of the survivors of my family fled back east, and I have many connections there."

"I don't know." But Solyra couldn't bring herself to turn down a new avenue of investigation. Given that her mother and father were probably impoverished, therefore living in the kind of community where immigrants lived, there was a chance, a very slight but real chance, that Figgo could turn up something.

"I'll be much obliged for anything you do toward finding them."

"I would give anything to be with my parents again, Solyra," he said. "I never will, but I truly hope... No, hope is treacherous. I will do my best to help reunite you with your mother and father."

Solyra blinked back tears as he took a pencil and paper from his satchel. "Please, tell me about them," he said, pencil poised over the paper. "Their names, descriptions, anything that might help." A little taken aback at his promptness, Solyra gave him the information. He wrote it; she read it over.

"That's correct," she said, handing the paper back.

He put the paper and pencil back in his satchel. "Why are your parents missing, Solyra?"

Solyra gave a forced laugh. "My husband separated us. He wasn't a very nice person, you know."

"Why did he separate you?" Figgo's questions were a little merciless, quite intrusive, and very gentle, for all that lay between them.

"So he could... I guess to be mean."

Another long silence, then, "He wished to control you?"

"Yes, that's right. And now you know my deepest secrets, Figgo. Not that they're especially deep. I misplaced my own parents and I let my husband whore me for a business deal. Therefore.... Oh, never mind."

She sipped her root beer with a shaking hand. She'd stopped herself just in time from saying, *therefore, you can rest assured that Terring will never, ever love me.* Which would have been an utterly insane thing to say.

She put her glass down. "Please don't worry about the business having a bumpy start. Really. We've made a lot of progress, and I'm sure the rest will work out over time. Anything that's gone awry is certainly not your fault."

"It is at least partly my fault, Solyra. And I have been unjust to you."

Solyra took his words with the gobsmacked silence they deserved. She found herself disagreeing — but maybe Figgo was saying something else that even he didn't fully understand.

"I think you have been just to me," Solyra said.

"For one thing, I should never have threatened you about..." Solyra could sense him groping for words, the way his stick had groped for a chair when he came in. "About your husband's conduct." He blushed, but went on. "Terring told me about your quarrel with him. He was very upset. He said you spoke lightly of it. Yet the more I thought about it, the more uncertain I became. I hope you will not be offended that I asked Tad to tell me more. He did not reveal to me any more than Terring did. Any more facts, I mean."

"It's all right."

"Yet he made me see that I did not understand what really happened. I never even tried to see how you might have felt about it. Me, of all people, not understanding what it means to be coerced...."

"My conduct was hardly for a noble cause."

"Solyra, I am very sorry for my injustice to you."

Solyra was moved nearly to tears. She was also painfully embarrassed; she wondered if Figgo could feel the heat radiating from her own blush.

"Maybe justice isn't that important. I hope not, anyway."

"Justice is...." He adjusted his goggles, his hand trembling. "Justice has been... Everything I have."

Solyra swallowed and tried to think of what to say. She hadn't sent any congratulations about his exoneration; Terring said he wanted to put it all behind him. Yet, even with the court's decision, even if he had never actually wielded a ma-chete or thrown a girl-child on the ground — even if he'd saved his country, in the end, he still had to deal with what he had done. He had mapped Death-bringers' raids and ridden through them at the commander's right hand.

The ideal of justice allowed him to keep not only his honor but his sanity. He'd sacrificed the few for the many. Therefore, he was not guilty. Therefore, he might deserve to go on living, to exist.

"But justice is not everything," Solyra said softly. "There's more. Much more that's good, under the great big blue sky."

Outwardly, they might have looked like two people en-joying a relaxing drink together. To Solyra, and to Figgo, she sensed, this moment between them was almost unbearably poi-gnant. It broke as gently as a sigh when Figgo stood and tapped his way out.

A MISSED CHANCE

"I DON'T BELIEVE THE FULGUS are alive," Diaa said as Zago climbed onto the seat Tad had made for him in the wagon out of feed sacks and fleeces. The rest of them rode saddle horses. The other group going to the ranch, including Figgo, had left the day before, but Solyra and her companions decided to travel overnight so the food they were bringing would stay fresh until dinner. The rising moon and the signposts Baloos's crew had erected would show the way.

"They are sentient," Zago said as the wagon rolled into motion. "I hear them."

Solyra rode up alongside him. "So do I," she said. She couldn't count how many times they'd had this conversation. The only thing new this time around was Diaa taking her side, instead of waffling and wondering. "The wind whispers in the trees; the sands sing; chickens that you eat cluck and mate and lay eggs—which you also eat. What makes fulgus different? And we're not even destroying them. We're just putting them to use. Like a donkey or a horse. Fulgus have it better than a lot of animals."

"I can't explain it. They're different."

Solyra looked at him in the rays of the moon. She hadn't re-alized how much the journey had changed him, physically, un-til the fever reduced him to his former bendy softness. Bulked up, he was like any man. Less substantial now, he'd regained that mystic grace whose beauty she'd never before appreciated. The moonlit pools of his dark eyes made her wonder if he did see something, or hear something inaudible to the more sturdy souls of his companions.

"I don't think we're hurting them," Tad said, "even if they are alive."

"No." Zago was silent a while. "Funny thing is, I love in-stalling them. That moment of contact, before they're caged… And to do a frame — most of us keepers never get the chance. It's something to tell grandchildren, if we could have them."

"Why can't you?" Tad asked.

"Keeping fulgus does something to your body," Zago an-swered. "None of us have kids. I don't mind."

"Neither do I," Diaa said. She cuddled up to him.

Zago smiled with the universal smugness of a man desired. "It's just as well. We keepers are loopy." He gave a laugh that struck Solyra as false. "In case you haven't noticed."

Solyra exchanged a look with Tad. Neither of them trusted Zago's sudden compliance.

"How would you liberate them, anyway?" Tad asked.

"I don't know," Zago answered. Of course, he would see right through the question, and lie.

"Break them?" Tad pressed.

Zago shrugged. "I'm not sure that would work."

His face was so easy to read, it gave Solyra a pang. It also made her resolve to keep a sharp eye on him, when they got to framing the fulgus. If all fulgu keepers got the urge to "free" their charges, no wonder their occupation had a high mortality rate.

"Poor Peg," she said, pointedly, "if she were here, she could attest to how dangerous it is to open a fulgu outside a proper installation."

Zago's mouth trembled, and Solyra shuddered at the memory of that horrendous day. But she didn't regret her words. She didn't want a repeat.

>> <<

THEY REACHED THE RANCH HOUSE in early afternoon. The steward reported that Terring and his crew wouldn't return from the field until dusk.

"Who's up for going out there?" Solyra asked.

"I'll go," Zago said immediately.

"No, you can't," Diaa said. "You need to rest. Solyra, don't let him go."

Solyra wasn't about to. Zago had slid more than climbed down from the wagon, and his face was wan. "She's right, Zago."

Diaa whispered to Solyra, "May I stay here? I'll take care of him."

"That would be great. I'll be back soon; I just want to see how far they've gotten."

Solyra and Tad rode only a few miles before they came to the beginning of the frame. Wire netting stretched taut between the posts as far as Solyra could see. A sturdy cable stretched between the posts above the netting. During the install, the balloon carrying the partially activated fulgus would be tethered to the cable, the balloon gliding from post to post so that the fulgus could be placed in the cap-cages as quickly as possible.

Tad split off when they met Carl and Baloos checking a load of netting spools. A little later she passed the chief podder, Pinkin, who ignored her wave. She didn't take it personally. Jaleen had warned in one of her letters, "He's dedicated." Not much further on, Terring stood under a canopy, leaning over a table.

Solyra would have liked to think that Terring was squinting

into the sun as he faced her, but his back was to the sun. He was scowling. She could hardly blame him. He hadn't gotten a one-two from Tad only. Her ugly revelation about how she and Dahn had stolen his account, together with her vow to Zago would have broken even Gobi's patience.

She had to put that all aside, however, even if he couldn't.

And she really couldn't hold her spirits down. It would be a year or more before harvest, but seeing the actual frame that she'd traveled so far and worked so hard to make possible was exhilarating.

She dismounted and a hostler took Toggly to a makeshift canvas stable. "What progress!"

Terring nodded and even he couldn't be but so much of a grouch in the face of that truth. "Yep. We've got an excellent crew." He paused. "Carl did well by us. He knows his business, that's for sure."

Solyra tried and failed to keep the told-you-so from her grin. She surveyed the neat line of posts. "Tell me where we are."

They went to the table, which was covered with a topographical map pinned to corkboard. Solyra ran her fingertips over it and could feel a grid and swirls embossed in the paper. It was a map Figgo could read.

"We — you and I — are right here." He pointed to a green-headed pin nearly in the middle of the map. "This is the ranch house." A larger green rectangle. "The white pins in a line are posts netted already. The red pins—" Terring ran his finger along the line "—are not yet netted. Or at least they weren't this morning. At the end of the day, if all goes as planned, all the red pins will be changed for white."

"I never would have expected the frame to go up so fast." Solyra had almost begun to think that the whole thing was a fantasy, that she would go on bumbling through life forever without achieving anything. But Terring read her thoughts — or at least part of them.

"Sometimes I have to pinch myself to make sure I'm not dreaming." For all the fatigue on his dusty face, he looked happy.

Solyra decided not to mention her uneasiness about Zago. No point in reminding Terring of her ill-considered promise. He might prevent her fulfilling her other ill-considered promise, that Zago take part in the installation. At least podder Pinkin didn't seem like the type to put up with any irregularity. He would surely keep Zago in line.

"Terring, I have to say, I'm thrilled."

Terring relaxed into a smile. "We'll start the install nearest the ranch house and work our way over. That balloon Lady Liberty gave you saved us at least a month, by the way."

"I'm feasting the crew tonight," Solyra said. "I know we have to get an early start, but it won't hurt to have a little celebration—a pre-celebration, before we do the install."

"Why not? But no booze. "

"No booze," Solyra agreed.

She headed back to the ranch house. The crew totaled several dozen men and women, and although most of the food she'd brought was already prepped, it was the biggest meal she'd bossed so far. Zago had managed to get the pump working so they didn't have to unload the water they'd hauled in, but it still took her and Diaa and the small house staff the rest of the afternoon to get everything ready.

The effort was well worth it. Many of the men and women came and thanked her personally for the food. Even Zago and podder Pinkin were getting along.

Several council leaders from the region had arrived that afternoon, and the high spirits, if not the food, must have made a good impression on them. A buzz of good-natured conversation filled the big, crowded room. It made Solyra think of the Beechen Lodge and, weirdly, she felt a jab of nostalgia.

"The dinner was excellent, Solyra," Terring said. "Just the right thing."

"Sometimes I think I'd be better as a restaurateur than as a business woman."

"Well, just say the word." He looked away from her, at some point in the room. "My brother's ready to buy you out any time. Name the figure, and you've got it—in reason—and, of course, we'll work out royalties. You could be heading back east next week."

Solyra's smile froze. Terring's offer took her totally off guard, but that wasn't what made her feel as if she'd just swallowed one of the plums whole, pit and all. She didn't know what made her feel that way. Terring had just offered to make her dreams come true.

Hadn't he?

"I'll think about that," she said with an air of lightness.

"Please do," he answered, and added, "The sooner, the better."

Figgo leaned over Terring and said, "Zago got the pump working again."

"Yes," she answered absently, "it saved us a lot of work." Then she gave smiling excuses and left the table.

Once out of the room, her steps quickened. She needed to get to her room. She desperately needed somewhere to hide.

A copper tub stood in an alcove of the room, the water heater already stoked. She lit it and while the water warmed she undressed, shook out her clothes, put her sweaty linens to soak. Then she filled the tub and stepped in.

She didn't have to take up Terring's offer, she told herself, closing her eyes and leaning against the sloped tub back. She could stay with the business as long as she wanted. As Figgo had said more than once, the contract was good and tight, and no one could kick her out. However, in interest of telling the truth at least to herself, she had to admit that Terring's proposal dampened her mood.

He wanted her gone. It would be easier, she supposed. If she stayed, he and she would have to wear smooth business faces. In time, the cold contempt in his eyes might not hurt so much.

That was unlikely, though. Because every time she met that look, it stabbed deeper and deeper.

As they'd traveled over the prairie and into the desert, a feeling had grown inside her. She hadn't dared to call it love. She'd thought she would wait and see. She'd thought that Terring and she were slowly forgiving each other, slowly drawing closer to each other. She might even have had a fantasy, a romantic fantasy, that they were courting each other, subtly, gently, in a secret game of their own. The day in the lake had been a revelation for her: Terring had shown her the ecstasy and release her body and his could enjoy together.

But it wouldn't mean that to him. He took his pleasure easily, whether with her or a faded roadhouse sexworker. He had been like a sated person giving a hungry urchin a cracker, though he wouldn't have known that. He wouldn't have felt so deeply the joy of that dalliance. Certainly he wouldn't comprehend how the memory of it could hurt so badly.

Then that day under the cottonwoods, in the warm soft water — had he been about to say, I love you?

And she'd panicked, and blathered out a self-slandering truth. To test him? Or to push him away. To make him leave her be.

She was tormenting herself by chasing schoolgirl dreams. She was a widow, with a widow's lust finally catching up to her. And that was a good thing. It was healthy. But it wasn't love.

Here she was, crying in her bathwater, lying yet again.

THE LIBERTY'S BALLOON

CARL'S CREW HAD LAID THE envelope—what most people called the balloon—flat on the ground near the first frame post. Blue with a sunburst at the top, it looked large, even in its flaccid state. It also looked perfectly neat, except for the inevitable wrinkles due to its shape. Meanwhile, Carl oversaw the charcoal-fueled air heater. Terring watched for a while, then paced along the frame, checking the post caps here and there. He'd already checked each one last night, and spot-checked again on arriving this morning. With an effort he made himself stop.

When he got back to the balloon, Carl and Tad were feeling the pipes, valves, hoses, and fittings that fed the hot air into the balloon. His crew fussed over the envelope to make sure no parts of it stuck together, and bustled to ensure that all the lines were laid out perfectly, so they wouldn't tangle as the balloon rose.

Terring rode again to the second post. He wished the balloon crew could do for his nerves what they were doing for the balloon, smoothing out the wrinkles, making sure all the lines were free of tangles. His own fulgu frame had been only about a quarter this length, and another engineer had been in charge, not Terring himself. A cloud of dust in the direction of the ranch house heralded the coaches bringing the spectators. He wished they weren't coming. He just wanted to get the job done and over with.

But despite the hazards and all the many, many things that could go wrong, he felt as exhilarated as a bride on her wedding day. Or at least, what he'd heard about brides on their wedding days. And the spectators in this case were a decorous lot, merry as they'd been last night, joining in a roof-raising chorus of ululating, led by Diaa.

The dinner was the first time Terring had seen Solyra with the local leaders. The Liberty was struggling, and several leaders were unhappy about the fulgu frame. Terring had expected tension, even hostility. Instead, he'd witnessed genuine warmth and cooperation. Part was due to the innate courtesy of the people. But another reason was that, when Solyra was with people, she was with them completely. She listened intently to every word that was said. Even if a disagreement followed, at least people knew they were understood.

He had not granted her that. Figgo, of all people, had, and last night he'd let Terring know his — their mistake with her. Figgo's hard-heartedness, as he called it himself, was because he had been unable to face the mirror that Solyra's dilemma held up to himself. Reliving his own betrayals during the trial, and a conversation with Tad, had forced understanding on him.

Moved and surprised as Terring was, to hear Figgo reveal so much of himself, he'd also received the message that Figgo was too polite to convey: that he himself had been, simply, a knucklehead. He'd barely slept last night, and not only because of the impending frame installation. He'd gone over and over, futilely, that day at the pond she'd blurted out that cursed confession. In his memory, it was obvious how frightened she had been, despite her jaunty words and her laugh. And he'd turned his back and walked away! He should have seen through it, he should have seen through it all. He'd known what Dahn was like. How could he ever have believed that Solyra was in league with such a man? He'd thought her tainted by Dahn and, as he'd told himself, he loved her despite it all. Now his noble love showed as a shoddy thing.

But he still loved her.

He loved her enough to throw away his own chances of happiness by telling her about his brother's offer. But instead of making her happy, he'd extinguished her. Again.

The coaches emptied at the roped off area near the first frame post. No canopy had been set up, as that would block the view of the balloon, and most of the people sat on rugs, with a few of the elders on cushioned benches. As everyone settled in, Terring rode to join them.

Solyra looked both nervous and joyful. Just like on that fateful day Terring had told her their deal was off. And she was wearing the blue dress, now transformed into the frock coat. How had he ever thought it ridiculous? Solyra looked every inch a Liberty governor, and every inch a woman as she delivered a flowery welcoming speech.

A silence brought Terring back to reality. It was his turn to speak. He faced the squinting, sweating assembly.

"Many of you know what I'm going to explain," he said, "but bear with me, and listen carefully." He looked over his audience intently, as if drawing every bit of their attention with his eyes.

"This morning, the very most delicate part of raising this frame will take place. Everything absolutely must go like clockwork."

Tad, translating into Zhi'nging'ha! for those who didn't read common sign, broke off to mutter to Terring, "They don't have mechanical clocks in these parts."

"Right. For those of you who don't know what a clock is, it's a machine for showing time. Every one of its parts has to work with the others, all in order, for every minute ticked off."

Terring heard one of the leaders whisper to Solyra, "Mint dickoff?"

Solyra's eyes crinkled. "It's how they count time," she whispered back. They. As if she'd never had a clock herself.

Terring felt something between a smile and a grimace stretch his face. Blast it all if he wasn't nervous. "The point is, everyone has to do their part precisely with the other members of the install crew. Spectators will stay behind the red line."

He pointed to a line of red rock dust that Onyx had laid down in front of the enclosure.

"Carl and his crew will handle the balloon."

Heads turned obediently to where Carl and a dozen others stood around the recumbent, still-flabby balloon.

"As she fills with hot air, Pinkin, our chief podder, and our keeper Zago will partially activate the fulgus and place them in the basket. Once the balloon is fully inflated, Carl will hook the balloon to the guide cable with two wires. The balloon then moves the fulgus from frame post to frame post with the utmost speed and the least jostling.

"When the balloon basket is at a post, Zago will fully activate a fulgu and install it in the post-cap. Pinkin will secure the cap. Then the whole thing is gently moved to the next post.

"Where are the danger points in this operation? Everywhere. But there are two highly hazardous points."

Only the murmur of Carl's crew as they attached the air hoses to the balloon met his dramatic pause, then a throaty, roaring sigh as the valves were opened.

"Main hazard one. A basket of inert fulgus is dangerous. Unfortunately, that's not what we have."

Another dramatic pause. Terring heard Carl, "How full is she?" and Baloos responding, "About a quarter there." It took all of Terring's will power not to turn around and look.

"Our balloon basket will carry partially activated fulgus," he continued. "That means our load is very, very volatile. The hazard is raised exponentially."

Tad labored at translating "exponentially," settled for "a thousand-fold."

"Frankly," Terring said, "I wonder how folks like Podder Pinkin and Keeper Zago and their assistants have the nerve to do their jobs."

Podder Pinkin and Keeper Zago and their assistants didn't look at all daunted. If anything, they looked entranced. Once they started the install, their faces would be obscured by goggles and the mesh veils now bunched atop their helmets.

"Main hazard two," Terring continued. "The balloon. Solyra Liberty's vessel is excellent. Problem is, it's a little more buoyant than we need, even for a load of this weight. Carl will try to regulate the hot air accordingly, and the guide cables will hold, we're sure of that, but Carl's crew will have a job every time they unhook the cables as they reach each post, and re-hook them past each post. I have complete confidence in them, but again, they will need to devote their utmost competence and concentration to the task at hand."

A little whisper went over the crowd and a few people pointed. Terring couldn't resist turning this time. The flaccid envelope had grown lumpy, then puffy. He turned back to the crowd and gave a piercing whistle. Everyone stared at him.

"Now, even if you didn't take in a word of that, here's what every single one of you needs to know." Tad grew more emphatic, adding gestures: pointing to the audience and pounding a fist twice on his palm.

"If I or any other of the crew yell 'Down!'," Terring continued, "everyone will hit the ground and cover their eyes. Stay down and keep your eyes covered until I say you can get up. Doesn't matter what's happening. Even if everything seems to be just fine, even if we're way down the line, if someone yells 'Down!' you all hit the dirt and cover your eyes. Every one of you, including crew, engineers, keepers and spectators." Terring saw out the corner of his eye, Pinkin and Zago exchange a long look. "Drop whatever you're doing and hit the dirt. And cover your eyes, unless you want to take a chance on being blinded. You get up again only when I say so."

Tad translated, emphasizing the word "down."

Terring yelled, "DOWN!"

Solyra and Diaa, Figgo, and all the workers went down.

"Get up!" Terring yelled. Some of the spectators—who hadn't dropped—giggled.

The giggles withered under Terring's glare.

He roared, "DOWN!"

Everyone dropped so fast, Terring's voice was still echoing from the redrock when he let them up again. Had Terring not been so nervous himself, he might have laughed. They drilled several more times.

"That's all right, I guess," Terring said when everyone was good and dusty. "Remember, if you please, not to cross the red line. And we'll begin."

When he turned again, the balloon was nearly rounded and had risen from the ground. It was small, as balloons went, but inflated it looked enormous. Onyx and Ebony hooked the cables to the frame's guide wire as the balloon firmed.

"Check inflation," Carl directed, and his assistants prodded and poked the envelope.

"Inflation achieved."

"Air off."

"Air off," the crew echoed. A few more commands and checks back and forth, and the hoses were removed and the inflation level checked again.

"Basket secure?" Carl asked.

Ebony and Baloos ran their hands over the lines, testing each. "Basket secure, aye," Baloos said.

Terring shouted in his sea captain's voice, "Non-crew, get back!"

It was the last order before the install. An eon passed, though it was only moments, before Carl said, "Ready for install."

Zago and Pinkin, with only glints of their goggles showing from behind the safety mesh, quietly examined each fulgu, the four apprentices looking on from behind their own mesh face covers.

Some fulgus went in the basket as they were. Presumably they were the ones already partially activated. Others, they cranked open slightly using instruments that looked, as Solyra had explained to one of the dignitaries last night, like oyster knives with gears. She'd then had to explain what oysters were. They placed the partials in the basket with extreme delicacy. Metal "wool" shaped like egg crate lined the basket itself. The assistants put in more sheets of it as each layer filled up. Finally, they secured the load with a metal grid.

Pinkin rechecked the safety lid that fastened the fulgus in the basket.

"Ready, fulgus?" Carl asked.

"Fulgus ready," Pinkin said.

To a pattering of applause, Pinkin opened the first post cap.

>> <<

ALTHOUGH THE BOTTOM OF THE balloon was barely off the ground, Solyra gasped. The big blue globe with its brilliant sunburst was glorious.

"Ready, fulgus?" Carl asked.

"Fulgus ready," Pinkin answered.

The spectators burst into applause, which quickly sputtered out under Terring's glare.

The crew ignored the acclaim, except for a few grins and nods. Zago and Pinkin and their assistants gave no sign of even hearing it. Pinkin had removed the safety lid and they bent over the basket, deep in their fulgu world, Solyra guessed, listening to whatever they imagined their charges had to say. The next several hours of installing the fulgus in the frame caps would be the pinnacle of their careers, or the end, if things went wrong.

It was hard to imagine something going wrong. But Solyra wished she could see the keepers' faces, especially Zago's. The balloon floated steady, the cables taut, the basket in easy reach of the keepers. Solyra imagined that the balloon could go much higher, over the mountains and even higher, were it not for the cable. She turned to Figgo, next to her, and whispered, "Wouldn't it be glorious to fly into the sky in that basket?"

Diaa giggled. Figgo didn't answer at first, then he said, "I shall miss you, Solyra, if you leave."

Of all the things he could have said to her, that was the last thing she'd expected. Even after their conversation over root beer. She hardly knew what to say —

Zago shouted, "Down!"

Terring echoed in a roar: "DOWN!"

Everyone hit the dirt — except Solyra, Zago and Terring.

Solyra leaped forward as Terring pulled Zago away from the balloon.

"Get down, Solyra!" Terring cried.

Zago had chosen his moment just as Onyx unhooked the cable. The balloon bobbed loose. He maneuvered and tugged. Solyra leaped onto an empty netting spool, and grabbed the cable—

And the balloon rose.

Solyra opened her mouth to scream, but didn't, even when someone grabbed at her legs and ended up with an empty boot. She soon drifted out of reach, floating into the sky.

Panting and gasping, she hauled herself up the rope to straddle the basket. Lucky she still had the upper body strength she'd gained on the road...

Except now she was straddling a basketful of partially activated fulgus.

She wondered why she didn't at least whimper with fear. The balloon glided higher, anchorless, beyond any chance of being pulled back. She should have been terrified, but she wasn't, though her heart beat hard and fast.

The breezeless air kept the balloon more or less in place, hovering high above the crowd. Some shouted useless things like "Come down!" "The fulgus are dangerous!" "Don't fall!" Others simply gaped.

It all seemed far away. It was, literally, about eighty foot-lengths away, but in a sense much further.

It was earth, and this was sky.

Solyra felt … happy. Euphoric, in a quiet way. Maybe this was what Gobi and Diaa talked about, the mind being like a clear blue sky.

Other than the people below, all was quiet. She looked up and smiled at how the balloon was like her own private little sky within the great big sky. The air was so still, she hardly moved, an almost comic contrast to the crowd milling below.

The world looked both smaller and more vast. Smoke from the cooking fire rose lazily into the morning from the distant ranch. The wind vanes on the water pump winked. A little herd of antelope grazed where no one but she could see them, in a rough little meadow pocketed by a fold at the foot of the redrock. She didn't need to shade her eyes—the balloon did it for her—in the soft air of morning. Except her backside was hot.

She needed to uncoil the fire rope, hook it to the basket's edge and let Carl and his crew pull down the balloon. Before a breeze came along and carried her away.

First, though, she had to decide if she really did want to get down.

The balloon would drop, sooner or later. Or it would crash into the side of a cliff. Or explode. Solyra looked between her legs and saw the fulgus cracked open a little wider. In the shade of her body, they glowed. In fact, she reckoned it wouldn't be a good idea to let Carl haul her down, what with the fulgus ready to open up any minute now. Zago must have activated them more than needed for an install. They were deadly dangerous now. Carl and the twins had herded spectators and crew away from the ground below, but that wouldn't necessarily save them.

If she tossed them out of the basket—away from her friends, of course—one by one, besides burning her hands, she'd lighten the load and go higher, and higher, and higher for as long as the air in the balloon stayed hot, and with the sun shining so hard, that might be a while.

And when she finally dropped, that would be the end of her.

She didn't want to die, but the lure of just flying away....

She looked up. She looked down.

Diaa yowled and stretched up her arms as if she could grab Solyra right out of the sky. Zago called, but his voice carried only as a mew. Carl and Tad, surrounded by their crew, looped cable in various patterns, pointing and gesticulating, probably trying to come up with an absurd plan to lasso down the balloon.

Figgo spun slowly in place, his caftan swirling, his arms raised, face upturned, lips moving, goggles flashing rhythmically as they caught the sun. He looked as if he were dancing; maybe he was chanting, I shall miss you, Solyra, if you leave. I shall miss you, Solyra....

Terring was there, too.

His face glistened. Was he crying? He shouted, "Solyra!"

Solyra craned toward him and the basket rocked. A soft breeze sprang up, drifting the balloon. The people below ran after it.

A murmuring filled her ears. The voices of the fulgus. Theirs was an exquisite song, spun of earth and sky and sun, pure energy, disembodied—

"SOLYRA, DON'T LEAVE ME!"

Terring's voice cut through the fulgu song as an almighty sobbing shout, yet it came to Solyra as if he were whispering in her ear.

"I LOVE YOU!"

Solyra uncoiled the fire rope and hooked it to the basket. Still, she couldn't rush. She couldn't upset the basket and spill the now gaping fulgus on her lover and her friends. Careful to tilt the basket as little as possible, she bunched her frock coat over the cable to pad her hands and climbed over the edge.

She slid down that cable so fast, the coat's fabric smoked. Terring caught her legs, before her feet touched ground, her hands still seized on the cable. The balloon tugged in the quickening breeze.

Solyra stretched between earth and sky.

"Let go, Solyra!" Terring cried. "Let go, my love."

Solyra let go and slid into Terring's embrace.

The balloon bobbed up and glided off into the blue sky. The murmur of the fulgus became a distant, eerie cacophony of whistles, hoots, moans, wails, and rattles.

"DOWN!" Terring roared.

He and Solyra didn't hit the ground, though. They only hugged each other harder and hid their eyes on each other's shoulders. Bursts of light danced on their eyelids.

Solyra felt every line of Terring's body against hers: his chest pressing hers through the thin fabric of her linen shirt, one of his legs between hers, one of her legs between his, one of his arms wrapped around her shoulders, the other hugging her at the waist, and her arms reaching up to his shoulders. Then his lips and hers crushed together, the sweat from his neck wet on her hands, and she was filled with desire, filled as full as a fulgu was of light and heat, full of energy, even as the debris of the fulgu pods pattered around them.

When they finally broke apart and opened their eyes, their business was fragments of fulgu shell and silk balloon strewn for miles over the desert.

Everyone still crouched, eyes covered.

Terring grinned. "We could make love right here and now, and no one would be the wiser."

Solyra laughed, throwing her head back, predicting,

accurately, that Terring would nibble at her throat. "That would be wrong," she said. She looked at him again, and tears washed her eyes. "Though making love with you would be very right."

Terring gave her another long kiss, then they broke apart. "Everybody up!" he shouted.

Slowly, the crew and spectators stood and brushed themselves off. Even as they began taking in the disaster, so did Solyra. She saw the dismay on the faces of the crew, and as the spectators began streaming to the crew members who were their brothers and sisters, fathers and mothers, daughters and sons, Solyra knew that relief would soon turn to anxiety. Miraculously, no one had been injured, but their only chance of prosperity was utterly destroyed. The Liberty was doomed.

Then Figgo's observation, which had seemed painfully obvious the night before, hit her.

Zago got the wind pump working again.

And he got the pump working in the root cellar where the fulgus had been stored. And he'd revived the spring, by the rock where he was wounded. Solyra's eyes filled with tears again, even as she laughed.

To Figgo, it was a hope he hadn't dared express. To Solyra it was a certainty. The water had come back.

The people of Solyra Liberty were no more out of work than Solyra and Terring were out of work. They had a town and a Liberty to bring back to life.

SOLYRA'S LIBERTY

SOLYRA STEPPED FROM THE HOUSE, her gown's crystal beads softly clinking. As the crowd cheered, Terring, already waiting, grinned and took Solyra's hand and kissed it, then they turned back toward the bachelor and bride houses.

Zago came out next, and Diaa, and they took each other's hands.

The onlookers chanted, "Zago, Zago, Life-bringer, Water-waker!" A blush tinted his cheeks, but his face brimmed with happiness. Diaa had her followers, too: her ululating yowl of joy was echoed by all. Including Figgo. He had planned to go back east, but thanks to Zago Water-waker, his kin were returning from exile. Solyra hoped that some day soon, they would come with her parents. Figgo had spread the word.

Carl came out of the bachelor's house, and then Tad came out, not from the bride's house — he'd dead refused that — but from another house next to it. The crowd showered Carl and Tad with affection. It wasn't the wild acclaim they'd given Zago and Diaa, but Solyra reckoned they hardly noticed. Free to love, they both looked dazed with joy. People cheered their kiss, rather than threatening them with death and shame.

As the triple wedding procession moved down the street, the crowd burst again into shouts and ululations. Drums played, flutes warbled, and the air swirled with "flower petals," snips of colorful silk, the newly planted flowers still only seedlings.

Gobi awaited them at the main square. He wore his usual plain brown robes, but his smile provided all the festivity his appearance could want. Behind him, on a table covered with richly embroidered cloth, sat the laughing fat man and the half-naked woman. And behind them, the fountain that had been dry burbled and sparkled with water.

Solyra gazed at the statues, but in her mind, she was in the river under the cottonwoods, with Terring.

Last night they had gone there and made love...

A cheer went up. Solyra blinked and came to staring at the half-naked goddess. Gobi must have said the blessing while she was lost in her delicious daydream.

The crowd laughed and cheered as the children pressed the fountain's outlets, sending water everywhere. In a sweet rain, Solyra and Terring embraced.

ABOUT KEATES NELSON

KEATES NELSON CHERISHES HER HOME state of Virginia, but she and her husband also love to travel. On the road or curled up on the couch with her oversized, fluffy cat, she'll read just about anything, from biography and history to classics to gritty Westerns to speculative fiction and, of course, romance.

VISIT KEATES AT KEATESNELSON.COM

www.ingramcontent.com/pod-product-compliance
Lightning Source LLC
Chambersburg PA
CBHW021002260626
47169CB00006B/1897